TOURNAMENTS OF THAW

BOOK 9 THE THAW CHRONICLES

TAMAR SLOAN
HEIDI CATHERINE

SEQUEL HOUSE

LEXIS

The sight of her village, little more than a scrape of dirt on a canvas of more dirt, has Lexis's lips twitching in an unfamiliar motion. As the edges turn up, she realizes she's almost…smiling.

She quickly dampens the foolish action, allowing its momentary lightness to flicker in her chest. She's thirsty and hungry, and although being home isn't likely to help with either of those, she has good news.

Her feet lift a little higher, her steps reach a little further. She can't wait to tell Evrest.

A quick glance over her shoulder shows her three companions have adjusted their stride to match hers like the good soldiers they are, their mouths tightly shut against the dust that's always an inhale away. She knows they would've seen the village, too. Everyone is always on the alert in the Outlands.

It's how you stay alive.

Lexis wipes at the bead of sweat trickling down her temple, absentmindedly flicking her tongue to lick it from the back of her hand. She's not losing even a drop of moisture to this harsh, ashen land.

Raze steps up beside her, his blue eyes narrowed. He lifts his arm and points.

Lexis is about to snap that of course she's seen it, they were trained by the same man after all, when she looks a little more closely.

The People of Cy are coming out. But their shouts aren't words of greeting. Their hands aren't empty as they wave.

It seems Evrest wants to send a welcoming committee.

Reaching behind her, Lexis slips her spear out of the halter strapped to her back. The sounds of metal clinking and leather creaking tell her the others have their weapons ready, too.

Lexis grips the smooth wood in both hands, letting out a slow breath. A little shorter than most spears, but thicker, it became an extension of her from a young age. It's one of the few things in her life she's ever allowed herself to get attached to.

It's the only thing she can depend on to ensure her survival.

As she takes in the growing mass of people running at her, Lexis counts. Six warriors. Two more than they have. Three more than last time this happened.

A cool calmness steals through her. The dryness in her mouth no longer exists. The need for food is gone. It's like the five days of endless trekking to the People of the Cragg and back never happened.

Evrest will see what she's made of.

Lexis lifts her spear as she breaks into a run. "No mercy!"

There's a roar from their opponents as they increase their speed. There's silence from Lexis and her warriors as they sprint forward to meet them.

When they're only a few yards away, Lexis identifies each one of them, all from her village, all with war twisting their faces. There's Ivor, the man who showed her how to put stones in broth so you fool yourself into thinking the pot's almost full. Arc, who always puts his hand up for any sort of fight. And

Hesper, the woman who slept with Lexis and Raze when they were young to keep them warm on the rare nights a cool breeze crept in. And then three more who Lexis doesn't bother to name, realizing it's easier if she doesn't.

Not when she's about to try to kill them.

The battle cries become louder. The bodies closer. Lexis's thumping pulse feels like it's everywhere and nowhere at once, somehow simultaneously too loud and nonexistent in her heartless body.

It's Ivor who streaks out into the lead, his feral gaze trained on Lexis. Never losing momentum, she lifts her spear an inch higher and starts to bring it down in a wide arc. Lexis sees the split-second Ivor thinks he's figured her out. His gaze flares, and his hand flexes around the short blade he's holding.

Lexis brings her spear down, and Ivor almost grins as it sweeps past his face and misses. The blade darts out, a missile heading for her gut.

But it never connects.

As the spear hits the ground, Lexis pushes down. She vaults into the air, flipping right over Ivor. Her feet hit the dust on the other side and she lands in a crouch. She doesn't look over her shoulder as she shoots forward.

The cry behind her tells her Ivor will no longer be an issue. Raze has made sure of it.

Another face looms and Lexis doesn't give herself time to register who it is. She forgot how hard this can be.

How something in her fractures as each one of her people crumple under the violence of her spear. There's a scream from her right, and Lexis recognizes it before she means to. That's the sound Hesper made whenever she thought someone was attacking...which was most nights.

Lexis spins and swings her spear, that very same scream telling her exactly where Hesper is. It whistles through the air and sweeps through Hesper's legs as if they were twigs, and the woman crumples.

Before the spear has completed its arc, Raze kneels beside Hesper. He yanks one of the wooden stakes out of the pouches lining his belt and slams it down, his face cold and hard. Hesper screams again, this time in outrage. The sleeve of her tunic has been pinned to the ground.

Following the momentum of her spear, Lexis scans for her next victim. Fearless, is what people call her. Dauntless.

Ruthless.

Rather than focus on what she's lost, she concentrates on the victory thrumming through her veins. She's winning. She's untouchable.

And she has Raze.

No matter where she steps, even when it feels like she's made the move before she's thought of it, he's there. Her shadow. Her armor. An extension of the fighting machine she was raised to be.

It would almost be beautiful if it wasn't so terrifying.

If it were destined to stay like this.

Around her are the grunts and snarls of battle. Someone cries out and Lexis realizes it was one of her own men. Arc stands over him, blood glinting off his serrated blade. With a growl, she leaps, her spear lancing forward, the tip slamming into his throat.

Arc staggers back, choking and gasping as he stumbles and sprawls flat on his back. Before his battered throat can try to pull a breath, Raze stabs another of his stakes into the ground, just beside Arc's ribs. A gargled cry tries to climb out his injured neck and Lexis sees why. Blood blooms across Arc's shirt. Raze has sliced open a gash with the tip of his stake. Deep enough to hurt, but too shallow to do permanent damage.

A warning. And a punishment for killing one of their own before the Tournaments.

Lexis does a slow spin. Everyone is down. One person is dead. Raze already has his back to hers, waiting to see if anyone is foolish enough to try to get up.

"Finish it."

Lexis freezes. That voice. Those words.

She turns to find Evrest, their leader, standing not far away. For pointless seconds, she desperately wishes she heard him wrong.

But his cold gaze is unwavering as he raises his fist. "Do you think the people of Askala will hesitate when we arrive to end their selfishness? Do you think the one who becomes Commander will get there by showing mercy?"

Mercy. The ultimate weakness.

This is why Evrest ordered the People of Cy to attack their own. It's the ultimate training exercise.

To find who is the strongest. The fastest.

To find who will do what it takes.

Wanting this over and done with, Lexis does one final spin, her spear slicing through the air. This needs to be hard enough to hurt, but not hard enough to do damage.

But time slows, not willing to give her the blissful respite of a fast knockdown.

The wood of her weapon connects with the side of Raze's head, the reverberations feeling like they climb straight up her arms and into her chest.

There's the inevitable *crack*.

Raze crumples, having never raised a hand to stop the strike.

He collapses in the dirt, face impassive. Lexis's movements are automatic, having been programmed into her fighting moves long before she can remember. She leaps and stands above him, her spear held high.

Poised. Ready to strike.

Her hand loosens around the spear, her mind screaming for

her to throw it away. A traitorous bead of sweat zigzags down the side of her cheek like a tear.

"What are you waiting for?" Evrest demands. "For him to beg for his life?"

Raze never moves. Never takes his gaze from hers.

He knows this was always destined to be his fate. His eyes will her to do it.

To not be weak.

"Exactly," Evrest growls in disgust. "He's nothing but a stupid mute. Finish him."

Glad she left her heart somewhere back in her childhood, Lexis brings down her spear. The scorched soil beside Raze's head fractures, the soft crackle enough to make her feel sick. The sharpened length of wood impales into the barren soil, standing straight and tall in victory.

Her twin brother lets out a breath, his head nodding once. Although Raze hasn't spoken most of their life, his voice whispers through her mind.

You did good.

The sound of clapping has Lexis looking up. Evrest's eyes shine with something she doesn't see very often in her father.

Pride.

His gaze flickers at the carnage that surrounds her, his hard eyes almost dismissive. Like someone didn't just die in his little training exercise. Like his son isn't the one he just ordered her to finish. "What news do you bring?"

Lexis straightens. It feels like a lifetime ago that she considered smiling. "The People of the Cragg have agreed. They will take part in the Tournaments and honor whoever wins as the Outlands' one ruler."

Her father's nostrils flare as his chest expands. "Only one more to go," he states resolutely.

The People of Fairbanks.

The weakest of all the Outlands' factions.

The poorest.

The ones who nobody cares whether they even come to these very necessary games.

Lexis nods. "We'll leave at first light."

WINTER

*W*inter stares out the broken window, each fragment in the glass a symbol of the jagged scars across the damaged Earth. Pressing her forehead to the warm surface, she wonders how much longer she can avoid joining the sea of human misery in the wastelands that stretch before her.

The building groans as if it hears her thoughts, reminding her that it can't hold her people much longer. That soon it will crumble and fall, joining the rubble of the city that is no more.

In ancient times, Fairbanks was densely populated. This building had families with food in their cupboards, water in their taps and light that would pour from circles in the ceiling like stars in the night sky. These same walls were witness to the tears and laughter of the inhabitants as they told stories, kissed their children, read books, and argued over things that didn't matter, as well as things that did.

But not now. As the paint peeled away, so did the memories these walls held, replacing them with a new kind of life. One where it's not so much about living as it is about surviving.

All these walls see now is a desperation born out of generations of humans depleting the planet as they watched the temperatures soar and oceans swallow up the land. And Winter is just as desperate as anyone else. Named after a season that no longer exists, in a time long forgotten, she can't imagine a future that stretches beyond the very minute she's breathing in now.

"You know you'll wear out that view if you stare at it too long."

Winter spins around to see her twin brother, Gray, smirking at her. Tall and broad, with a smile made for breaking hearts, this guy is everything she's not. If Gray were the sun, Winter would be the moon. If he were the rain, she'd be the storm. Her brother is no survivor. He's one of the few people out here who knows how to live. And he does it with a twinkle in his eye and a spark in his heart. The shining light that contrasts all her dark shades.

The better half of herself.

"I saw a bird earlier," she says.

"Was it a raven?" Gray pushes a lock of black hair from his dark eyes. "Or maybe a pterodactyl? I hear dinosaurs are due to make a comeback."

Winter swats away a mosquito. She understands as much about dinosaurs as she does people. Insects, on the other hand, she knows only too well.

"Did you leave a window open?" she asks as the mosquito returns to land on her arm. She slaps it hard, killing the bug and leaving a red smear on her skin.

Gray shakes his head as he joins her at the window. "What did that poor little guy ever do to you?"

"Try to bite me and give me a fatal disease." Winter grimaces. She's not even being dramatic. People die from mosquito bites out here all the time. Almost as many as those who perish underneath falling buildings.

"Oh, watch out. There's another one." Gray waves his hand, trying to shoo it away.

"Go bite him instead," she tells the insect. "He's the one who let you in."

"Everyone knows you're sweeter than me." Gray drapes an arm around her as they look out at the nothingness stretching before them.

What Gray said is in no way true, but Winter doesn't bother to correct him. He's not only sweeter than her, he's smarter. And stronger. And pretty much every other good quality she can think of.

"Did you hear that?" Winter asks when the walls groan again. Known as Polaris, this building is the last one standing in Fairbanks in its complete form. Which means it's only a matter of time before it falls.

"It's nothing," he says. "Polaris is just talking to us."

"And what's it saying?" she asks.

Gray tilts his head as if he's listening, nodding as he rubs at his chin. "It said that it's big and strong and we're going to live safely here for the rest of our days."

Winter sighs, wishing she could believe him. "And how many days might that be?"

"Hey, don't worry so much," he says, being serious once more. "Every building groans."

"Yeah, right before they collapse." Winter doesn't have to point out the fallen slabs of concrete and twisted steel beams that surround them. She knows he sees the devastation. It's his eternally optimistic spirit that remains blind. He really should've been called Gold, not Gray.

"Where will we live?" she asks him. "When—"

"Right here." He tugs playfully at her long dark braid. "This is our home. I just told you we're safe."

"I mean it, Gray." She shrugs him away. "We need to start thinking about it. Nobody else here is. Polaris will fall in the next storm. That's what it's telling us."

"We've been doing repairs every time a crack appears," Gray

reassures her. "We've made sure it's strong. It's not going to fall. We're fine!"

"But what if it does?" She shakes her head at his naivety.

"Then we'll live in the rubble." Gray pokes out his tongue, refusing to take her seriously. "We'll scurry like rats, eat cockroaches for dinner and catch rainwater in our hands. We'll find a way. We always have."

"If we don't get out soon, we'll be the rubble." Winter crosses her arms, the image of her future just as blurred and looming as it's always been. If only Gray would take off his rainbow goggles and talk to her about it, they could figure out their next move.

"Trakk said he saw two huge rats earlier." Gray changes the subject. "Want to go see if we can find them? I have a feeling it's our lucky day."

Winter lets out a long sigh. "You think every day is our lucky day."

"Then one day I have to be right, don't I?" He laughs. "No matter how bad things are, there's always one day that turns out to be the best of your life. Maybe it's today."

"That's kind of depressing." Winter shakes her head, refusing to catch his smile. "Please let this not be as good as it gets."

"It's not that bad, is it?" Gray takes a step back, and guilt punches its way into Winter's gut. She shouldn't dampen his spirits like this when all he ever does is try to build her up.

"Let's go catch a rat." Winter throws her brother a smile as she pushes away from the window. "Maybe we really will be lucky and this time we'll catch two."

"Who knows, maybe we'll catch three!" Gray is already heading to the door, pleased to think he's managed to cheer her up.

Passing the kitchen table, Winter scoops up her netting and winds it around her head, watching as Gray does the same. If gravity doesn't pull Polaris down, the weight of all the insects inside it will. And that's nothing compared to what's outside.

There's nobody to tell that they're leaving. Their father is dead, as is their older sister. And their mother is asleep. She's always asleep. She says she's tired, but Winter knows it's because she has nothing to wake up for. She might not find it so easy when they have to flee this building and make new beds out of concrete. Or worse still, dirt. Because it's becoming more and more obvious to Winter that's where they'll inevitably end up.

The Outlands.

A place run by savages who think power is won by strength instead of honor. A place that Winter knows she'll have to face one day in that future she can't imagine.

Winter and Gray slip out of the apartment they've called home their whole lives and head down the dark corridor. It's even hotter out here, the lingering stale smell of decay a permanent reminder that Polaris's better days have been left behind. Most of the other apartments are nothing more than empty shells. Others are filled with the last people who'll breathe the air inside them.

Winter knows that on the rare occasions the Outlanders spare a thought for the People of Fairbanks, they think of them as weak. Maybe they are. Or maybe they're just too busy trying to hold onto what they have here to worry about proving their strength to everyone else.

They lighten their steps as they pass Brik's apartment, not wanting any trouble. Fairbanks doesn't have an official leader, but if they did, Brik would be it. It's a position he earned from being taller, meaner and more tattooed than anyone else. He's not weak. But then again, nobody from the Outlands has ever met him to find that out.

Thankfully, all remains quiet on the other side of Brik's door and they manage to creep past.

Reaching the stairwell, they begin the pitch-black descent. Ninety-six stairs. Eight landings. Anti-clockwise to go down, and clockwise to go up. Winter knows these stairs as well as she knows each line and curve of her brother's eternally smiling face.

"Took your time," says Trakk, who's waiting for them in the bright sunshine as they step outside. Lanky and dirty, and covered in red spots, Trakk doesn't wear netting, saying the insects don't bother him. He'd rather put up with the inconvenience of being a human pin-cushion than the discomfort of a net.

Gray punches his friend playfully on the arm. "I didn't realize you were going to wait."

Trakk nods at Gray then quickly loses interest, his eyes finding their way to Winter, instead.

"Hey, Winter." Trakk winks at her. "You look nice today."

She holds up a hand. "Not going to happen, Trakk."

"I only said hello," he sulks, swatting away a mosquito.

She resists the urge to grin, preferring to save her smiles for when they count. Trakk's not a bad guy, he's just not her guy, so she doesn't see the point in giving him hope.

"You really should wear a net," she tells him. "You'll catch a disease and die from one of those bites one day."

"As opposed to dying from what?" Trakk rolls his eyes. "Falling buildings? Lack of clean drinking water? Starvation? I'm good, thanks."

"You're about as cheerful as Winter is today." Gray's dark eyes dart between his friend and his twin.

"We prefer to leave the sunshine to you." Trakk grins. "You do it so much better. I swear sometimes I think it shines out of your—"

"Are we ready to go?" Winter asks, keen to get moving and skip all this macho banter.

Needing no further encouragement, Trakk lets out a loud whistle, the same one he insists on using whenever he's about to run, saying it will come in handy one day.

He takes off. Winter follows, pushing off the ground, filling her wasting muscles with energy she doesn't have. The promise of food is a powerful motivator and her feet find purchase on the rubble as she scrambles up a large slab of concrete, leaping off the end to land on a narrow beam. Gray is right behind her as they navigate the familiar yet ever-changing ruins of their city.

Ducking. Balancing. Weaving. Jumping. Barely stopping, rarely faltering, never doubting. They move with ease and confidence built from years of having to judge distances, weigh up risks and calculate rewards. All in fractions of seconds. You hesitate and you lose. And the prize for losing out here is death, if not from a cracked skull then from starvation. Food is rare and if you want to fill your belly then you have to be fast.

"Watch out!" Gray calls from behind as Winter flies off the edge of a beam.

She flicks up her gaze to see a pillar that's chosen exactly this moment to fall. Pulling her head back half an inch, she gasps as it sweeps past, missing her by the narrowest of margins. She lands on the ground on all fours, glancing back briefly to see Gray avoid being knocked sideways.

He gives her a wide grin and a thumbs up, but Winter doesn't have time to return the gesture if she wants to keep up.

"This way!" Trakk shouts. "I see one!"

They pick up their pace, the direction of their feet at the mercy of Trakk's sharp eyes. Once he's locked on a rat, he won't give up. He's almost as fast as the vermin itself and it occurs to Winter that perhaps that's exactly what they've become.

The Rats of Fairbanks.

Eating whatever scrap they can find. Breeding beyond their capacity to care for their young. Trying their best to keep a low profile from predators.

Trakk climbs a mesh wall and dives off a ledge. Winter

follows without hesitation, not even taking a moment to see what lies below to catch her fall.

A tree looms up at them. A rare specimen in Fairbanks and Trakk grips one of the branches to break his momentum, the force swinging him back as it bends to take his weight.

Winter reaches for a branch of her own, followed by Gray, and soon the three of them are clinging with white knuckles as leaves rain down, the tree's only protest at being disturbed.

"Look!" Trakk points and Winter sees a rat scurry into a gap between the roots of the tree. "I think it's a nest."

Gray is the first to drop to the ground and unwinds the netting from his face. Trakk and Winter are right behind him. Winter removes her own netting just as an explosion of brown fur erupts from between the roots, scrambling in all directions to get away. There are enough rats here to feed Fairbanks for a week. If only they can catch them…

Winter holds out her netting wide and in a well-practiced move she launches herself, taking two rats prisoner, cursing as one makes a slippery escape. Scooping up the net, she knots it to contain her bounty, then stretches the remainder wide and dives again. Over and over, she moves until there's no netting left and she has four good-sized rats, their desperate squeals unable to penetrate any feeling in her heart. There's no room for sympathy when survival is at stake. Lifting the netting above her head, she slams it on a rock and the squeals fall silent.

Pausing for the first time to catch her breath, she sees Gray has a similar squirming haul. Trakk has managed to knock out two rats of his own using a small rock, their bloodied bodies lying beside him. Never in all their years of hunting have they caught as many as this.

"Did I do good?" Trakk looks at Winter, pride shining from his eyes.

As much as she knows she shouldn't give him hope, this time

Winter can't help herself and she unleashes a smile so wide it makes her cheeks ache.

"You did better than good, Trakk."

Gray sets down his net and goes to her. "I told you it was our lucky day."

She can't deny he's right. For all the hard days that have come before this one, and all the impossible ones she knows lie ahead, right here, right now, she's having the best day of her life.

RAZE

*R*aze angles the knife he's holding so it scratches a little deeper into the small piece of wood in his hand. He's never seen any of the things he carves, only heard of them or seen images in the few books that come through their village before they're used as firewood, but that's what he likes about it.

There's no expectation of what it should look like. Nothing to get wrong.

Sitting on a rock at the edge of Fairbanks, some annoying bug whining past his ear, Raze keeps his gaze down. Lexis is only a few feet away, pacing, although this was supposed to be their last rest stop before they enter the death-trap of a city that is Fairbanks. She takes four steps one way before spinning and tracking back over the same compacted dirt.

There's an inner compass inside Raze, where Lexis is his true north. He knows where she is at all times. Without her, the always-there jittery feeling grows. It stretches, clamps around his chest and digs its claws in. It's the same monster that clamped around his throat when he was a child, stopping any words that wanted to come out. When it gets really bad, it hurts. It's hard to breathe. Impossible to think.

But being beside Lexis, always being ready to protect her, that keeps him focused. Calm.

It's what he's supposed to do.

Not far away sits Jacobi, his eyes hooded as he watches his comrades. In his hand is the brown colored bread that's made from whatever tree bark they can find. It's tough and bitter, but Jacobi looks like he's ready to leap and slice at anyone who considers even looking at his portion.

Which is exactly what he'd do.

On Raze's left is Arc, stretched out as his head rests against a rock. His eyes are closed as if he's asleep but Raze knows he's not. His breathing isn't slow enough, a little uneven. And his hand hasn't relaxed around the serrated blade that rests on his gut.

No one trusts anyone in Raze's village. The People of Cy are smart like that. They know what humans are capable of when it comes to ensuring their survival. They know because they embody it.

But Raze trusts Arc even less than any of the others, and that was before he killed Giff. It's no coincidence the man's death left an opening for Arc to be part of this team. That he's here now, pretending he's not a threat as they get ready to enter Fairbanks and relay the message.

The Tournaments have been announced. The winner, the lone survivor, will be the one true leader of the Outlands.

And when Lexis wins, she'll lead the Outlanders to victory over Askala.

It'll mean an end to the hunger, the permanent thirst, the lifespan that barely reaches beyond adulthood.

Not that Raze will get to see that. Or experience it.

The thought barely makes him blink. Raze likes certainty in his uncertain world. There's a calmness about it he rarely gets to experience. A surety. And sacrificing his life for his sister is a given.

Angling his knife again, Raze continues with his carving. He's created countless sculptures that fit into the palm of his hand, all of objects and animals that never got to see what a world would look like after humans destroyed it. There was the elephant with its fascinating, ribbed trunk. So many flimsy and fragile flowers. The strange little furry creatures—dogs—that humans had the luxury to keep as companions rather than food.

This one is a seashell. Small and curved, it will take time to hollow out. This was the first object Hatch taught him to carve, and it remains one of Raze's favorite forms.

As oceans rose, they acidified, dissolving and disintegrating anything with a calcified shell. Within a generation, millions of animals were left homeless—dead—as their protective layers were burnt into a rust-red layer at the bottom of the ocean. How odd to think the ocean used to be blue...

Lexis stops and Raze is instantly on his feet and by her side, the half-formed shell tucked deep in his pocket.

"Let's move," she says resolutely. "We tell the People of Fairbanks the news and we leave."

Raze nods, glad the break is over. The less time they spend in this crumbling city, the better.

Lexis leads the way, and Raze is about to shadow her side when Arc shoves past him.

"Get out of the way, mute."

Raze holds his ground, making his body as unmoving as a tree. He looks at Arc coolly, knowing he doesn't need words to communicate his message.

Arc's lip curls. "You're nothing without her, you know that?"

The good thing about being a mute is that people don't expect an answer. Not that there's anything Raze could say anyway. It's the truth. He accepted that a long time ago. But he can't help himself. He looks down, just below Arc's chest, pausing at his ribs. At the place his stake skimmed only yesterday, slicing Arc open just enough to let him know Raze is as deadly as any of them, mute or not.

Arc pushes his face a little closer. "If you weren't so necessary, I'd end you now."

Behind Arc, Lexis's hand clenches and unclenches around her spear, but Raze shoots her a flicker of a glance. They learned at a young age he's better off if she doesn't try to defend him.

Plus, the other truth is that Raze isn't expendable.

Not yet.

Arc rams his shoulder into Raze's chest as he shoves past. Raze absorbs the impact, his feet remaining firmly where they are. Beside Lexis is where he belongs.

Her lips thin, his twin turns away and starts clambering over the first of many hill-sized hurdles they're going to have to cross to get to the People of Fairbanks. Arc leaps forward so he can join her, hauling himself up so they're side by side. Raze is next, with Jacobi bringing up the rear. As much as Raze would rather not have had that, he's not willing to put any more distance between him and his sister. He'll just have to keep an eye on Jacobi as much as everything else. There's a coiled quietness about the man. He's like a sleeping serpent—ready to strike.

They reach the top of the first hill of twisted metal and crumbling concrete and stop, getting their bearings. Sweat is beading on Raze's forehead, wasting what little moisture his body has.

The only remaining building is about a mile away. "That's where they'll be," mutters Lexis.

The safest dwelling in the least safe place to live. Although it's only a matter of time before it joins every other building in this disintegrating city, it provides shelter from the weather and the incessant insects that do little more than suck blood and spread disease.

It also provides a vantage point to watch out for intruders.

Lexis must also realize this because she points out a path through the piles of dead buildings. "We want to keep the element of surprise."

"What are they going to do if they see us?" Arc asks in distaste. "Demand we leave?"

Jacobi chuckles at the thought of these weak remnants of society trying to fight those who have risen to the top of the food chain in the same way the giant leatherskin sharks rule the ocean. With strength and ruthlessness.

Lexis glares at the two men. "We're here to invite them to the Tournaments, nothing more."

Arc snorts, no doubt scoffing at the word 'invite.'

No one expects the People of Fairbanks to take part. They know just as well as anyone else they'd be nothing but fodder for all the other factions.

Arc curls his lip as he slaps at a bug on his neck. He peels the mosquito off his skin and pops it in his mouth. "Let's get the inviting"—he practically spits the word out—"over and done with."

For once, Raze agrees. The sooner they do this, the sooner the Tournaments can begin.

Without bothering to wait and see if the others agree, Arc takes a single step down the rubble hill. The chunk of brick his foot lands on slips away and Raze watches in quiet fascination as Arc tumbles down, a small part of him hoping this is the end of the sly bastard.

Except, then the world is falling out from beneath their feet, too.

Like that one brick was holding the entirety of the hill together, an avalanche of decay is released. Cement groans as the ground becomes shifting slabs and twisted metal, a tumbling mass that feels like it's trying to pull them down. Raze acts before thinking, not that he needed to. He knows what his role is.

As everyone else windmills their arms and tries to fight the inevitable, Raze leaps forward. He tucks himself into a ball before he hits the sliding rubble, but it doesn't stop the sharp points and rough edges from scraping and bruising his skin. He ignores the pain like he's been trained to, like they've all been trained to, as he bumps and rolls his way down. The moment he hits solid ground, Raze is upright. He squints through the dust and gravel coming at him like a wave, spotting the one he's looking for.

Lexis.

Two steps to the right and she's barreling at him, the only one who's managed to stay standing. Arc and Jacobi are little more than a tangle of arms and legs and grunts. Lexis stumbles, the momentum becoming too great, so Raze darts forward. She slams into him, stopping her downward trajectory that would've seen her sprawling. Possibly hurting herself.

The rumbling of the concrete landslide comes to an end, the billow of dust clogging Raze's lungs.

Lexis pushes back to look at him. There's a flicker in her gaze before she turns away. "Let's keep moving. This time, we stay low."

She turns to look at the others as she steps away, and Raze is glad the flickers are becoming little more than a twitch of eyelashes. Although Lexis stopped verbally objecting to his role in her future, there is still the thinning of the lips, the troubled frowns.

It seems she's almost accepted his destiny, just like he has.

Arc waves an arm like he knows what manners are. "I'll let the daughter of Evrest go first."

With straight shoulders, she passes him, and Raze is right behind her. He keeps his gaze lowered, although disgust is hot and heavy in his gut. Arc was only willing to go first when he thought that was safest.

They weave their way through the decomposing landscape. Raze's eyes glance left and right compulsively. It feels like the hulking, broken buildings could finish what they've started and fall on them any moment. He shifts closer to Lexis, coiled and ready to push her out of the way if necessary.

Suddenly, they all stop, nostrils flaring.

"I smell food," growls Arc. His feral eyes light up as his chin angles higher. "Meat."

Meat. A food they rarely hear about, let alone get to taste.

The scent slides across Raze's senses, making his mouth water.

Jacobi's gaze is no longer hooded. He breathes in deeply, as if just the smell of protein gives him strength. "The Ghosts of Fairbanks are eating better than us."

The People of Fairbanks were labeled Ghosts a long time ago. Ghosts because it's only a matter of time before they're all dead.

Lexis's eyes harden. "We give them the message, then we ensure the strong are the ones who eat."

GRAY

*G*ray's mouth waters as he flaps his hands trying to waft the delicious smell of roasted rat meat away from the direction of Polaris.

Seven rats.

The most they've ever caught before today was three and they'd thought that was an incredible haul. This is a sign that things are going to get better. Surely, even Winter can see that? The way she's smiling as Trakk turns the rats over the small fire is the happiest he's seen her in a long time. Maybe ever.

Gray's netting is lying on the ground next to Winter's beside the fire, ready to wrap up the rats to bring home. Neither of them was keen to put it back on given they're stained with rat blood. For once, being bitten by an insect seems the more attractive option. Unless it turns out to be the time it makes them sick. But that won't happen. It's their lucky day!

"We need a plan," says Trakk, looking up at Winter. "How many are we giving to Brik?"

Gray frowns at the way he becomes invisible to his best friend when his twin is around. It's not jealousy that has him concerned.

It's fear.

Winter is beautiful in a way Gray wishes she wasn't. It makes her too much of a target when the best strategy to survive out here is to blend in. The way men look at Winter tells Gray she's nowhere near close to succeeding at that. But, thankfully, she knows how to look after herself. Plus, she has Gray and Trakk. They won't let anything happen to her. Trakk would never hurt her, despite how he clearly feels about her.

He pulls a smile back up to his face. "First, we eat one each," he says. "That leaves four. We'll save one for Mom and one for your family, Trakk. That leaves two for Brik."

"Brik's not getting two!" Trakk shakes his head. "One is more than enough."

"How about we don't give him any?" Winter suggests.

"Do you think we could get away with it?" Gray's face lights up with the possibility as he scans the ruins, keeping guard. "Seven rats would be a feast!"

"Someone will have smelled this by now and told him," says Trakk. "Too risky. Let's stick to giving him one."

Winter sighs, accepting that Trakk's right. "True. If we come back empty handed, we're dead."

Trakk laughs at this. "What? You were planning for a long and healthy life? Face it, we're as good as dead out here, anyway."

This comment annoys Gray. "Why do you always have to be so doom and gloom? Maybe we'll live a whole lot longer than you think."

"Yeah." Trakk shrugs. "We might even make it to next week."

Gray refuses to join in the joke. "Well, I plan to live at least until my hair matches my name."

Winter giggles at this.

Gray sees a flash of movement behind one of the crumbling buildings and holds up his hand. Unsure if it's just another piece of the foundation slipping away or if they have a visitor, he cocks his head to listen.

Trakk and Winter fall silent.

They'd thought they were far enough away from Polaris to do what was needed before they got caught. The plan was to cook the rats, smother the fire and return home before anyone had a chance to investigate what smells so good.

"Who's there?" Gray calls out, cautiously. "I hear you."

Trakk lifts the rats from the fire by their charred tails, wrapping them in the netting while Winter kicks dirt over the flames. They need to be ready to run. Because if this turns out to be one of Brik's men, they won't get a single bite of the meat they'd worked so hard for.

A girl steps out from the shadows. She's about the same age as them and the first thing Gray notices is that she's not from Fairbanks. Nobody around here dresses in clothes stitched together from animal hide.

But it's more than her clothing that sets this girl apart. It's the glint in her eye. She has the look of a predator, making her seem part animal to all the undeniable parts of her that are human.

She takes another step. With blonde hair cropped short, a lean body lined with muscle and smears of dirt across her face, there's something about her that has Gray pausing.

Lifting a hand to the rapid beating in his chest, he waits.

"Do we run?" Trakk asks from behind him.

"Not yet." Gray can't take his eyes off the girl. There's no doubt she's a savage but she's also undeniably beautiful. Not in the same way as Winter with her bright eyes and soft edges, this girl has a hardness about her. Something that tells Gray he shouldn't trust her, yet he finds himself moving toward her all the same.

"Gray!" Winter hisses. "Stay back."

He hesitates, still certain the girl won't hurt him, but aware that Winter believes his optimism will be what gets him killed one day.

The girl holds up her palms to show she's unarmed but even Gray knows that doesn't mean much. Enemies can't be relied upon to show you all their weapons. He can't even be sure she's come alone.

She motions for him to meet her halfway.

"Don't trust her," says Winter, not bothering to keep her voice down. "It's a trick."

People from the Outlands rarely come to Fairbanks, too afraid that a building is going to fall on them, or they'll be eaten alive by insects. This isn't exactly a normal situation, which means Gray has no idea how to behave.

The girl waits for him to decide what he's going to do. But just like it's not in Winter's nature to trust her, it's not in his not to. He hates the idea of thinking the worst of someone before they've even had a chance to open their mouth to speak. There's no way this girl has come all this way to kill him. What would be the point?

Walking further away from Winter and Trakk, he goes to the girl until they're only a few feet apart.

They stand there for the longest moments, staring at each other. She's even more beautiful up close. She's also a whole lot more frightening.

"I have a message for you," she says.

"For me?" He smiles as he indicates himself, but she gives him an icy glare.

"For the People of Fairbanks," she clarifies. "There are going to be Tournaments to decide the true leader of the Outlands. You're invited to participate."

"Why would we want to do that?" He's genuinely puzzled. Of all the things he'd expected her to say, it wasn't that. "We don't want to rule the Outlands. We're happy here."

The girl lets her hands fall to her side and Gray notices she's clenching her fists.

"I need to speak to your leader." She leans to look over his shoulder.

"You won't find him out here." Gray has never known Brik to leave his apartment. Why would he when everything he needs is brought right to him?

"Then take me to him," she demands.

"I told you." Gray crosses his arms. "We don't want to rule the Outlands. We're happy as we are."

"But maybe I'm not," says Winter.

Gray spins around to see his sister standing beside him, her shoulders pulled back, her eyes flaring with defiance.

"Go back to Trakk." Gray tries to step in front of Winter, but she jostles him out of the way and retains her position, the movement seeming to set the Outlander on edge.

There are footsteps and a spray of rocks, and before Gray has time to react, a guy has appeared, standing protectively beside the girl with the golden hair. They're almost mirror images of each other, their only differences being the ones that make them either distinctly male or female.

"You've got to be kidding me," says Winter. "I thought we were the only twins around here."

The blond guy stares at Winter but doesn't say anything.

"How many more of you are there?" Gray asks, trying to see around the corner they appeared from.

"More than there are of you." The girl tilts up her chin like a dare.

"We have more men," Winter says, not missing a beat. "You just can't see them."

"That's a lie." The girl says this with such certainty that Gray suspects they were being watched well before they were approached.

"What are you really doing here?" A sense of unease slides down his spine.

"I already told you," she huffs. Patience clearly isn't this girl's strong suit. "We're inviting you to the Tournaments. Bring me to your leader so I may explain."

"Our leader doesn't take visitors." Gray knows they'd be fools to allow their enemy into Polaris. Those concrete walls are their best line of defense. They've gone to great effort over the years to turn it into the fortress it is today. "But we'll pass on the message."

"How do I enter your Tournaments?" Winter asks.

Gray sucks in a deep breath. He hadn't thought Winter was being serious. Surely, this doesn't sound interesting to her?

Winter's question seems to amuse the girl, and she gives them her first wry smile. "It's a fight to the death. Are you still so keen?"

To Winter's credit, she doesn't flinch. "And what's the prize?"

"I told you. The last person left standing gets to rule the Outlands. There'll be no more war between the factions. We'll work as one to take Askala and nobody ever has to go hungry again."

"We don't consider ourselves part of the Outlands," Gray tells her.

The girl's smile falls. "That doesn't mean you're not."

"We're not at war with anybody," he points out, trying a different tack.

"Aren't you?" The girl arches a brow at Gray, and he notices how blue her eyes are, a contrast to the familiar depths of his sister's dark irises.

The blond guy, who has so far remained silent, taps his sister on the hip and nods in Trakk's direction.

"Tell your friend we know he has seven rats," says the girl. "There's no point trying to hide any of them."

Gray takes a step back, reaching for Winter's hand. These

people haven't come to issue a peaceful invitation. Winter was right when she said this was a trick.

"You can send as many fighters as you like," the girl says. "The Tournaments will begin once everyone's arrived. We must talk to your leader."

"Why do you care so much if we enter?" Winter jams a hand on her hip and glares at the girl.

She shrugs. "We don't. But all the other factions have agreed to participate. Whoever wins will expect you to join their army. Or..."

"Or what?" asks Gray.

She smiles sweetly at him. "Or we'll kill you in your beds at night."

Gray swallows. Is she serious? The People of Fairbanks have never bothered any of the other factions before. Why can't they continue to just let them live out here in peace? He's not joining anyone's army. And nor is Winter. She might have indicated she's not happy out here, but he is! They have a roof over their heads, rainwater, the occasional meal to keep them going, and most importantly, they have each other. He'll just have to try harder to find a way to make sure Winter's happy, too.

"I think we'll have our meal now." The girl clicks her fingers and two more people emerge from the shadows. Both men. Both savages. Neither of them the sort Gray wishes to share his oxygen with, let alone his food.

"We can spare you one rat," says Winter.

The girl frowns as the three men beside her bristle.

"Each," Gray adds, thinking that if they give away four, at least they're still left with one each. He doesn't mind sharing his with his mom. Winter can still have hers to herself.

"Thanks anyway," the girl smiles. "But we'll have all seven."

"But..." Winter's jaw falls at the same time Gray's heart sinks. These people plan to take all their food, with no concern for what that might mean for them.

Trakk lets out a loud whistle, the first time it's ever been genuinely useful, and Gray glances at his sister.

They nod.

It's time to go.

Winter is the first to push off, as always, Gray preferring to stay behind her where he has at least a small hope of keeping her safe. They run to Trakk, who has the rats slung over his shoulder like a sling. He'll lead them on the best path through the city. Nobody knows this place better than he does.

But the savages are right behind them, faster than Gray would have expected for people who've traveled so far. He doesn't turn to check, knowing that a split second could be all they need to catch up.

Trakk moves through the ruins, his feet seeming to have suction cups on the soles as he navigates them over, under, through and between various obstacles. He's faster than he's ever been and Gray has to drive himself forward to keep up. Their only hope is that their pursuers are even more depleted of energy than they are.

Winter slips on a piece of tin, almost toppling. Gray is by her side in a moment, steadying her, then pushing her forward as they scamper down a large sheet of steel that was possibly once the side of a truck.

There's a pressure on Gray's back and he realizes that stumble may have cost them dearly. The golden girl has hold of his shirt. He pushes forward, hearing the fabric tear as he knew it would. Ancient cotton is far more delicate than the thick hides the girl wears, which is just another blessing to be thankful for right now.

Trakk runs straight at a solid wall, his feet expertly finding the smallest divots to use as footholds as he defies gravity and scampers up. Winter is next, and Gray draws in a breath as he slams himself against the concrete and hauls himself up, his muscles burning as they beg for some kind of relief from this sudden onslaught of activity.

Using a metal bar jutting out of the wall to pull themselves over the top, they land on the other side, grinning at each other. This is what they train for. This is what keeps them alive! They're unstoppable! Unbeatable! He knew this was their lucky day.

"I think we lost them," says Winter, breathing heavily.

Concrete dust rains down, and they know it can't be good news. A flash of blonde hair appears above the wall and Trakk doesn't even need to whistle to let them know they're moving again, this time sliding down a steep slope with their feet struggling to keep up with the speed of their bodies.

"The black hole!" Gray cries out when it looks like Trakk is going to take a left instead of charging straight ahead.

Trakk lifts a hand above his head to show he heard, and launches himself forward.

It's a risky move, but this is their only hope of outrunning these relentless savages. This is their home turf and there has to be some advantage to that.

Increasing their pace, they run straight at a gaping hole in what used to be a concrete floor. It's pitch dark below, giving the appearance of dropping into infinity. It takes guts to jump into it. Gray will never forget the first time he did it as a young boy.

They run straight at the black hole, flying off the edge and into the nothingness, their feet hitting the ground below that they knew would be there. All they need is for the savages to take a moment before they jump, and it will be enough to give them the lead they need.

Springing to their feet in the darkness, they run toward the stairwell ahead. Ten steps north. Twelves steps west. Sharp turn left and... up.

They take the stairs two at a time. One flight up and the light starts to filter in. Another flight up and they burst out into the sun. Now it's just a simple dash through the ruins and finally… finally…the hulk of Polaris is in sight. And it seems they've managed to lose their pursuers.

For now.

Trakk bursts through the entrance to the building, waiting for Winter and Gray to follow, then slams the door closed and bolts it.

They're all panting heavily now, each breath a trial of its own as they drag it in.

"Trakk," Gray says, struggling to speak. "Go hide them."

Trakk nods before heading up the stairs. They can't lose the rats now. Not after all that. They've fought too hard to keep them.

"Then tell Brik we have visitors!" Gray calls up the stairs. "We'll guard the door."

There's a thump on the other side of the metal surface, followed by another.

"Do you still think it's our lucky day?" Winter asks.

Gray nods in the dim light. "We got away, didn't we?"

Winter lets out a long sigh. "It seems we're about to find out."

LEXIS

*O*f course, the Ghosts of Fairbanks ran like the cowards they are. Lexis steps back, eyeing the decrepit apartment block. The fools thought they could escape, taking their rats with them, but the People of Cy are trained warriors. All they had to do was focus on their prey's frantic footsteps and panicked breathing to lead them through the dark parking lot.

She considers kicking the door again, but she knows there's no point. All she'll do is cause more damage to shoes that are hard to replace. Her annoyance only peaks when she feels the sting of an insect bite on her arm. Evrest's instructions were clear.

Invite the leaders of each faction to send their best warrior to the Tournaments.

Her father does not accept failure. What's more, Lexis refuses to be one.

And whoever that guy was, he's obviously not the leader. No one as trusting as him could be. The way he'd just walked up to her, unarmed, almost smiling. It's not something Lexis has ever seen in her lifetime. It had been…unsettling. And in her world, anything unknown needs to be considered dangerous.

Ignoring the itching that's already radiatir
bump on her arm, Lexis narrows her eyes
building. Tangled lengths of razor-wire decor
in haphazard lines, obviously to deter an
consider climbing.

And yet, the windows on the second floor are unp.
Fools. All they have to do is find a way to get to them.

Arc and Jacobi stand back, arms crossed and lips curled.
They won't be wasting any more precious energy as Lexis
figures out their next move. A few steps to the side and Raze's
hand clamps onto her arm. She turns to find her silent twin
scowling at the ground. She glances down, seeing what he has.

Nails protrude from the soil. Thin, sharp spikes waiting to
pierce a foot. Covered in mottled rust, they were almost camou-
flaged in this dirt-stained world. Lexis's gaze scans further,
seeing that a three-foot stretch of ground has been seeded with
a network of nail spikes. She pushes the one closest to her with
a toe, but the sharp spike barely moves.

"The bastards have embedded them into the ground, somehow," she mutters to Raze. If they manage to find a way to
climb, falling will be deadly. "The only place clear is the path to
the front door."

Raze's lips thin. The front door that's been bolted from the
inside.

He takes a few careful steps backward, no longer looking at
the building, but rather their dilapidated surroundings. He indicates with his chin to the left.

Lexis nods. "I was thinking the same thing. There will be
more than one way to get in."

"Then let's find it," growls Arc. "And finish this."

"And get us some meat," adds Jacobi.

Lexis's stomach cramps with familiar pains. Hunger. They've
spent the past two weeks trekking all over the Outlands to
extend the invite to all the factions. It's meant more energy

...ied...but on the same rations. And there are roasted rats ... e that crumbling concrete coffin. There's no way Lexis is ...aving without some of that precious protein in her stomach.

She lifts her hand, signaling for the others to follow her. There's a path that heads down the east side of the building. One that's obviously been used before. Lexis is conscious Raze is right behind her as she makes her way around. Her very own human shadow. It's comforting and disquieting all at the same time.

The narrow alley that greets them is bordered by the building and a pile of rubble about three men tall, but there are no more nail spikes. Raze brushes her hand, glancing at the small mountain then the windows lining the wall on their left.

He's pointing out the dangers he can see. If that pile shifts, they'd be crushed. And each of those windows is an eye of the enemy. Lexis nods curtly. "You focus left, I'll focus right."

Even as she says the words, Lexis knows Raze's sharp gaze will be everywhere at once. Making sure she's safe. That she returns unharmed.

Their father saw how close their twin bond was when they were quite young. He recognized it for the resource that it is. Together Lexis and Raze are twice as strong. There are two minds keeping them safe.

And one of them is twice as likely to win.

Lexis starts down the path, every sense on alert. There aren't any noises coming from the building, which only makes her more tense. The Ghosts inside are probably quaking in fear, waiting to see if Cy's people will find a way in.

But they may be foolish enough to try to attack. Lexis doesn't want anyone injured before they show the Ghosts what a mistake it is to even consider that.

The only sound is their shoes crunching over gravel, the only movement is theirs. The further they walk, the more trapped Lexis begins to feel. The building on the left has swallowed them in shadow, the rubble on the right looks as stable as the weather.

Raze comes up beside her, his face tight. Lexis is about to take another step when his arm shoots across her chest, stopping her.

"What?" she asks. "What have you seen?"

A quick scan of the windows reveals they're empty. An eddy of dust picks up over the rubble with the puff of a breeze, but there's nothing.

"It's clear. Come on, we need to keep going."

Raze shakes his head vehemently, glaring at the ground in front of them as he tries to communicate something. Except Lexis can't figure out what. The way ahead actually widens and clears a little, there are no nail spikes, no rolls of razor-wire.

Lexis tries to push his arm away, but Raze keeps it high, a barricade stopping her from passing. She frowns, for once, wishing her twin could just tell her.

Jacobi shoves past them. "We don't have time for your freak brother to try and spell out that he needs to take a piss."

He takes one step forward, then two.

And disappears.

The sound of splintering wood is quickly followed by a scream of pain. A cloud of ashen dust rises and promptly settles, revealing the pit that just opened like a giant mouth. With Jacobi at the bottom.

Another howl of pain rises and Lexis's eyes widen when she sees why. Jacobi is sprawled several feet below, one of the multiple spikes pointing to the sky protruding through his thigh.

Lexis lets out a slow breath. Raze saved her. Again.

Just like he's supposed to.

She glances around, finally seeing what he did. The path stopped at the point they're standing, never continuing beyond the pit.

Arc leans over the edge, peering down in disgust. "They've booby trapped the place."

Jacobi's frantic eyes find them, filled with pain as blood blooms over his leg. "Get me out of here!"

Simultaneously, all three of them step back, knowing they won't be doing that. Lexis turns away, indicating they need to go back to the front of the building.

There's no point trying to save Jacobi. He's as good as dead.

His howling voice follows them as they retreat. "Bastards."

Lexis's jaw clenches. Jacobi can say that, but he'd do exactly the same thing in their situation. He probably wouldn't even experience the twinge of remorse she can't suppress.

Jacobi's cries quickly fade, no doubt as the blood drains from his body. Lexis glances at Raze, seeing the blank look he's spent so long perfecting schooled across his face.

But she knows her twin. When Raze stopped talking, they found new ways to communicate. A look. The slightest hand motion. A twitch of the lips.

It means she sees past the silent barrier Raze has erected around himself. His chest is expanding and contracting in slow, measured movements. He's counting his breaths, which is what he does when he's turning inward.

Blocking out the painful world his sensitive soul was born into.

They reach the front of the apartment building again with its deadly garden of nails. Lexis's gaze does another quick sweep, but she can't see a way they could scale the walls without risk of serious injury.

She sighs. "We need to try the other side."

"There'll be more surprises," says Arc, a hint of anticipation in his voice.

Lexis looks away. She could never stomach Arc's love of violence. She's about to continue walking when a movement above catches her attention. There's someone at the window.

A man, not one of the three people they came across. Not the ones with the rats. The one with the sliver of a smile. This man is older, harder, dirtier, with tattoos that snake across his torso and cover his face.

Lexis cranes her neck back and throws her voice out. "We come with a message for your leader."

The window opens a fraction. "Yeah, that's me. Brik."

Expanding her chest as the words she was sent form in her mind, Lexis watches the man closely. This message is about to change the trajectory of all their lives.

"The time has come to end the injustice. We need a Commander to unite the Outlands. To take what Askala is keeping from us. The People of Cy invite your strongest to take part in the Tournaments. The winner shall be accepted as the sole leader of the Outlands."

"So you savages can kill everyone but your own?" Brik shouts. "No one is that crazy."

"All the other factions have agreed. The strongest will be crowned Commander. He or she will be given everything they need to mount an attack."

This is what drew the other factions. In part, because of the promise of power and authority. But mostly, for the promise of food and water. The Commander will never worry about starvation or dehydration.

"Well, they'll be heading to their deaths," shouts Brik. "Your people will make sure of it. Now, leave us alone."

Lexis clenches her hands. If these people want to be cowards, so be it. But it means they don't deserve the food they've holed themselves up with. "Throw us the rats and we'll leave without any trouble."

"Rats?" Brik asks in surprise. "There aren't no rats."

Arc sucks in a breath through his teeth. "Liar," he hisses.

Before Lexis can say anything else, Brik slams the window shut and is gone. Probably to hide the rats.

Or eat them.

Lexis glances at Raze. "One more try and we leave."

Raze nods curtly. Finding food always involves some risk in the Outlands, and several roasted rats is worth a little more energy.

Especially when the meat will only be wasted on the Ghosts of Fairbanks as they rot in their multi-story death-trap.

The trodden path follows around the other side of the apartment building. They approach the narrow alley with caution. Just like before, there's a crumbling wall on one side, and a hulking pile of rubble on the other.

This time, the path continues right to the end.

Every step is measured, every inch around them is studied, but Lexis is still surprised when they make it to the corner of the building unhurt.

Raze holds his hand up as he quickly glances around the corner to make sure it's safe. Lexi chafes at having to wait, that Raze is the one to take the risk, but Arc simply crosses his arms. He's more than willing for her twin to be the first to discover any more traps.

Raze turns back, nodding. Lexis takes a look herself, seeing that the path continues to the back of the building. About three quarters of the way down is a scraggly tree, barely alive after all the bark has been stripped from it. But just before it, is what they're looking for.

Another door.

"I'm gonna get me some rat," Arc mutters with relish and Lexis's stomach leaps at the prospect. Meat. Fat. Marrow. Just thinking the words gives her a burst of energy.

They creep down, staying close to the wall. The debris has crowded in closer here, as if it's trying to sneak up on the building and devour it. They walk single file, Lexis at the front, Raze behind her, Arc at the back.

Light footed, they silently make their way toward the door. Although it seems the Ghosts only had one trap, they're no longer making any assumptions. Lexis is only a foot away, her hand reaching out for the doorknob when she feels something press against her shin. The slightest of pressure, it still has her freezing.

She glances down, at first not seeing anything. A short shuffle of her foot, though, and the light glances off what she missed. A wire. Sheer and thin and barely there, stretches across the path, disappearing into the rubble.

"The debris!" shouts Arc.

Lexis spins around, looking past Raze to see what has Arc panicked. The rubble. It's moving.

Toward them.

As if it had been held back by that single thread, the mountain of crushed concrete, glass, and metal tumbles over itself, crunching and grinding. Raze grabs Lexis's arm, about to yank her back the way they came, when a beam slams into the ground, blocking their path. The rumbling grows louder. Closer.

They spin around and Lexis sees Arc's furious face. He starts to run the other way, not bothering to check whether Lexis and Raze are coming, too. Arc is just about to gain momentum when he jerks himself to a halt. A jagged hunk of concrete ploughs into the ground, right where he would've been if he hadn't stopped.

Her breathing harsh and choppy, Lexis realizes they're being enclosed. Trapped. Dust rises ahead of the wave as the blocks of concrete tumble over each other. Before Lexis has a chance to decide which direction is going to be easiest to navigate, Raze has engulfed her. He wraps his arms around her and pushes her against the wall beside the door. In a blink, her sight is eclipsed by her twin, all she can do is hear the approaching destructive tide, taste the ash-flavored dust.

Lexis freezes. This is what's supposed to happen. If she's in danger, Raze protects her.

No matter what.

Yet, nothing has ever felt more wrong.

Before she can decide what to do next, the avalanche stops. The sound dies. The only thing that touches her are the particles of pale dirt wafting in the air.

Raze holds her for a few more seconds, making sure it's safe. He finally releases her when she starts to push. Lexis glances past him. The shifting debris lost momentum. About two feet short of the people it was supposed to crush.

Arc unfolds from the ball he'd tucked himself into beside them. As the dust returns to the ground, they look around. The debris is now piled higher, closer, meaning getting out is going to be a treacherous climb, but they're alive.

Arc shakes his fist at the building. "Your traps are just as much a failure as you are!"

A quick scan shows the door is still relatively unobstructed, meaning they could still get in.

And eat.

Lexis reaches it, not surprised to find the door locked. She rattles the handle for good measure, noticing that a sprinkle of dust rains down on her from the doorjamb. The three of them wait, breath held, but there are no sounds of footsteps or shouts from the other side. The Ghosts aren't coming.

The sound that does reach Lexis, though, has her freezing.

Something's moving again. All Lexis gets is the briefest flash before Raze has engulfed her once more.

But she saw it. Massive and jagged, a boulder has toppled and is coming straight at them. Fast.

There's no time to run. Which is why Raze has her pressed against the door, his body a shield around hers. The only thing between her and the boulder.

No. Not this time.

Lexis spins around in the tight circle of Raze's arm, grabs the doorknob and starts shoving. The door doesn't budge, but she didn't expect it to. It would be bolted just like the first one.

But it's the doorjamb around it that's as decayed as the rest of the building. That she's hoping won't hold.

"Help me push," she shouts desperately.

Raze hesitates. To do that, he'd have to let her go. He'd have to stop protecting her and risk trying to save them both.

"Now!"

Lexis shoves hard just as Raze slams his shoulder in. The door collapses in and they stumble through after it. Raze's arm shoots out, grabbing Arc and yanking him into the building, as well.

A split-second later, the boulder thumps into the side of the building, making it shudder. There's a low moan from the walls around them...then nothing. A shard of light spears through the half-blocked doorway, dust coiling through it like smoke.

Arc glares at Raze. "I was just about to jump through on me own. I ain't owing no freak."

Raze turns his back on him, dismissing the statement. Lexis doubts he wants any ties to Arc, no matter what.

Now that the shock has worn off, Lexis glances around the stairwell they're standing in, anger burning away the fear. The razor-wire and nails, the pit, the bastards were funneling them here. So they could pulverize them.

Although, now the fools have a great big boulder resting against their building. She doubts they planned for that to happen.

They must decide whether the Ghosts need to be taught a lesson, or whether they should just leave. The half-dead people inside were never meant to come to the Tournaments, anyway. Extending the invitation to them was purely to demonstrate that the Tournaments are fair. That every faction was given a chance to enter.

Her gaze settles on Raze and she knows what he's thinking. She nods once, every muscle locked into place. "We're getting those rats."

Suddenly, the deadly, grinding sound of another avalanche is rumbling across Lexis's ears. She turns to the pile of rubble beyond the door, only to find it's not shifting.

But the sound continues, ominous and lingering, like a giant, heaving groan.

"Run!" shouts Lexis to Raze and Arc. "Get out of here!"

It's not the pile of rubble that's moving.

It's the building.

WINTER

*I*t's happening. The thing Winter has dreaded all her life.

Polaris is falling.

Even Gray and his optimistic spirit won't be able to deny it this time. The groaning sound is beyond anything they've heard before. Crumbs of ancient plaster are raining down, turning their hair white just like the savages who caused this chaos.

"We have to get out of here!" Winter cries to Gray from their position at the door.

"We need to get Mom." Gray turns and heads up the stairs in the exact opposite direction they need to move. "Come on!"

"Gray! No! We'll all die." She hates the thought but can't deny it's how she feels—that it's not worth sacrificing their lives trying to save someone who gave up on living a long time ago.

"We can get her! It's okay!" Gray disappears into the darkness, leaving Winter with a decision. Does she follow the path her feet want to take and head out of this death trap to safety? Or does she follow her twin? They came into this world together. Perhaps it's only right they also leave it the same way and become the Ghosts they know the other factions believe them to be.

The only problem is that she doesn't want to die. She wants to live to grow the gray hair her brother jokes about. She wants to defy Trakk's prediction that they need to live for the moment as they're unlikely to be given too many more.

She's stronger than that. Better. She has stuff to do...

People are barreling down the staircase, bumping into Winter in their haste to get out. All she has to do is allow herself to be swept up in their urgency and carried out to safety. Nobody has to know it wasn't her own choice.

So, why can't she do that?

"Damn you, Gray!" she shouts as she pushes past the people to get up the stairs. "I swear if I die in this building, I'm going to kill you!"

"That makes no sense," says a familiar voice in the darkness.

"Trakk!" gasps Winter. "Gray's gone to get Mom."

"Hurry then." Trakk slips his hand into hers and pulls her further up the stairs.

She grips him tightly, accepting the comfort his touch provides, not caring in the least what message it sends him. At this point, she can only hope they live long enough for him to even have time to consider taking it the wrong way.

The stairs vibrate under Winter's feet as they leave the stairwell and run down the hallway. Brik's door is wide open, something Winter's never seen before. It seems like their leader has finally decided to leave his precious apartment to make his escape.

Above the terrible rumbling comes the sound of screaming from other open doors. But they have no time to check on anyone else now. Winter's still not even fully committed to the task of reaching her mom. Trakk's a far better person than she is. He hadn't hesitated and it's not even his family member they're trying to save. As for her foolish twin…she'd always told him he was going to die of optimism one day.

A piece of the ceiling in the hallway breaks free and crashes to the floor. Winter and Trakk manage to press themselves against the wall just in time, breathing rapidly. If their reflexes weren't so finely tuned, that may have been it for them.

"We don't have time!" Winter calls. "It's no use!"

But Trakk hauls her down the rest of the hallway and into her apartment where Gray is trying to carry their mom out of her bedroom. She's clutching at the doorway, shrieking that she doesn't want to leave.

Gray is too strong for her and he pulls her away, throwing her over his shoulder as she thrashes and scratches, trying to break free.

"Leave her!" Winter shouts over the noise of Polaris's march toward death. Only this time her words aren't formed from her own selfish fear. Their mother has never wanted to be anywhere else than right here. It's not right to take her out if she's adamant she wants to stay. They have so little control over their lives. Surely, the one thing they're allowed to choose is their own death.

But Gray refuses to give up, holding tight to their mom, somehow still believing that he can save someone who doesn't want to be saved.

"Leave her," Winter repeats.

Gray looks at her, his dark eyes filling with uncertainty. The hesitation is only a split second, but it's enough for their mom to use all the strength she has to twist herself out of his grip and run back to her room.

Winter follows her, knowing they only have a minute at best. Probably not even that. The thunderous noise of the building's death throes aren't filling her with much confidence.

Her mom is sitting in the far corner of the room, her knees

pulled up to her bony chest. She's shaking and crying, clearly petrified.

Winter kneels beside her, knowing this is likely the last moment they'll spend together.

"Please, Mom," says Gray from her other side. "Come with us."

A wave of calm washes over their mother as she looks between each of her children.

"Go," she says. "Show them we're not Ghosts. Be better than me. Go!"

"No, Mom," begs Gray, lifting her hand to his cheek. "Come with us. We can do this. We can all get out."

"Umm, guys, we need leave," says Trakk from the doorway. "Kind of like, now."

"Go!" Their mother repeats. "Please. Do it for your sister. Live the life she couldn't. Honor her name."

With one last look at her mother, Winter tries to pry Gray away. But he's too strong, his face full of the same anguish she's feeling in her heart but doesn't know how to express.

"Help me, Trakk!" She looks to the doorway, surprised to see their friend has gone without them.

Then she hears him whistle.

The sharp sound seems to snap Gray to attention, his mind conditioned to know exactly what it means.

It's time to run.

Winter tugs on his arm again, finding that now she's able to pull him away.

Trakk whistles again. It's a sound that has both of them running to find their friend standing at the apartment door, his face filling with relief as he sees them.

But as they're about to step out into the hallway, Trakk stops, spreading his arms wide and holding them back as a groan fills their ears. Louder than any of the deafening sounds that came before it, this one means business.

They took too long. It's too late. They're all going to die.

Winter presses herself to Gray's side, determined not to be separated from him in the moments that are sure to follow. She gasps as everything that remains of Polaris on the other side of the hallway, falls away. It's hard to process what she's seeing. It's like the ground has opened up and is swallowing half the building as it slides to the ground with incredible speed. She covers her ears as a thousand thunderstorms crash in at once, followed by a massive cloud of billowing dust that threads its way into her lungs, choking her with the taste of bricks, concrete and ruined dreams.

Winter blinks, shocked. Somehow, their half of Polaris remains standing.

For now.

Trakk rakes his hands through his hair as the three of them step back a few paces, shielding their faces.

There's no hallway to run into now. No path to take them to the stairs. Who knows if the stairs are even still there.

"We're climbing down," Trakk shouts over the rumbling and crashing. "Now!"

He disappears into the dust and Winter squeezes Gray's hand, finding herself unable to be sorry she followed him up here. They may not have been able to save their mother, but there's no way she'd ever be able to leave Gray to save herself.

"You first," she urges. She doesn't trust him not to return to their mother. She has to see him go before she takes that first step.

"No." He puts a hand on her back, pushing gently. "I always go last."

"Not anymore." Her voice is firm. He has to know she means it. "If you want me to leave, then this time you go first."

Gray knows her well enough to realize when she's digging her heels in. He nods, lets his hand fall from her back, then steps forward into the dust.

Just before Winter's about to follow, she turns in the direction of the apartment. Sometimes children have to let go of their mothers, just like sometimes mothers have to let go of their children. It's the way life is out here. They don't have the luxury of seeing each other grow old. Difficult choices have to be made.

Pressing her fingers to her lips, then holding them out in her mom's direction, she forces herself to leave. Her mom's right. She needs to live for her sister, but most of all she needs to live for herself.

Winter's not a Ghost. She's a survivor. And it's time for this survivor to kick some butt!

Feeling the steep drop with her feet, she crouches and takes hold of the edge of the building, swinging herself down.

She finds a ledge that will take her weight, immediately scrabbling with her fingertips for her next move. She's scaled a thousand walls with Trakk and Gray. They've climbed and clambered and grappled and crawled their way through the ruins, knowing they were training but never certain what for.

With no idea how far down Gray and Trakk are, she keeps moving, her muscles screaming for mercy as she pushes herself well beyond her limits. Was it really only a few hours ago she'd thought this was the best day of her life? And she still hasn't had anything to eat. Lucky day, her ass!

Coughing as toxic dust infiltrates her lungs, Winter climbs down another level, swinging herself into the apartment below. There's screaming coming from inside, but Winter ignores it. All around her, people are suffering. Not in the slow agonizing way they've become accustomed to in their lives, this pain is more acute. It's like everything they've ever fought for has come down to this. Don't these people realize they're the fortunate ones to still be alive? They, too, could get themselves out if only they tried.

She climbs down to the apartment below, this time finding

an empty shell, which is far easier to deal with. Again, and again, she climbs until she's certain she has to be close to the ground, wishing she'd remembered to count the levels. It's impossible to see in all this dust. All she knows is that the building she's clinging to feels like it's moving beneath her. If she doesn't get to solid ground soon, then it's lights out.

"Winter!" Gray calls through the dust. "Are you there?"

"Gray!" she shouts back as she grapples for her next hand-hold. "I'm okay!"

But as she fails to find anything to cling onto, she wonders if she really is okay. There's literally nothing to grab hold of, except thin air.

"Say something, Gray!" She needs to hear his voice again so she can judge how far down he is.

"I can see your feet," he calls up to her. "Jump!"

Winter doesn't hesitate. She trusts Gray with every cell in her body. Letting go of the edge of the building, she falls, pulling her body into a crouch to help with her landing.

She hits the concrete below with a thud, the force reverberating up her legs and being absorbed by her hips. The dust begins to clear and she can make out shapes large and small. Shapes that are new to Fairbanks because now the ruined city has claimed a new casualty.

Polaris.

Gray is by her side in a moment, helping her to her feet. He tugs at her hand and she runs with him, aware of the heaving sound behind her.

The rest of the building is falling and if they don't get out of the way, they'll be buried underneath until their bones turn to dust.

They clamber over the mountain of chaos, careful to avoid the many jagged shards of glass as they squeeze through what used to be ceilings, floors, furniture, and walls. Everything is broken, lying damaged in haphazard piles. Winter tries not to look too closely at the arm sticking out from underneath a particularly large slab of rendered wall. The scale of this is hard to comprehend, despite the reality of it before them.

When they're a safe distance away, Gray pulls Winter to his chest and they turn to watch as the only home they've known collapses. It falls in, rather than out, sending out a new plume of destruction. Winter closes her eyes, unsure if she's trying to protect them from the dust or the horror of what's taking place.

There are other buildings around here that remain partly standing.

But not Polaris.

It had stood the test of time, outlasting every other structure in this doomed city. Generation after generation of humankind had managed to destroy the planet they lived on, yet somehow the building had survived.

Until now.

The horrible crashing noise continues, before falling silent almost as suddenly as it began. Winter dares to open her eyes a crack, dreading the sight she knows lies before her. The dust shields the worst of the horror, but as she looks through it, she sees light where there should be shadows.

Their home is gone, taking their mother with it.

"Do you think it hurt?" Gray asks. "Do you think she's gone now?"

"She's gone," says Winter. Nobody could have survived that.

"It's what she wanted, wasn't it?" He holds her just that little bit tighter. "We did the right thing…"

"Gray, if we insisted on taking her, we'd all be dead right now." She tries opening her eyes, but there's still too much dust, so she buries her face back in Gray's chest. "She wanted us to live. She couldn't handle the thought of losing another child."

"She was a good mother." Gray presses his face to the top of Winter's head, drawing comfort from her.

Winter murmurs in the absence of the answer she wants to

give. Their mom hadn't been a bad mother in that she'd never hurt them, but it's going too far to call her good. They'd had to raise themselves after their sister died, bringing her food and trying to coax her from her bed. If Winter's truthful, she and Gray were more the parents to their mom than the other way around. Children are far more resilient than people think.

"We need to find Trakk," she says when the building makes another terrible noise and something crashes to the ground. They know only too well that over time there will be more movement as the rubble settles into place. It won't be safe to go anywhere near it for a long while yet.

Or possibly ever.

They stumble over toward the sound of frantic voices and Winter loses her sense of direction. She's so tired now. And hungry. And thirsty. A flask of water would be worth a thousand rats.

About two dozen people are gathered on what was once the broken-up road in front of Polaris. It's a horrific sight. They're covered in dust and blood, some trying to help each other, and others struggling to help themselves. There's the sound of crying, whimpering and groaning to replace the booming sounds of the collapse.

"Where's Trakk?" Winter asks, scanning the faces.

"I haven't seen him since he climbed off the ledge." Gray's face pulls into a frown. "But I'm sure he's fine. He'll be here somewhere."

Winter nods, wishing she could believe him. She's not even sure he believes himself.

Trakk hadn't hesitated to help Winter when he'd found her on the stairs and heard that Gray had gone back up the building. There's no way he'd leave them behind. They have to do the same for him. They need to find him, no matter how long it takes.

They weave through the people, trying not to get drawn into

their terror. They know them, of course, but in the fractured society they live in, Winter can't say she's grown to care too much for any of them.

Except Trakk. The guy who's made it clear he loves her so much more than she loves him. But just because she feels differently, doesn't mean her feelings aren't strong. If Gray is her whole world, then Trakk is her compass. She'd be lost without him.

"He's over there!" Gray points to a half-standing exterior wall of Polaris. It's about the only thing left pointing toward the sky, with the building having fallen the other way. "I knew he'd be okay."

Winter breathes out a sigh to see Trakk is squatting beside a gaping hole in the ground, an injured man lying beside him. It's hard to tell who it is from this angle.

They waste no time in reaching him. That wall could topple at any moment and he's directly in its path.

"Get back from there!" Winter shouts. "It's not safe."

"Help me move this guy," says Trakk, trying to lift the injured man by his armpits.

It's only then that Winter recognizes him underneath the dirt caked to his face. It's one of the men who emerged from the shadows and tried to take their rats. An Outlander. The enemy. And it seems that Trakk has decided to save his life at the risk of his own.

"Did you pull him out of there?" Winter points at the hole in the ground. The hole that all the People of Fairbanks knew was there because they built it. It seems the trap worked, along with all the other traps they'd painstakingly set up over the years. Which would be brilliant, except for one thing.

They hadn't counted on the traps bringing down Polaris along with their enemy.

"He was half out already," says Trakk. "I just helped him with the last bit. We need to move him out of the way."

Before Winter can say this isn't such a great idea, Gray has picked up the man by his ankles and is helping Trakk carry him away. The man is badly injured with blood running from a large wound on his thigh. Trakk's shirt is tied around his leg like a tourniquet, but Winter doubts the effort's been worth it. The guy is barely conscious. There's no way he'll survive.

Winter follows them, picking her way across the rubble. When they're a safe distance, Gray and Trakk set the enemy down, leaning him against a piece of timber so that he's sitting up.

"You're going to be okay," Trakk tells him. "We're safe here."

The man murmurs something intelligible, so Trakk leans in closer.

"My name's Trakk," he says. "I'm going to help you. What's your name?"

The man tries to speak again.

"It's no use," says Winter. "You did all you can."

"He can still be saved," Gray insists. "We have to try."

Trakk holds his ear to the man's lips, asking him for his name once more. What does his name even matter when in a few moments he's going to be a corpse?

"Jacobi," the man manages to spit out. "My name's Jacobi and you really should have given us those rats."

There's a sharp movement and Winter steps forward, trying to pull Trakk away, only to find he's limp in her hands.

"Gray!" she cries, as her twin rushes to help.

Life blurs as she looks from the slumped over form of Jacobi and back to her friend with the handle of a small knife sticking out of his chest. She can't put these two images together. Or perhaps it's that she doesn't want to.

"He stabbed him," says Gray, his voice breaking with agony. "He stabbed him."

Winter falls to the ground, cradling Trakk's head in her lap as tears pour down her cheeks. This can't be happening.

"I love you, Trakk," she says, not caring how he might wish to interpret these words.

He stares up at her with unseeing eyes and she knows she spoke too late. So afraid was she of giving him false hope that she'd failed to let him know how much he meant to her. That's not a mistake she ever wants to make again.

"Is that bastard, Jacobi, dead yet?" she asks, unable to bear the thought of him breathing air while Trakk is not.

Gray picks up a large piece of concrete and goes to Jacobi. Winter looks away and winces as the sound of rock meets bone.

"He is now," says Gray, an unusual tone of dread to his voice. It seems even her brother with the beautiful soul has limits to how far his kindness will stretch.

Winter hadn't known Gray had that in him. She's not even certain she could have done that herself.

Maybe they're both stronger than they realize. Maybe the idea of a fight to the death isn't so crazy after all. It's not like they have anything left to lose.

But there are two problems with that. Firstly, there's no way Gray will agree to enter the Tournaments.

And secondly, even if she pulls off a miracle and manages to convince him, one of them will end up dead.

RAZE

*R*aze leans against the rusted old car, breathing heavily as Lexis and Arc do the same. A new mountain of rubble has been forged. A mountain of death and destruction, dust hanging in the air like a sickly fog. Pale particles flutter on eddies, looking to land and stick to anything they can find. Raze can feel the dust coating his skin, his hair, his lungs. It feels like it's choking him in the same way the fury and the fear are. He wants to cough, but he can't.

Not with the Ghosts of Fairbanks so close.

The desperate run from the collapsing building had been frantic and terrifying. The air was alive and roaring, the ground shifting everywhere he stepped. Raze's heart had felt like it couldn't go fast enough, and yet it still stalled and stuttered every time his sister slipped and righted herself.

He'd stayed behind Lexis every step of the dangerous run, the whole time looking ahead for the safest escape route, looking behind at the building that was cleaving in two. It was as if Mother Nature was tearing it apart with her bare hands.

But it wasn't the destruction, or roar that shook the very air, that scared him. Raze is used to living in an unsafe world, forever trying to find a moment free of fear. Up until then, nothing has stopped him from keeping his twin safe. But today, something did. Someone did.

Lexis.

She'd pushed him away, refusing to let him protect her.

Lexis has never done that before. They both understood their roles. Hers is to win the Tournaments.

His is to make sure she's the last person standing so she does exactly that.

Although her actions meant they were able to get into the building before the boulder crushed them, Raze's world is now founded on the same shifting rubble they were running over. His one foundation is gone. He needs to know that Lexis will be able to let him go when it's time.

Now that they're far enough away from the destruction to be safe, Raze grabs his twin by the upper arms, gripping tightly. For once, he wishes he could talk. Shout. Scream.

But his throat dried up years ago, the words refusing to come.

So he stares at Lexis. Hard. *You weren't supposed to do that.*

She glares at him defiantly, knowing exactly what has him so mad. "I saved both of us!"

Raze considers shaking her, the fury fast incinerating the fear. *That's not your role!*

But Lexis raises her chin, her gaze unflinching for long seconds. Then her eyes slide away and her shoulders drop with resignation.

She knows he's right.

Arc spits on the ground, ignoring them as he looks toward the rubble. "Serves them all right."

Lexis's hands clench. "We did what we came here to do. It's time to go home."

Raze couldn't agree more. It feels like far more than just the landscape has been disturbed.

Forever altered.

By silent agreement, they loop back. It means heading toward the rubble, but it's the shortest way out of Fairbanks. And the less time spent here, the better.

Establishing a loping rhythm, Raze follows Lexis as she leads the way, Arc behind him. They cover the ground they'd just practically flown over, but this time with more care. With every cautious step, the crumbling world around Raze feels even more fragile and fractured than it did when they first arrived. It's what keeps his pace steady, no matter how clogged his lungs feel or how dry his mouth becomes.

He knows the sooner he can get his sister out of here, the better. Back in their village, things will go back to the way they always were.

They have to.

They fall silent as they pass the place where they lost Jacobi, tucking themselves behind a wall as they listen for the voices they'd heard earlier when they'd passed through here.

Raze had been the one to hear them that time. He lives in silence, which means he's far more attuned to sound. Particularly those made by the greatest threat of all—other humans.

He'd grabbed Lexis's arm, and they'd ducked behind the wall.

Someone had spoken, and Raze had instantly recognized the voice, despite only hearing it once before.

It had been her.

"It's no use," the girl had said. "You did all you can."

It was the girl who defines beauty. She'd taken Raze's breath away when he first saw her. Thick, dark hair. Fine, smooth features. Eyes the color he always imagined the Earth was before it was depleted and decimated—a rich, sweet brown.

The other one—Trakk—had been sitting beside an injured man as he leaned against some timber. Raze's eyes had widened. The man spat out his name just as Raze recognized who it was beneath the dust and dirt.

Raze already knew what was about to happen, but for some reason, he'd still winced when he saw the flash of blade. Trakk's eyes had widened with shock before fluttering closed, never seeing his blood spill over the hand that impaled him.

What had he expected Jacobi to do? These were the people who built the trap that injured him in the first place. He was probably dragging himself out, bleeding and injured, just so he could exact revenge.

He still gave Trakk a quick, clean kill, allowing that small scrap of mercy. Or maybe that one jab was all Jacobi's battered body could manage.

Raze had been about to turn and leave when the beautiful girl realized what he already knew. Her friend was dead.

She'd collapsed beside him, taking his head in her lap. Raze had watched in shocked silence as she curled over, moisture leaking from her eyes, scraping two lines through the dust caked on her cheeks.

She was…crying.

Raze has heard of it. Of how useless and weak it is. He's sure he did it himself when he was a child.

But the beauty before him was the same age as him. Old enough to enter the Tournaments.

"I love you, Trakk," the girl had whispered brokenly.

These words had turned Raze to stone. Love. A concept more alien than crying. And yet this achingly beautiful vision had loved the bite-riddled boy she'd been holding. She was mourning him. And the emotion was so strong, she was completely oblivious to everything around her. Raze could probably have had a knife to her throat before she even knew he was there.

Except that thought vanished before it barely registered, railroaded by one simple question that continues to plague him even now.

Apart from the sister he shared a womb with, when Raze is

gone, will anyone mourn him?

The one called Gray had picked up a rock, his face twisted as he slammed it down on Jacobi's head.

The crunch was sickening, but unsurprising. Jacobi knew he was dead from the moment he fell in the pit. He just made sure he took someone with him before he left.

A hand drops on his shoulder and Raze recognizes his twin's touch. He glances over his shoulder to find Lexis. They need to be quiet as they leave.

Raze nods, angling his chin to say he'll follow her.

One last glance reveals the beautiful girl brushing a lock of hair from the boy's forehead, her fragile features molded by grief. She remains where she is, even though her own life continues to be in danger.

Raze has never seen anything more confusing. Poignant. Almost…touching. A part of him wants to go to her. A part of him he thought was dead.

Abruptly, he turns away.

This girl will soon be a Ghost of Fairbanks, literally. Their one last bastion of protection is gone, leaving them homeless and defenseless. What's more, many of them would've been crushed to death.

The few remaining people who tried to survive in this deadly city will likely be dead within weeks. Maybe days.

Seeing that Lexis is further away from him than she has been in a long time, Raze breaks into a jog to catch up. He reminds himself that beauty isn't able to survive in the Outlands. Just like love can't. Why tears are a waste of precious water.

He reminds himself that it's a good thing he won't ever see such unexpected loveliness again.

Raze is more than willing to do what needs to be done to ensure Lexis wins the Tournaments, in part because the life he'll leave behind is barely worth mourning.

He can't afford to find a reason to live.

GRAY

*G*ray peels Winter away from Trakk, trying not to notice how much more attached she is to their friend than she'd been to their mother. It seems some bonds are earned by loyalty rather than blood.

Although, Winter had been like this when their sister's body had been carried home, devoid of both her soul and the baby her belly had once held. Placed gently on Polaris's doorstep by the warrior who'd claimed to love her, Gray wonders now what became of him. Dead as well, most likely. No warrior in the Outlands lives long enough for wrinkles to crease the corners of their eyes.

"We can't leave the knife in him." Winter points a shaking hand at Trakk's chest.

Gray sighs, knowing what he has to do, and telling himself it can't be worse than finishing off that bastard Jacobi with the rock. He grips the handle of the knife and pulls it out of his friend. It slides with some difficulty, the only blessing being that it's causing Trakk no pain.

Wiping the knife on Jacobi's clothing, Gray puts it in the back of his pants. A weapon will be handy out here. Especially now.

"I can't believe he's gone," says Winter.

Gray nods. "The best person we knew."

"Apart from you." Winter leans on Gray for support.

"He was better than both of us." Gray puts his arm around his sister and pulls her close.

"Which is exactly why he died," she says. "We can't be so trusting. It's us against the world now."

"We still have them." Gray inclines his head toward the group of survivors huddled together on the rubble.

But Winter isn't having any of that. "We're not one of them. We never have been. There isn't really even a *them*. It's every person for themselves. It always has been."

Gray rubs at his chin while he thinks about this. She can't possibly be right. They're part of something here. Aren't they?

"We have a choice to make," says Winter. "You realize that, don't you?"

"What exactly are you talking about?" he asks, hoping she doesn't mean the Tournaments.

"We can't spend the rest of our lives hanging out with these losers." Winter steps away and sweeps out her hand. "Polaris falling was a sign that it's time for us to move on."

"Move on to where?" Gray rakes a hand through his hair, sending dust falling into his eyes. He lets go of Winter to shake his head.

"To the Tournaments," says Winter, her face solemn. She really isn't joking about this. "We have to go."

"You liked the sound of those Tournaments the moment you heard about them," he says, unable to accept that the idea holds any appeal.

She shakes her head. "Not the Tournaments. They sound awful. I like the sound of the prize."

"You want to lead a bunch of savages to attack a peaceful

island and take all their food?" His brows shoot up, leaving him blinking as more dust falls over his face.

Winter shrugs. "Why should they have food when we're all starving out here? Sounds pretty selfish to me. Do you know what they call us? Remnants! It's true. Trakk told me. We're the leftovers of the world in their eyes. Nothing more. That's even worse than being called a Ghost."

"And you think you can beat all those fighters and win?" He touches her on the arm, not caring what anyone calls them. They know they're better than that. "Come on, Winter! Be serious! They'd crush you. You wouldn't stand a chance."

"We might be able to win if we worked as a team." She shakes off his hand and pouts. "We're fast, Gray. We know how to move. We can judge distances better than anyone. We're strong, too. We outran those rat-stealing bastards earlier on. We can do it again."

He takes a step back. She's serious. She's actually serious. "Winter! We don't know who we'd be fighting! Maybe they sent their weakest out here with that message? Just because we know how to run doesn't mean we know how to fight."

"I want to do it," she says. "I think we should."

"Did you even listen to what that girl said?" he asks. "It's a fight to the death. Only *one* survivor. If we both enter, the best-case scenario means that only one of us ends up dead."

"Not very optimistic of you, Gray." Winter rolls her eyes.

"Optimistic? That was me being optimistic!" Gray kicks at the ground. "Because if you want the most likely scenario, it means that both of us end up dead. Is that what you want?"

Winter crosses her arms, the only sign he's made her uncomfortable. His hands explode outward. He doesn't remember a time he's been mad with his twin, but right now qualifies just fine. It's impossible to keep the glass half full when your sister keeps tipping it over your head.

"So, you're okay with that part of it?" he asks. "You do realize that dead is forever, don't you?"

Moisture streaks down the tracks her earlier tears left running down her face. She shakes her head as she places a hand on each of Gray's arms.

"I'm not okay with any of this," she says. "I just don't think we have much choice."

"We always have a choice." Gray fights back tears of his own. "Those savages chose to leave their friend here. Trakk chose to help him. Every day we make choices and sometimes they lead to survival and other times they lead to death, but it's the choice itself that counts. Don't tempt fate, Winter. Don't choose death when we still have a chance of life out here. We can be happy here. I know we can."

Winter has become distracted and Gray waves his hand trying to see if she was listening.

"Look," she whispers, pointing to a bundle of cloth poking out between the rubble. "It's our netting."

Gray's eyes widen. Is it possible Trakk carried the rats out here with him, then hid them while he tried to help the savage? If so, he may have just saved their lives. Some meat is exactly what they need right now to start their new lives.

They hurry over to the netting, but just as they squat down there's the sound of loud coughing behind them. Gray spins around to see Brik standing there with two of his loyal men beside him. All three are covered in dust but seem to have escaped without injury.

"What's going on here?" Brik asks, taking in Trakk and Jacobi's bodies.

"Trakk tried to save him," says Winter, standing. "But he stabbed Trakk. Then...then a rock fell on his head."

Gray swallows. Perhaps this isn't so much of a lie. The rock had fallen out of Gray's hands. He stands beside Winter, hoping

Brik hadn't noticed what they'd been looking at when they approached.

Brik nods, crossing his arms over his tattooed chest. "Didn't think either of you had the killer instinct. I would've killed that asshole myself if I had the chance."

Winter opens her mouth to speak but Gray puts a hand on her back to silence her. It's better for your enemy to underestimate you. Then you can take them by surprise. This thought has Gray's mind reeling. Is Brik the enemy? They're supposed to be on the same team.

"Where's the knife?" Brik asks, pointing at the wound in Trakk's chest.

Gray purses his lips as the hard edge of the blade digs into his back. They might be able to get away with hiding the rats, but the knife will be more difficult.

He pulls it from his waistband and holds it out, contemplating if he has the strength and courage to use it. But what would that achieve anyway? Brik's men would probably snatch it away and then both he and Winter would be killed.

Brik takes the knife. "Excellent. I could use one of these."

Gray grimaces in what he hopes might pass as a smile, reminding himself that it's all okay. They still have the rats and that's what counts. And they have each other. The knife was just a bonus. They can survive without it.

Brik tucks the knife in his own waistband and turns to leave.

Hope soars in Gray's gut as saliva floods his mouth. Soon, thanks to Trakk, he and Winter can eat. Then they can contemplate their next move.

"Oh," says Brik, turning back with a wolfish smile. "Just one more thing."

Gray hears Winter sigh beside him, and he clings to the possibility that Brik isn't playing the game he fears he is.

"You know anything about these rats those assholes were

talking about earlier?" Brik asks. "They seem to think one of us made quite the haul this morning."

Winter and Gray both shake their heads, possibly a little too quickly to be convincing. Handing him the knife was one thing, but handing him the only meal they're likely to get all week is a whole new level of not-going-to-happen.

"No idea who they were talking about," says Gray, trying to sound casual. "But I could eat about a dozen rats right now."

Brik looks at his men and widens his smile. He's enjoying this far too much not to know exactly what he's talking about. "Mason, can you take a look at what our friends here were so interested in when we arrived?"

Mason muscles ahead, but Gray and Winter hold their ground.

"Might need that knife, boss," says Mason, turning to Brik.

Gray sighs, realizing they've been beaten. Even their enemies knew that rats and revenge aren't worth dying for.

Stepping aside, Gray can feel the disappointment bouncing off his twin.

Mason crouches down and pulls the netting from the crevice, handing the parcel to Brik.

"Well, well, well," Brik says, holding the netting to his nose and inhaling deeply. "I smell dinner."

"You can't take them all," says Winter, making a grab for the rats as Brik pulls them away.

Fear surges up Gray's spine as he tries to hold her back. They've lost the rats but they still have each other. They can find some more rats later. That nest proved there's more out there. Winter has to accept their loss or it's not going to end well.

Brik reaches out a filthy hand and trails a finger down the streak on Winter's face. Gray knows it's only a matter of time before fresh tears forge a new path.

"I'll let you have one." Brik draws his hand from her face to her waist and pulls her close. She leans back, trying to keep her face away from his. "For the right price…"

"Just take them all." Gray yanks Winter back, her movements jolted like she's frozen in shock. "We don't need any."

Putting an arm around his twin he leads her away from the three men who are now howling with laughter, making noises that Gray never wants to hear in relation to his sister. This is why her beauty scares him. This. Exact. Reason. It's only a matter of time before Brik makes his request a demand.

"We need to leave here," Winter says through gritted teeth.

Gray nods, knowing she's right. But they won't be joining the Tournaments like his twin thinks.

"It's time I told you something," he says, knowing this day had been coming but still surprised that it's happening right now.

"What?" She blinks at him as she waits for him to speak.

He turns the words over in his mind, deciding in the end to come straight out with them. "We're not the only people in Fairbanks."

LEXIS

The wind feels like a battering ram as Lexis ploughs her way through the wall of dirt around her as the dust storm rages. They've got to be getting close to the village. To home. And the ration of water and food she's been thinking of for hours.

She and Raze will treat it like the celebration it is.

This mission was their last one. All the factions have been invited to the Tournaments now. Everyone wanted to take part.

Apart from the Ghosts of Fairbanks.

Tucking her head down, Lexis tells herself it's probably a good thing. She wouldn't have relished killing people so weak and vulnerable. The guy she saw, the one who looked like he might still have a heart despite a life in the Outlands, has a better chance of living longer in the remains of the city than in the Tournaments.

Lexis pulls the tattered material around her face a little tighter. The gritty dust still manages to get in her eyes, grind between her teeth, coat her entire insides, but without the cloth, she'd be blinded, suffocated by the relentless soil that never has a chance to settle. All she can do is keep moving forward.

She has no idea where Arc is after losing sight of him about an hour ago, but she doesn't really care. Survival is everyone's personal battle in the Outlands. Raze is walking in front of her, trying to act as a windbreak even though the gusts continually buffet in random directions. He was so angry that she tried to save him. Rightfully so.

She went against everything they've been taught.

She forgot her responsibilities.

The dust storm is so cloying that they're almost at the first hut of their village before Lexis realizes they're home. At least it means no welcoming committee this time. All Lexis wants is her allocated cup of water and three portions of bread.

There's no one around, but that's what she'd expect. Everyone would be holed up in their huts, away from the harsh, desiccating winds. They'd still know Lexis and the others are back, though. There's always someone on lookout duty, no matter how unsavory the task is during conditions like this. Usually, it falls on whoever has slighted Evrest.

Keeping close to the squat buildings in an attempt to shield herself from the worst of the storm, Lexis makes her way to their father's hut, Raze close by her side. She's disappointed to find Arc appear through the whorls of dust just behind them.

Lexis catches Raze's gaze. He's just as dust-battered as she is, his lashes and brows caked brown as opposed to the light blond that always sets them apart from the others in the village. He nods once, telling her he's ready. Even though his face is covered, she knows his impassive mask has already been put in place.

Because they're seeing their father.

Slipping through the door, Lexis lets her eyes adjust to the gloom. The first thing she sees is the statue of Cy standing proudly in the center. It gleams with the one material that no one has use for in the Outlands but was so valued by their ancestors—silver.

This is the man the new Commander will avenge. The wrong of his banishment, of turning their backs on the starving people of the Outlands, will be made right.

To the left, huddled and filthy, are her father's two wives, neither of them Lexis and Raze's mother. She died within a week of giving birth to twins. Already standing are his men. Each one a hardened savage who was chosen purely because they haven't broken during Evrest's trainings.

Lexis trusts them about as much as Arc.

If she wins the Tournaments, they will follow her as their new leader.

Unless they kill her before she can even get there and fight for the title for themselves.

Directly across from her, on the other side of the hut, sits her father. He pushes to his feet in slow, measured movements, his eyes flashing in the gloom. Evrest is a man who looks like he was fashioned from scars and sinew. From harshness and hardship. And was victorious.

He was the man who taught Lexis and Raze how to live with fear from a young age. Raze stopped talking. Lexis started fighting.

"Our warriors are back," he says quietly. Lexis has never heard her father shout. He always uses the same cool, detached tone. "What news do you bring?"

Lexis stands beside the door, not wanting to enter any more than she has to. Raze is closer than her shadow. Arc slinks in to join some of the men on the right.

She lifts her chin. "The People of Fairbanks were invited. They declined to take part in the Tournaments."

Her father huffs out a cold laugh. "Of course, they did. Cowards." He narrows his gaze as he glances around, dismissing Raze and registering only Arc is with them. "No Jacobi. I want a full report."

He wants to know whether his death needs avenging. Retribution.

"They had several traps set up to stop us from entering their building. Jacobi fell in one. We were almost crushed by another." Lexis raises her chin another notch. "We made it out alive. Their last remaining building did not."

Her father's nostrils flare as he sucks in a breath, icy flames flashing in his eyes. "They lost their home?"

Unprotected is one thing no one can be in the Outlands.

Lexis nods. "The Ghosts of Fairbanks are either dead or soon will be."

"You exceeded my expectations, Lexis."

All Lexis feels is relief. The report is complete, which means she and Raze can retreat to their tiny hut.

Arc clears his throat. "Except she tried to save Raze."

Every cell in Lexis's body stills. Arc betrayed her. Of course, he did.

"You did what?" Her father's voice is almost a whisper, but it still cracks through Lexis like a whip.

"A boulder was going to crush us," she says unflinchingly. Fear of the truth is still fear, an emotion she can't afford to live with. "I managed to push open a door."

"And you made sure the both of you survived," sneers Arc. "Rather than letting your freak brother do his job."

Lexis's teeth are clenched so tight they could grind the sand in her mouth to a paste. Her actions saved Raze, which meant Raze could save Arc.

But gratitude is about as useful as fear in the Outlands.

Lexis knows the slap is coming. She even braces herself for it. But the hand across her cheek still has her head snapping to the side. Pain blinds her for precious seconds, meaning she can't tell when the next one is coming.

"Do you forget who is depending on you?" her father asks evenly. *Crack.* Another slap slams across her other cheek.

"That everyone in this village is dead if you don't win?" Lexis's head is ringing and her father's face blurs. "That the Outlands need a leader who can ensure Askala's downfall, or all this has been for nothing?" His hand lifts even as his voice dips, except this time it's clenched as it winds up for another hit. "That every soul in the Outlands is doomed without this?"

Lexis tastes blood in her mouth, and she's almost glad for the moisture. She stands still, taking the beating. She closes her eyes, admitting that there's no preparing for this. The pain she can take. She's used to it.

But the shame of failure is almost too much to bear. All she can do is hope her legs don't give out under its weight, which would only add to the humiliation.

But the next strike never comes. Lexis opens her eyes to find Raze standing in front of her, holding their father's hand midair...right where he caught it, stopping it from connecting with his sister.

Alarm has the pain deadening. Raze is defying their father!

Evrest shakes off the shackle of his son's hand. He pushes his face close to Raze's, eyes alive with something Lexis can't name. "You'd protect her from *me*, mute?"

Raze's stony silence is his only response. Lexis holds her breath, having no idea what's going to happen next.

After a handful of seconds that last a lifetime, Evrest pulls back. "At least I know you'll do your job properly, mute."

With a disgusted glance in Lexis's direction, their father turns away. Lexis lets her breath out slowly and silently. That's the first time Evrest has stopped after a few strikes.

The speed that Evrest spins back around is the same speed that honed Lexis's reflexes over her lifetime. It's the sort of blurred motion that if you don't act before you think, you quickly learn you'll end up injured.

Although Lexis doubts Raze would've stopped this blow.

Evrest slams his fist into Raze's gut, face twisted with the effort he puts behind it.

Raze doubles over, a guttural groan wrenched from his lips. Lexis's heart clenches painfully. The fact Raze made a sound, as primal and wordless as it was, is proof of the pain their father just inflicted.

"Never touch me again, mute," Evrest spits out, the words dripping with threat.

Their father turns to the handful of people in the hut, extending his arms out wide, and Lexis knows he's smiling. "All the invitations have been extended."

There's silence, but that's what Evrest expected.

The air is thick with emotion. Anticipation. Excitement. The knowledge that destinies have been put into motion. That only one person will survive the Tournaments.

But also fear and dread and one more that Lexis didn't expect.

Denial.

She and Raze have prepared for this moment their whole lives. Trained for it. Shown no mercy and received even less.

And yet her actions in Fairbanks showed her she's not as ready as she thought.

When it comes to the moment she was born for, Lexis doesn't know whether she'll be able to do what it takes.

WINTER

*W*inter stands and waits, barely able to believe Gray has been holding out on her. She thought he told her everything.

"How can there be other people in Fairbanks?" she asks. "When did you see them?"

Gray shakes his head. "I didn't. Trakk did."

Winter looks toward Trakk's body, still slumped on the ground. It seems there was nothing about Fairbanks he didn't know. He was as much a part of this place as it was a part of him. Maybe it's fitting that he died here. Because he was never going to leave Fairbanks. Not ever. And now he never will.

"Why didn't you tell me?" She shakes her head, wondering what other secrets her brother has.

"Trakk wanted to tell you himself," he says. "I didn't want to steal his thunder."

Trying to swallow down the sick feeling that's building in the back of her throat, Winter grimaces. Maybe if she hadn't been so worried about Trakk getting the wrong idea, she could have spent more time with him. Given him the joy of telling her all the things he'd been saving up to share.

"Where do they live?" she asks. "Why haven't we seen them? How many people are there?"

Gray manages to find one of his smiles underneath all the dust and misery that's stuck to his face. "Which question do you want me to answer first?"

"All of them!" Winter throws out her hands. "Tell me everything you know. Don't leave anything out."

This is big news. Huge! There might be another way to live out here that doesn't involve joining a Tournament with a bunch of savages and being forced to kill or be killed. It totally changes the game.

"Trakk saw a woman with a scarred face when he was on one of his runs," says Gray. "This was years ago now, although he only told me about it very recently. He said it was like the entire half of the woman's face had melted away. She was wearing netting wrapped around her. It was billowing out from her waist like a skirt and she was searching in the rubble for something."

Winter is aware her jaw has fallen open as she listens, hanging on Gray's every word. She hasn't seen a woman like that around here. That doesn't sound like a face she'd forget.

"Trakk stayed hidden and watched her for a while," says Gray. "He wanted to see where she went."

"And where did she go?" Winter grabs at Gray's torn shirt. "Stop pausing. Tell me the story faster."

"She disappeared." Gray shrugs. "Trakk said it was like the rubble opened up and she became a part of it."

"So, she was alone?" Winter asks.

Gray shakes his head. "Trakk was sure he heard another voice when he first saw her. He thought there could be a whole community of them underneath this chaos somewhere."

Winter's breath catches in her throat at these words. "Somewhere? You mean you don't know where?"

"Trakk's been searching over the years, with no luck." Gray

glances toward their friend. "He started to wonder if he imagined the whole thing. That's why he told me. He hoped we might help him look. Only...we never got the chance."

"Oh, Gray." Winter takes two steps away then loops back. "Why didn't you ask him to describe where he was? To tell you where he's already looked?"

"I didn't expect this to happen." He hangs his head and Winter tries not to curse at his naivety. "I thought he could show us."

"You—"

Gray holds up his hand to silence her. "I know, Winter. My optimism is going to kill me one day. I get it. Either that or it'll be the thing that saves us."

"This city is huge." Winter goes to her brother, unable to help herself from wrapping her arms around his waist when really it's his neck she should be throttling. "Where would we even start?"

"He said there was a tree." Gray presses his cheek to the top of her head. "A large tree growing out of the rubble near where he saw the woman."

Winter nods. This is useful information but not useful enough. Trees have sprung up in the most unlikely places. There would be dozens, maybe even hundreds of them, if they searched widely enough.

Listening to the beat of her brother's heart, Winter waits for him to realize how hopeless this idea is. They'll never find these people. Nor do they know how dangerous they might be. Besides, there's no way to know that this woman hadn't wandered into Fairbanks completely alone and crawled into the rubble to die. They could spend their whole lives searching for something that doesn't exist.

Whereas the Tournaments are a sure thing...

"We should head north, then loop around to the east," Gray suggests.

Winter lifts her head from his chest and blinks up at him. "But the People of Cy live west? That's the wrong way."

The horrified look on Gray's face tells her she misunderstood. He hasn't realized what she has. He still thinks it's a good idea to leave here and chase after a woman who may no longer even be alive.

"We're not entering the Tournaments," he says. "No, Winter. It's madness. Let them fight it out amongst themselves. We can build a new life here."

"I want more than this, Gray." She winces as this truth escapes her lips. "I *need* more."

As much as she loves her twin, she can't spend her life with only him for company. She wants to see what's left of this decimated world. Dip her toes in the acidic ocean. Find out what made the girl with the hair of gold so fierce. Understand why the girl's handsome brother chooses not to talk. Maybe even fall in love... Not have children, though. That's taking it too far. There's no way she'd ever bring a child into a hell like this. The fact that her sister's baby never got to draw breath is proof enough of what kind of future a child has around here.

"I want more for you, too." Gray pushes away from her. "And I can give you more. We'll figure it out. Together."

"Do you really think we don't stand a chance?" she asks. "We've proven time and time again what we're capable of."

His brows shoot up. "Umm, do I need to remind you that Brik and his friends just walked up here, took our food, and we couldn't do a thing to stop them? And you think we have a chance against trained fighters? Brik barely left his apartment his whole life and we were no match for him."

"He had a knife..." She kicks at the ground, knowing he's backed her into a corner.

"We don't know what weapons they might have in the Tournaments," he says. "Why do you assume it's going to be a fair fight?"

Winter wants to scream at the top of her lungs. Punch at the concrete that surrounds her. Claw at her hair until she pulls it from her head.

There's literally no path they can take that will lead to anything other than their death.

They stay here and Brik will kill them.

They search for the scarred woman and they'll die of dehydration.

They head into the Outlands and they'll perish in no time.

They go to the Tournaments and they'll be slaughtered like rats.

"Gray." Her eyes fill with tears as she grabs at the front of his shirt. "I know it might not be a fair fight...but it's still a fight."

"What do you mean?" Tears of his own gather in the corner of his eyes as he does his best to understand what she's not even sure she understands herself.

"I want to go down fighting," she says. "If I'm forced to die, then I don't want it to be like Trakk. Or Mom. I want it to be with my fists in the air and blood on my hands. I know we don't stand much chance, Gray, but it's still a chance. And that feels like a whole lot more than what we have out here."

"I can't let you." Gray's voice is heavy with the strain. "I can't."

She shakes her head. "But it's not up to you. You don't have to come with me. That's your choice. I respect that. Can't you just respect my choice, too?"

"No." His face is like thunder. She barely recognizes her free-spirited brother underneath the anger he's directing at her. "We stick together, Winter. It's how it's always been."

Winter lets out a long, slow breath. She has no idea how to resolve this difference of opinion.

A massive clap of thunder has them spinning on their feet.

Thinking that more of the building has fallen, Winter steps instinctively away from the ruins. But when the sky opens up and rain pours down, she realizes it was actual thunder they'd heard.

She and Gray both tilt up their faces, smiling as heavy rain runs over their depleted bodies, washing away the dust and sending precious droplets into their mouths. Storms aren't unusual out here, but normally they'd be attuned enough to their environment to have had more warning than this.

Water pools on the rubble surrounding them and they rush to it, sticking out their tongues and catching mouthfuls of cool liquid as it runs away in rivulets. It's a relief beyond anything they could have asked for. A gift from a dying planet, sure to keep them alive at least for another day.

When their thirst has been sated, they lift their faces and grin at each other. And even though the decision about their future still looms in front of them, there's relief in having had a brief reprieve.

"See!" says Gray. "This is a sign! The universe is telling us to stay. This is our home."

Grief punches Winter in the chest. He read her smile all wrong. It's no wonder she rarely uses it. Look at the trouble it gets her into. Now Gray thinks she's happy to stay when all that changed was that now she has enough water in her system to make it to the Tournaments alive.

Gray sees her face, his own expression falling to match hers. What do you do when the one person you never want to be separated from chooses to walk another path?

The rain stops as quickly as it started, sending steam rising from the rubble.

"Gray," says Winter. "We need a way to decide."

"Rock, paper, scissors?" he huffs.

She knows he's not serious, but even if he were there's no way she'd leave her future in the hands of random chance. Just like the Tournaments, she wants to play a part in her fate.

"I'm going to give you a race," she says. "If I win, you're going to let me leave for the Tournaments without making it any more difficult for me."

"And if I win?" he asks.

"Then I won't go." She crosses her arms, banking on the fact that although Gray's stronger, she's faster. "I'll stay here and build a new life with you."

"You promise you won't go?" he asks. "I'm not going to wake up one morning to find you missing?"

She thinks about this, wondering if it's a promise she can keep. Gray may have kept a secret from her, but she can't bear the thought of lying to him. But if he beats her in this race, then it means she's not as fast as she thinks she is. Which also means he's right—she doesn't stand a chance to fight for her life.

Winter puts her hand over her heart. "I promise."

Gray shakes out his hands and stretches his legs. "Where are we racing?"

"To the black hole." She grins at him, pleased he's accepted her challenge. "First one to the stairs, wins."

Instead of nodding to show he understands or waiting for her to say it's time to start the race, Gray takes off. She knows he's teaching her a lesson. That not every race she runs in life will be fair—the Tournaments included.

She chases after her brother, hoping she has time to gain the ground she just lost.

The entire direction of her life depends on it.

It's time to fight.

RAZE

*R*aze's gut still aches as he steps out of their father's hut. It had only been a single punch, but Evrest wanted to make sure he felt it. His father's fist had been a boulder slamming into Raze's solar plexus—the soft spot right above the stomach—just like he taught them.

Raze focuses on his breathing, blocking out the pain and humiliation.

In. Out. One.

The sneers from the men and women in the hut, his own people, don't matter.

In. Out. Two.

Learning to live with pain has only made him stronger.

In. Out. Three.

Evrest reminded Lexis of what she must do and why. That's what matters.

Outside, the winds have started to ease, the particles of dust no longer feeling like needles against his skin. A red haze hangs in the evening gloom.

Lexis presses a hand to his arm. "Now, we can rest."

Raze nods. Water. Food. Sleep. The trifecta of bliss.

They've only taken a few steps when they both still. The murky air reveals what they didn't see when they arrived.

The village has been prepared for the Tournaments.

Beyond the closely built huts is the large clearing that's always been there. Their village is surrounded with nothing but barren wasteland. Except several yards away, a circle of stones is visible.

The Ring.

Like they're being drawn by invisible ropes, Raze and Lexis walk toward it. They stop at the edge, seeing that the rocks surround a large circle that has been dug out, the ground below a handful of feet down. It means every person will need to descend into the Ring and its inevitability, reminding Raze of a place that humans used to call Hell.

Lexis looks at him, just as silent as he is. This is where it will happen.

She moves closer to him, wrapping her arms around his waist. Raze pulls her in close, his heart aching far more than any other part of his body.

How does he tell her? How does he let her know it's okay?

Death is inevitable, and it happens sooner than anyone would like in the Outlands. But with the Tournaments, Raze can do it on his own terms. This death has honor. Purpose.

He'll die for Lexis. For the future of the starving people of the Outlands. They won't need to struggle, to fight, to kill for a piece of bread made from nothing but bark.

And it'll mean peace for Raze. Peace from hunger. Thirst. Disappointment. Fear. Pain. How does he tell Lexis there's a part of him that welcomes it?

He pulls back, staring at her intently. *You need to see this through.*

Lexis, as strong and ruthless as the land that molded them, swallows hard. Her eyes glisten, wrenching at Raze's gut.

But he doesn't back down or look away. *This was always how it was going to be.*

Her eyes flutter closed, shutting away the agony that was swimming in their blue depths. Her lip trembles and she clamps her teeth down on it.

Within a breath, Lexis opens her eyes again. The coldness is back. The knowledge she has to do this. "When the time comes, I'll make the right choice," she says resolutely.

Relief washes through Raze. Turning, he tucks Lexis under his arm. Now, he can actually sleep tonight.

As the sun continues to sink on the dirt-smeared horizon, they gaze at the Ring and the surrounds. Five lines have been gouged into the soil, radiating away from the circle, creating a space for each faction to camp around it. Each will become a petal around this flower of death.

They're as prepared as they can be for the coming together of more people than have ever gathered in the Outlands. The thought has Raze coiling and tightening. More people. More stares.

Plus, tensions will run high. Every faction will bring their own food and water, which will mean bartering. And stealing when a deal can't be reached. And fighting when accusations are slung.

And killing outside of the inevitable slaughter that will happen in the Ring.

Raze grits his teeth. All the more reason for the Tournaments. They're the only way to end the death and desperation.

Raze is about to turn away, his dry mouth and empty stomach screaming at him for relief, when he pauses. Shapes form on the hazy horizon, refusing to be dissolved by the wind. Lexis tenses beside him, slipping out from beneath his arm as she stares.

"They're already arriving," she says quietly.

The outline of about fifteen people forms, steadily gaining

substance as they continue to make their way to the village. Raze and Lexis stay still as they watch and wait.

It doesn't take long for the faction to become recognizable. The tattered robes of the People of the Never are unmistakable. Of course the nomads of the Outlands would be the first to arrive. It's not like they had a home to leave.

The closer they get, the more tense Lexis and Raze become. The Never people have always been dangerous looking. Their flowing clothes are little more than shreds of material sewn together, their faces are as caked and dry as the earth their bare feet are trudging over. It's widely known they live by stealing from every other faction.

Lexis slides her spear out of its halter on her back as they approach. Raze uses the time to study their enemy. Sixteen of them, mostly men, some women. None of them particularly young, although they all hold clubs of various sizes, each one a piece of driftwood they've collected in their wanderings.

They stop in front of Lexis and Raze, a man with a beard as matted as his hair stepping forward. "We've come to fight in the Tournaments." His lip curls. "And win."

"Then you'll be disappointed," Lexis replies coldly. "If you'd prefer to live, then you're best off leaving now."

The man's hand flexes around his club. "The Savages of Cy aren't the only ones who've been preparing for this."

Raze keeps his surprise hidden beneath his blank mask. It makes sense that the nomads with their endless wandering have heard of the need for a new Commander even before the invitation. Of the necessity of the Tournaments.

But, how many other factions have also been training?

With a hard glare, the Never people turn away. They settle on the slice of ground next to the village, no doubt so they can try to steal their food. With a quick glance at each other, Lexis and Raze turn away, heading to their hut. Inside, two small cups sit in the center, a stack of flatbread slices beside them. The water is warm and gritty, but Raze savors it as it slides down his throat. The bread is tough and fibrous, but he grins at Lexis as they chew on it.

His twin smiles back. "Eating is almost as much of a workout as training with Evrest," she jokes.

Except with less bruising.

The food and drink are over much quicker than Raze would've liked, but at least he'll be getting two out of the three comforts he was looking forward to. He sits down with his back leaning against the wall, facing the doorway. Lexis settles next to him, also preparing for the long night ahead.

There will be no rest tonight. Not when the remaining factions will continue to arrive.

The People of the Rust will probably be next, named because they live by the blood-colored ocean, their hair bleached by the acidic sea. The last to arrive will probably be the People of the Cragg, the ones who have the furthest to trek. On clear days, the mountains of the Outlands can be seen on the horizon, arid and desolate. The people who call them their home look like they were molded from the same stone as the jagged hills. And their hearts are just as cold.

And once the Cragg are here, then four out of the five factions will be present. The ones who will compete in the Tournaments. Every faction except the Ghosts of Fairbanks.

Raze lets his head rest back against the rough wall. That's the one piece of comfort he can wrap around himself on this night before the Tournaments.

He won't have to watch the beautiful girl being slaughtered.

GRAY

Gray's lungs are screaming. His legs are threatening to give out. But he can't give up. Not now. Not ever. If he lets Winter get to the black hole first, then she's as good as dead.

He's still in front, proving she's not as cut out for this as she thinks she is. She'll complain when he wins, saying he had a head start, but he doesn't care. She's fooling herself if she thinks there won't be any bending of the rules in the Tournaments.

With feet pounding the concrete as he runs across what was once a towering wall, Gray feels a sense of overwhelming sadness. This must be one of the only times in his life he's run without Trakk leading the way. But now's not the time to get emotional. If he doesn't push harder, it will be Winter he's mourning instead of Trakk. If Gray's still even alive to witness her death. So much is riding on this race.

As he approaches the ledge of the wall, he knows he'll have to choose which route to take.

Turn left and it's safer. A longer but steadier path with far less chance of stumbling, which would help him gain back any time he loses. Turning right is risky. That path will mean climbing the same wall they climbed earlier when they ran away from the savages. Which means landing on the other side and running down the slope that's resulted in more than a few sprained ankles between them over the years. It's a shorter route, but so much more chance of something going wrong.

The symbolism of all of this isn't lost on him, each path representing exactly what it is they're fighting for here. A risky but rewarding life versus a safer yet slower journey to the end. Which means he can be sure Winter will turn right, certain that he'll go left.

Reaching the ledge, aware of Winter close behind him, Gray glues his eyes to the gap between the pillars that will take him left, changing his mind at the last moment and dodging right.

He can do this! It was the route Trakk took them on this morning, which means it has to be right.

If he can make a perfect run, he'll shoot out at the bottom of the slope right in front of the black hole. He'll be unbeatable. And that's exactly what he needs.

He slams into the wall, wincing as his forearms take the brunt of the force and he scrambles for a handhold. Pulling himself up, he begins his climb, pausing for only a moment to see how far behind Winter is.

But he's shocked to see that she's not behind him at all, and his pause turns to hesitation as he processes the fact she decided to turn left. What is she up to? Winter never takes the safe road. The whole reason for this race is evidence enough of that. Is she letting him win? Has she changed her mind about the Tournaments and is trying to save face?

Shaking his head of these thoughts, Gray climbs higher. Whatever the case, he still needs to win.

He's almost at the top of the wall when the jagged piece of brick he's clinging to with his right hand breaks free, sending him wavering. He grips the wall with his left hand, hoping he doesn't lose one of his footholds as he tries to regain his balance. Falling to the bottom won't mean his death, but it will mean certain loss, which in this case is just as bad.

Just as he's about to topple, his fingertips find the metal bar that juts from the top of the wall and he manages to grab hold and steady himself. Using it to pull himself higher, he gets to the top, swings his leg over and hauls himself to the other side.

Not quite a perfect climb but it still should be perfect enough. Bracing himself for impact, he lets go of the wall and falls.

His knees buckle on landing as pain shoots up his legs, but his ankles seem to be intact. No sprains. He's in good shape, apart from the pounding of his heart and aching of every muscle in his worn-out body. Now just the final slope and he's there. And most importantly with no sign of Winter anywhere close. He's got this!

Gravity urges him down as he tries to balance the desire to go fast with the need to not tumble down. If his descent spirals out of control, he'll end up with worse than a sprain—he could break his neck.

Shuffling his feet, he leans back on the harsh angle of the slope, using his hands behind him like an upside-down cockroach. He moves at what feels like lightning speed, so close to the finish now that he can taste it. The black hole is right before him and the path that Winter would need to take is completely still. There's not even the hint of movement of her running down the final stretch. He must've made it here in record time.

When he nears the bottom of the slope, he rights himself and lurches forward, taking the final steps in giant leaps as he throws himself into the black hole, squeezing his eyes closed as he sails through the air.

It's a hard fall and he topples backward, landing on his butt. With no time to process the sharp pain, he immediately scurries to his feet. Launching himself in the direction of the stairwell, he holds out his hands in the darkness, ready to make contact with the solid surface of the finish line.

"Yes!" he screams as he surges ahead, only to land on something soft that pushes him back until he's left stumbling in the blackness.

"What took you so long?" Winter asks.

Gray steadies himself, heaving for air as he tries to accept what the sound of his sister's voice means.

Winter beat him. And not just by a little bit. Somehow, she beat him by a lot.

"How?" he asks, as a sick feeling churns in his gut. "How?"

"When Polaris fell, it opened up a new path," she says, barely sounding out of breath. "I pretty much just walked straight here."

"But…" Gray clenches his fists, fighting the urge to cry. "But that's not fair."

"Nor are the Tournaments," says Winter, her voice coming close as she moves toward him. "You told me so yourself."

Gray steps back, not wanting her near just now in case he decides to throttle her. Collapsing to the ground, he cradles his head in his hands, unable to accept what he knows he must. His whole world just cleaved in two in the exact same way their home had. And he hadn't seen that coming, either.

"I won, Gray." Winter's voice is full of both fear and excitement. "You have to let me go."

He shakes his head, even though he knows she can't see him. "You're not going."

"We had a deal," she says. "I'm going to the Tournaments, whether you like it or not."

"No," he says, knowing there's no way he can let her do this. "You're not. We are."

LEXIS

*T*he midday sun is harsh and heavy, but then again, it always is in the Outlands. It's just another way Mother Nature can punish them after everything humanity did to her. Lexis straightens her shoulders as she stands, knowing her pale hair will be attracting attention, but shouldering both discomforts as if they don't exist.

Raze is tall and strong beside her in their section around the Ring, far more ready than she is as they watch the others take their place.

The People of Never. The People of Rust. The People of Cragg.

And the People of Cy.

One segment remains empty, a testament to the cowardice of the Ghosts of Fairbanks. Lexis barely glances at the garish gap, like a hand missing a finger. The Ghosts made the right choice. The guy with the smile never would have made it past the first Tournament.

Beyond the competitors are the spectators. The witnesses to the decision of who will decide the future leader of the Outlands. They shuffle, kicking up dust, faces alive with anticipation. Lexis isn't sure what they're looking forward to more—the prospect of war or the battles they're about to cheer.

Evrest strides out of his hut. Clad in animal hide, his scarred face twisted into a scowl, he walks straight to the statue of Cy standing at the head of the Ring. He pauses beside it, acknowledging the one who must be avenged, before leaping down. The crowd hushes as he stops in the center, doing a slow spin to take in the competitors and the spectators behind them.

With a dramatic wave of his arm, he points to the dead soil at his feet. "This is where the victor will stand," he states, even now, not bothering to raise his voice. "The strongest. The fastest. The one who will do what it takes."

A couple of people shuffle closer so they can hear him, glancing warily at each other as they find themselves nearer their enemies.

"This is where the new Commander will be born, rising from the blood of the weak."

A murmur flutters through the people around Evrest, and Lexis isn't sure if the spectators or the competitors are more excited.

"There will be seven Tournaments. Seven rounds that will test our new Commander, that will prove his or her worth."

Lexis knows all this—these are the words that used to be her bedtime stories. She glances around, chafing at having to stand still. From the moment the sun rose and the other factions arrived, it feels like splinters have crawled under her skin and are digging their way to her heart. Determined to pierce her soul.

Each moment is bringing her closer to seven fights to the death.

Seven fights that Lexis must win.

And winning means losing Raze.

Her restless gaze means she's the first to see them. The two bodies that materialize like the ghosts they are, walking toward them. Raze must sense something because his head moves slightly, doing his own scan. He stops and stills in the same way Lexis did a second earlier, having seen it, too. For a moment, Lexis thinks she hears him draw in a sharp breath.

The twins are here. The ones who are like them.

And yet are nothing like Lexis and Raze.

The two steadily approach, their steps even and measured, their faces stony and silent. They stride into the empty section, completing the circle of factions.

"We've come to win the Tournaments," the girl announces, her voice so full of confidence that Lexis recognizes the uncertainty beneath it. For some reason, it lights the smallest spark of respect.

Courage in the face of the impossible is the hardest to find. The one that counts the most.

Lexis should know. It's the only way life or death decisions can be made.

Evrest nods before turning away, obviously not bothering to even note what they look like. He doesn't expect them to be alive for very long.

Doing another slow spin, his chest expands with satisfaction. Every section has someone in it, each faction with five contestants. All except for the People of Cy and the Ghosts of Fairbanks. They only have two. The People of Cy because that's all they need.

The People of Fairbanks because that's all they have.

"The one rule of the Tournaments is that there are no rules," Evrest states in his emotionless way. "The first fight is slated for...now."

Lexis freezes. The first Tournament is now? She hadn't expected it to be so soon. And yet, it's exactly something Evrest would do. It means no one is prepared.

"Every contestant who wishes to take part must enter the Ring. If anyone is cowardly enough to try to climb out, they'll be pushed right back in"—Evrest's eyes glint—"with a blade. There must be one kill for the round to end. Whoever makes the kill will be awarded immunity in the next Tournament." Her father continues his slow rotation, telling Lexis that he isn't finished. His lips twist in a cold smile. "Whoever loses, their faction is excluded from the Tournaments."

There's a murmur as the information sinks in. Lexis wonders if the others realize this decision is actually an act of mercy, something her father has never afforded her. The weakest faction will be expelled, meaning they won't have to suffer further deaths.

Lexis's gaze flies to the twins, the Ghosts. They should never have come. They're the weakest of all the factions. And there are only two of them.

Every other faction will be targeting them.

She finds the dark-haired guy looking at her. For some reason she wants to apologize to him. To acknowledge he would've been better off if he'd never met her.

Then the guy does something Lexis would never have expected. His lips soften. They tip up. And he nods.

She looks away, confused. Then annoyed. The last thing she needs right now is to lose her focus.

Lexis returns her gaze to her father. To the fate she was born into.

To kill.

To be the last one standing.

To be the Commander.

Evrest stops his slow pirouette, facing her as he says his final words. "May the Tournaments serve you well."

Her father leaps out of the Ring and stands beside the statue of Cy, keeping his gaze straight ahead as silence descends around the circle of stones.

Lexis swallows, wishing she could grip Raze's hand, but

knowing the time where she could turn to him for comfort just ended.

They're about to leap into the Ring, to start the journey from twins to enemies. Lexis locks every muscle, feeling the necessary ice flow through her veins.

Let the Tournaments begin.

EVREST RAISES his arm and muscles tense as the silence multiplies. Lexis isn't sure who is breathing less—the contestants or those who have come to watch this bloodbath. She wraps the dead air around her like armor, ignoring the thump of her heart —that organ is her ultimate vulnerability. For the period of this Tournament, it doesn't exist.

Without warning, her father slams his arm down, his hand slicing through the air like a guillotine. "Tournament one begins."

Lexis moves instantly to the words she's been waiting for all her life. She strides forward, Raze beside her, to the edge of the Ring. Unlike the other factions who do the same, there's no hesitation as she leaps the few feet to the dusty ground below. She never acknowledges that Evrest's hard words just called for the extermination of one of the bodies now in the ring of death.

Instead, she treats them as what they really are. The call for victory. For a champion of the Outlands to rise above the others.

The factions create five points within the Ring, everyone contracting closer to those they trust. Eyes dart frantically around as minds rapidly make decisions that are going to mean living or drying.

The Never people bare their teeth, their breaths hissing through the yellowed gaps. The Craggs expand their broad, naked chests, trying to make themselves look as big as possible.

The People of Rust are moving the most—heads twitching as their fists compulsively clench and unclench.

It's the twins of Fairbanks who are unmoving. They stand close and for some reason Lexis suspects their hands are clasped. If things were different, she would be clinging to Raze with all her might, as if that strangled hold could ensure he'd make it through this alive. Although the Fairbanks siblings' faces are shuttered, Lexis knows fear—she was raised by it. Those two are terrified.

And so they should be. They'd have to know they're the obvious target. The easy one. The Craggs shift subtly, angling toward them. Every other contestant is vigilant enough to notice the change, and they follow suit.

A new focus has been found in the Ring.

There's a shuffling of feet and muttered words from above as the spectators chafe under the tension that's building. Everyone is waiting to see who will make the first move. Immunity is the ultimate prize in a Tournament like this. But everyone wants to be alive to claim it.

Something flutters through Lexis's frozen veins. The feeling is as unwelcome as it's unwanted. She tries to ignore it only for it to slither into her mind. The Craggs are planning on attacking the Ghosts of Fairbanks.

One of the strongest factions is about to target the weakest.

Lexis admits what the tendril of emotion is. The one she's working so hard to shut down—anger, maybe a sliver of hatred. Purely because she's never had the luxury of protecting Raze and his sensitive soul, and now she's supposed to sit back and watch this happen.

Dammit. The Fairbanks twins should never have come.

The Cragg at the front, no doubt their leader, curls his lip and growls low in the back of his throat. Although it's his only movement, Lexis recognizes it for what it is. The call to kill.

Her decision is made in a blink. Removing the Craggs is

logical—they're the only real faction that presents a threat to Lexis and Raze. One death and they won't have to face them again.

In fact, she welcomes attacking the mountain of a man she's set her sights on.

The man's gaze flickers the moment she moves, registering Raze right behind her, then latches back onto Lexis. She sees the moment he registers she's coming for him. She watches his face cement into the granite that is his home.

And her heart hardens into the same cold stone.

"Slab!" shouts a woman beside the Cragg leader. The four people behind him fan out, forming protective wings on either side.

Slab roars, the Ghosts of Fairbanks forgotten, as he leaps to meet his opponent. In her periphery, Lexis notes that everyone else steps back. Two factions have chosen to fight, which means the others will stand and watch, waiting for one to win.

And the other to be expelled, with one less member alive.

When Raze overtakes her, Lexis's frozen armor almost fractures.

No…

He never glances at her, his focus on Slab as he shoots past, but she already knows what his intent is. It's a move they've practiced before. One she hates.

One that will no doubt work perfectly.

Slab angles slightly away from Lexis, adjusting his trajectory as he recognizes Raze will reach him first. His shoulders flex as he decides he has a bigger, deadlier fight on his hands.

Lexis's heart clenches against her will. She's not supposed to feel this. To care about what's going to happen next.

Raze lifts a leather-wrapped fist as he homes in on Slab, never slowing down. Slab sees the attack and prepares for it, angling his body to deflect the blow as his own meaty fists rise to mete out their own punishment.

Even though she knows it's about to happen, Lexis still grimaces when Raze stumbles. It's a slight slip of a foot, little more than a momentary loss of balance. But Slab is enough of a warrior to recognize the opening.

Just as he's supposed to.

Slab's over-sized fist ploughs into Raze's face. Although he twists his head at the last second to protect his nose, the punch still glances off Raze's cheek, the powerful hit ricocheting down his body. He crumples, even though Lexis knows he's been dealt far more painful hits, far too many times, and he's kept his footing.

But that's not the plan. Not the decoy.

Not the move that will ensure she wins.

Slab follows Raze as he slams into the dirt, his fists becoming pistons as they macerate Raze's torso. Lexis's twin is silent as punch after punch lands on his ribs, his solar plexus, his unprotected stomach. He pretends to fight Slab off, even landing a couple of punches of his own, but none of them stop the onslaught. They're not supposed to.

Slab is focused on pummeling his way to victory, assuming his people will protect his back. Although that's exactly what they do—falling into fighting stance as they realize Lexis is still coming—it's a foolish assumption.

An underestimation of what Lexis was raised to do. Of what she's capable of.

A single strike to the first Cragg and the woman falls to the ground, unconscious. Lexis knows she could take this woman out. Kill her with a single punch to the temple or by jamming the heel of her hand into her nose and compressing the cartilage into her brain, but she doesn't. Slab is her target.

He's hurting Raze. And he was going to attack the vulnerable Fairbanks fools.

Well, Lexis is not only going to win this round. She's going to do it by taking her most formidable opponent out.

Lexis doesn't even bother hitting the next man who launches at her. She feints right, then side steps around him to the left. She leaps, swinging her leg high and it slams into Slab's head. With a grunt, he tumbles to the side.

Lexis jumps over her twin, registering that he's already rolling away, no doubt trying to get up. They've been taught that no matter how injured you are, never stay down. It's a death wish.

In the very same way Slab is now down. He sprawls in the dust, trying to right himself but never getting a chance. Lexis vaults onto his chest, trapping his arms beneath her legs. She grips his head, shuttering her mind and heart as she prepares to snap his neck.

A body slams into her, knocking her off the Cragg leader. Lexis hits the dirt only to use it as a platform to leap back onto her feet. She spins around to find someone has taken her place kneeling over Slab.

It's one of the Rusts. His bleached hair as stark as his face, his body twitches with excitement. He's going to steal Lexis's kill!

Except a Never woman appears behind him. "No Rust is going to win immunity," she screeches.

Her scrappy, dirty robes flutter as her fingers spear into the Rust's hair. The man's eyes widen but it's too late. The same muted snap that Lexis was waiting to hear a moment ago spears through the Ring.

The body of the Rust man goes limp. The Never woman leaps to her feet, her hands raised in victory. Her people, just as dirty and scrap-covered, shout in triumph as they surround her. They dance around the dead body, celebrating their win.

And their immunity from the next round of Tournaments.

Keeping her face impassive, Lexis returns to Raze's side. Her twin is holding himself too upright, stiffness etched into his muscles as he stares straight ahead. He's in pain, but she's the only one who knows it.

Just like it's been every day of their life.

The other factions retreat back to their space in the Ring. The Never continue to celebrate. The Rust's pale faces are stamped with shock. They've just been expelled from the Tournaments. The Craggs are huddled close, the leader back in their fold, stony gazes cold with fury.

Lexis stands proudly beside her brother, reminding herself they're the People of Cy. It was their fighting skills that took the Cragg down. If the Rust, then the woman of the Never, hadn't waited for the final moment to strike and take the kill, they would be wearing the cloak of immunity right now. Lexis would have the first kill of the Tournaments to call her own.

But Evrest won't see it that way. Stealing is a legitimate way of winning. Cheating is necessary. The Never woman is the winner because she did what it takes.

Which means Lexis failed. Raze took a beating for nothing.

Lexis's own body tightens. She should've done what everyone else was going to do. Attacked the Ghosts of Fairbanks.

She won't make that mistake again.

WINTER

Winter thought she knew what it was like for her heart to pound. When she'd run through Fairbanks with Gray and Trakk, her ribs had barely managed to contain the thumping in her chest as blood was sent pumping through her veins.

But this is a whole new level. When that beast of a man from Cragg had set his sights on Winter and Gray at the start of the Tournament, she was certain it was all over. They'd been the obvious targets. Of course, everyone wanted the easy kill first. It's what Winter herself would have done, if only any of these warriors had looked like they might fit into that category.

Gray wraps an arm around Winter's shoulders as they stand in their segment outside the Ring. He's shaking even worse than she is despite the Tournament being over.

They're safe.

For now.

Winter shrugs off Gray's arm. They can't let the others know how much they mean to each other. It's a weakness that could be used against them.

The golden girl is smart. She proved that just now when she

went for the strategic kill over the easy one. Which means that to beat her, they need to be even smarter.

"One Tournament down, six to go," says Gray.

"We shouldn't have come here." Sharp regret slams into Winter as she looks at the mangled body of the Rust who tried to steal a kill and instead lost his life. A body that could so easily have been hers. Or worse still, Gray's.

"If we leave, they'll hunt us down to make an example of us," says Gray. "We actually have a better chance of living if we stay."

A sick feeling builds in the back of Winter's throat. Having a better chance of living if they stay for these death games is saying something. But Gray's right. There's no escape now. They chose to be here. *She* chose for them to be here. And now they're paying the price.

Leaning over, she retches. But with no food in her stomach, all she manages to do is make a heaving noise as her body contracts in spasms.

Gray puts a hand on her back. Again, she shrugs him off, but this time it's not because she's worried what anyone else thinks. It's to protect her own heart. Or perhaps it's to protect his.

Their bond has always been their strength, but right now it's their weakness. Because when one of them dies—which is certain to happen any day now—the other is going to be irreparably broken.

And she was the one who signed their death warrant. If Gray had his way, they'd be picking their way over the rubble of Polaris right now. Instead, here they are.

Trapped.

Doomed.

Destined for death.

They're no different to the rats Winter had captured underneath her netting in Fairbanks.

"We need to get out of here," she says, barely able to form her words. "We have to find a way."

"Winter." Gray blinks at her, his eternal smile missing from his beautiful face. "It's too late for that."

She opens her mouth to tell him how desperately sorry she is when she's silenced by a commotion in the Ring as the Rust's body is collected by his people. The Never are jeering and laughing, proud of their victory, no matter what means they'd used to achieve it. The Rust ignore them, focusing instead on packing up the camp they'd set up for themselves. It seems they want to exit the Tournaments almost as fast as they'd lost the first fight.

It's only then, as Winter looks around at the other segments surrounding the Ring, that she realizes they're the only faction to have arrived with nothing except the clothes on their backs. She'd foolishly assumed some kind of shelter would be provided, but it seems not. All she and Gray have is a wide patch of dirt marked out by a deep gouge in the soil. At least there don't seem to be any insects out here and it's unlikely the temperature is going to dip. They can survive, even if they're not going to be comfortable. As long as they can find food and water…

The man who'd announced the beginning of the Tournaments walks to the center of the Ring and spins around, assessing who remains in each segment.

Winter sizes him up, wondering if he could be related to the golden twins. He has the same upturned eyes as the girl twin, the same square chin as the guy.

He claps his hands once. "Tournament One goes to the Never," the man declares, spitting out the words like they're hot coals in his throat. "Immunity has been granted for the second Tournament."

The Never whoop and cheer, their tattered robes threatening to fall from their malnourished frames as they slap each other on the back. They might have made it through the first two Tournaments, but Winter doubts they're going to be the ones to make it to the end. Because something tells her that if the People of Cy had been the ones to win, they wouldn't be wasting energy cheering right now. They'd be far too busy strategizing their next move. Only a fool celebrates before the prize is in their hand. A lesson that was reinforced when Brik stole their haul of rats.

The man holds up his hand for silence. It takes some time, but eventually the Never settle down and show they're prepared to listen.

"The People of Rust have been eliminated and will not rule the Outlands." The man turns his gaze to the defeated faction. "Take your dead and leave the Tournaments immediately."

Winter scans the motley group with their faces turned to the ground, surprised to see one of them refusing to dip his gaze.

"Is that guy looking at me?" she asks Gray, wondering if she's imagining it.

Gray steps closer to Winter. "He is. And I don't like it."

She stares back, taking in the man's stocky build and fair hair. He looks a little older than her. In his twenties, perhaps? And he's watching Winter like she's fallen from the sky. Which if he'd seen Polaris crumble, then perhaps she had.

She shifts so she's standing behind Gray, breaking his line of sight. After what she's just lived through, she really doesn't have the energy to deal with a creep like this right now.

The man in the center of the Ring looks to the other factions. "The second Tournament will take place on the morrow."

"Tomorrow," Gray explains to Winter.

"I know that." Winter rolls her eyes, realizing that means they need to find a way to get out of here tonight. They absolutely cannot be still standing in this segment of doom when the sun rises.

"Three factions will fight," the man says. "The People of Cy. The Cragg. The Ghosts of Fairbanks."

"Just calling us Fairbanks is fine," shouts Gray. "No need for the Ghost bit."

Winter winces as the man glares at Gray like he just called him a dirty name. His gaze is a weapon of its own. Winter's sure he could stop a weak man's heart with just one of those looks. It's like he has no soul inside that muscled shell.

"Or Ghosts is fine," Gray adds, nervously. "Like, call us whatever you want, really. We don't mind. Ghosts. Warriors. Or fighters isn't a ba—"

Winter pinches his arm to silence him.

"Three factions will fight," the man repeats, ignoring Gray. "Two deaths from the same faction will end the Tournament."

Winter had thought the crowd was already quiet, but these words do the job of stunning them into the kind of silence she's never heard before. Fairbanks was a place filled with noise. There was the constant hum of the beating wings of a thousand insects, the groaning of a tired building that was struggling to stand, the whispering of the leaves in the stubborn trees that refused to become extinct.

But this is different. It's like people are too afraid to even breathe in case they draw attention to themselves. It's a strange thought to know that out of the competitors who stand strong around the Ring, that by tomorrow, two of them will no longer be alive to hold their breath.

The man waves his hands at the crowd and one by one they resume what they were doing. The Rust are preparing to leave. The Never are gloating about their win. The Cragg are surrounding Slab as he sits down to check his injuries. And the People of Cy are standing apart like it never occurred to them that they're a team.

Winter draws in a deep breath, still unable to control her shaking.

"Wait here," says Winter, seeing her chance and marching into the center of the Ring directly toward the man who doesn't seem to need a leader, having assumed the role for himself.

He's just taken a step toward his people when he sees Winter.

He stops still and watches her like she's an annoying mosquito he's waiting to swat.

"I made a mistake," she says, deciding a man with no soul is unlikely to be a fan of small talk. "I realize it's against the rules, but Fairbanks would like to withdraw from the Tournaments."

He blinks twice, his gaze trained on Winter, but doesn't reply.

She stares directly at him, willing him to agree to let them go.

"My brother and I don't want to be leaders," she ventures, remembering that her sister once told her that flattery is a powerful form of persuasion. "We've seen that there are other factions far better placed to lead. Like the People of Cy. You guys are great leaders! We're just wasting your time here."

His face doesn't so much as move at this compliment. The only thing he seems to be persuaded about is that he can't wait for this conversation to be over.

Winter clasps her hands together, hoping he hasn't noticed her inability to keep still. "So, if it's okay with you, my brother and I are going to head home?"

Still, the man says nothing, and Winter isn't sure what to make of that. Can she dare to take that as an agreement?

"Good chat." She swipes at a bead of sweat on her forehead as she takes a cautious step back. "So, we'll be off now. Good luck with the rest of the Tournaments and all that."

She risks a smile as she takes another step. But as she turns, she slams directly into Gray. She hadn't even realized he'd come up behind her.

"I told you to wait over there," she hisses at him.

Gray doesn't say anything. His eyes are glued on the soulless

106

man who's raised a hand to point beyond the markings of the Ring.

"Do you see that warrior there?" he asks in a voice that's managing to control the anger seeping from his every pore. "And that one over there?"

Winter looks where he's pointing and sees men with spears stationed at intervals around the Ring.

"Yes," she says. "I see them."

"They're waiting to kill anyone who tries to leave," the man says. "They'd take great pleasure in killing the likes of you. Even though Ghosts are already dead."

"I see." Winter nods her understanding, a sick feeling twisting in her gut. She knew it was too good to be true. There really is no way out of here. The pounding in her heart picks up once more to know that they're well and truly trapped.

"Sorry to bother you," says Gray, tugging at the back of Winter's shirt to urge her away from danger.

"You had your chance," the man says. "One of you could have walked out of here alive if only the other was brave enough to die."

Winter swallows. The thought had crossed her mind when that man-mountain had launched himself at them in the Tournament. She knew if she'd stepped toward her death that Gray would have been allowed to walk free. But Gray had held her back. Then the golden girl had intervened. And now a feeling of shame is piled upon Winter's regret.

"The rules are clear," the soulless man continues. "Once you enter the Tournaments, there are only two ways you can leave."

"Two ways?" asks Gray, his brows shooting up. "I thought death was the only option?"

This seems to amuse the man. "For you, it is."

"He means to succeed as Commander," says Winter. "That's the other way to leave."

"Oh." Gray winces. Now that they've seen their opponents in action, they both know how unlikely this is.

"Thanks for your time," says Winter, wondering why she's being so polite to a man who is sending them to certain death.

Gray tugs at her shirt again and this time she follows, gathering pace the further away they get.

"I'm so sorry." Winter's heart aches in place of the earlier pounding.

"You made your decision," Gray says. "I made mine. You didn't force me to come here."

She shakes her head at how generous he's being.

"What is he doing?" Gray frowns and Winter sees what has him distracted.

The man from Rust who'd been staring at Winter is setting up camp in the Fairbanks segment.

They jog forward and he stops his work to smile directly at Winter.

"Hello," he says, like what he's doing is the most normal thing in the world.

"This is our segment," says Winter, not needing or wanting a new friend. "Get out."

"Thought you could use a tent." He points to the tattered animal hide he's strung over some branches to form a shelter. "Can't have a woman as pretty as you sleeping rough."

"Back off, Rusty." Gray shoves the guy in the chest, sending him stumbling backward. "We don't need your help."

"I reckon you do need my help," he says, planting his feet on the ground. "You'll get eaten alive in that Ring without it."

"We saw how well your faction did in the first Tournament," says Winter, straightening her back. "We can manage just fine."

Undeterred, he extends his hand. "My name's—"

"Rusty," Winter answers for him. "First name Rusty. Last name Get-the-hell-off-my-dirt."

Instead of being insulted at her lack of interest in his name, he tips back his head and laughs.

"Knew you were a feisty one," he says. "The pretty ones always are. Evrest's daughter is feisty, too. Except she's way more scary than you."

"Evrest?" Gray asks, tilting his head toward the man who'd threatened to kill them if they left the Tournaments. "Is that his name?"

"Sure is," says Rusty.

"And the twins are his children?" asks Winter.

Rusty nods. "Lexis and Raze. Lexis is the apple of his eye. Raze is the turd that's stuck to his boot."

"How do we get out of here?" Winter asks, trying to get some more information out of this creep before they send him packing. "We need to get past those guards."

Rusty seems to find this funny. "Short of digging a tunnel, you're never going to get past them."

"Have you got a spade?" Gray asks.

Winter cocks her head, wondering if he's serious. A hundred shovels couldn't dig through this hard earth.

"You missed your chance today," says Rusty. "There are only two ways out of these Tournaments now."

"Yeah, we've heard all about them." Winter waves her hand to silence him. "I don't think much of the first option. And the second seems a little...ambitious."

"Not if you're clever about it." Rusty grins.

Gray's whole demeanor changes from hostile to...hopeful. He doesn't really think this guy can tell them anything that's going to help, does he?

"You're facing Cragg and Cy." Rusty returns to the tent and makes some adjustments. "What you need is an alliance."

Winter frowns, not having heard that word before. "What do you mean?"

"You need to work with one of the other teams." He grins at her. "You know, so they don't kill you in the first five seconds."

Winter looks across at the Cragg, wondering if there's any sense in what Rusty just said. Could she convince them to team up and take out Evrest's precious twins? It might be worth a shot given Slab has a score to settle after the way he was humiliated by them just now.

"Not them," says Rusty. "You're wasting your time there. The Cragg barely align with each other, let alone another faction. It's the Cy twins you want. Join forces with them and you might just live to see a few more days."

"Do you think we can convince them?" Gray is almost smiling, and it breaks Winter's heart. He can't really think that's a possibility, can he? The golden twins made their feelings more than clear when they delivered their invitation to Fairbanks. They're a lost cause and it's wrong to let Gray believe it might be otherwise.

"Gray," says Winter. "This guy's delusional. Don't listen to him. We're better off approaching the Cragg."

"But Lexis likes me," says Gray. "I know she does."

Winter almost chokes. "How do you know that? Is it the way she looks at you like she's trying to decide which one of your eyeballs she's going to poke out first?"

"She doesn't look at me like that," Gray protests. "I can win her over. I know I can. She's not all bad. I can see it. There's good in her."

Rusty slaps him on the back. "That's the attitude. You can win any wench over with a bit of persistence."

Winter bristles, realizing that's exactly what he's trying to do with her.

Stomping off, she heads directly for the Cragg, not wanting to be part of this conversation for another moment.

As she steps over the line marking out their segment, a murmur ripples across the camp.

She heads directly for Slab and pulls back her shoulders.

He looks up at her from where he's lying on the ground and lets out a sigh like her mere presence is a bore.

"I have a proposal for you," she says, jamming her hands on her hips.

"A what?" He bites down on a twig he has hanging out one side of his mouth. *Is he eating that?*

"A plan," she says, realizing she needs to use smaller words. "An idea."

"Git out of here." He waves his hands at her. "I don't make friends with ma supper. Makes the bones stick in ma teeth."

Winter presses on. "We team up. We work together to take out the People of Cy in the next Tournament. Get them back for the way they tricked you out there. They don't play fair. Then when the Never are allowed back in, we—"

"Git!" He pulls himself into a seated position, then stands to his full height, towering over Winter. This guy must be four times her size. "Git!"

"Think about it," she says, trying her best not to quiver in front of him. "It's a good plan."

"Git out of ma face before I stick ya ugly head right up ya ass," he growls.

"Sure." Winter gives him the same smile she'd offered Evrest and bolts back to Gray, deciding she far prefers her head in its current location.

"How did that work out for you?" asks Rusty.

Winter looks across at Gray, not wanting to answer that question. Rusty knows full well how that played out.

"Okay," she says. "We need to talk to the twins."

RAZE

*R*aze rests against the wall of the hut he shares with Lexis, the words Evrest just flayed them with like a fresh wound in his mind. His brain feels more battered than his body.

Their loss of the first Tournament was a humiliation to their father. Raze grimaces as he shifts his back against the rough timber, reminding him the bruises he sustained were a product of failure.

The next Tournament is tomorrow and they've been set a task. One that will right the wrong that happened today. A task he knows will be harder than it should be.

Glancing down at the small piece of wood in his hand, Raze desperately tries to think of something to carve. To escape into a world of creation rather than death for just a few minutes. But his mind keeps returning to Evrest's words.

Losers.

Failures.

I thought I beat it into you how important this is.

His shoulders sag as he realizes he won't be making anything today. How can something be born at a time like this?

The sound of footsteps has him stilling. Raze remains sitting although every muscle is coiled, ready to defend or attack. Their hut is at the edge of the village—the way he and Lexis chose it to be the moment they were old enough to live alone—and his people avoid him, which is the way he likes it. Loneliness is far preferable to having to constantly watch your back.

The footsteps continue, light and quick, suggesting it's a female. Raze knows it's not his twin—her movements are as familiar as his own. Plus, Lexis stormed off after their father's lecture, no doubt to the circle of dust the People of Cy call the Training Ground. She'll vent her frustrations on innocent slabs of rock or anyone foolish enough to accept her challenge and take her on.

Which means the person approaching is an enemy.

The woman who rounds the nearest hut has Raze's body coiling even tighter, squeezing his breath from his body. It's the female Ghost, the haunting beauty of Fairbanks. Her gaze scans the hut then falls on him, sitting near the door.

And stops.

Her dark eyes trap him, a stray strand of black hair fluttering over her smooth cheek. Raze tries to drag his eyes away, only to find he can't. This girl is soft and beautiful in a way he doesn't understand.

In a way he wants to.

So instead, he frowns. Doesn't she realize how dangerous it is for her to be here?

Those dark eyes crinkle as she smiles. "Hey, I thought we could talk."

Raze arches a brow. She's kidding, right?

When she doesn't move, he glares at her, frowning far more deeply and ferociously, then angles his body away. He doesn't need words to tell her to go away.

But the girl simply steps to the side so she's standing in front of him. With a grace Raze wishes he didn't notice, she folds down so she's sitting cross-legged in the dust.

Raze draws his leg in. Lexis is the only person he allows close to him.

"My name's Winter, by the way."

A season that's extinct, just like all the things he carves.

"And you're Raze," she continues. "You and Lexis are twins, just like me and Gray."

Raze keeps his mouth tightly shut. She's not telling him anything he doesn't know. Children are lucky to survive and grow to adulthood in the Outlands, twins even less likely. But being unique has never been a blessing in his world.

"Nice to meet you, too," she quips.

Raze focuses on the wood in his hand, flicking the blade in his hand so it catches the light. Mindlessly, he starts carving so he can remind Winter she's risking becoming as forgotten as the season she was named after just by being here.

But, once again, she doesn't take the hint. She arches her neck, trying to see what he's doing. "Where did you learn how to carve?"

From the one man who showed Raze some semblance of humanity. Hatch was one of his father's warriors. A big, scarred man who would spend his quiet hours whittling away at anything he could find. When young Raze had crept to take a closer look, he hadn't chased the odd, silent boy away. Instead, he'd taught him how to mold wood into the images that forever danced in Raze's imagination.

In some small way, Hatch gave Raze a voice.

When Raze doesn't answer, Winter sits back and tucks her knees up, wrapping her arms around them. "I saw what you did."

Raze pauses, the half-formed figurine he wasn't aware he was creating resting in his hand.

"You tripped on purpose," Winter says quietly. "So your sister could take the kill."

Returning to his carving, Raze tries to disconnect from the strange emotions that seem to be coiling around them. As his hands begin a familiar rhythm of chipping and carving, deeper for shaping, shallower for detailing, he reminds himself this girl is the enemy. As is her brother.

Fate has ordained it that way.

"I know how you feel. You were protecting her." Winter tugs on a thread at her knee. "I'd die for Gray. It wouldn't be a choice. That decision was made when two of us grew in a womb instead of one."

Raze is glad he doesn't speak. If he did, he'd have no idea how to respond to that. He's never had a conversation like this.

More than a handful of words.

And those sentences are softly spoken, almost gently.

A conversation with someone who understands the bond he and Lexis have.

He focuses harder on his carving, surprised as to what's emerging, but almost helpless to stop it.

Winter rests her chin on her knees, those dark eyes seeking his once again. "That's why I think we should work together."

His gaze flies to hers. Few things surprise Raze anymore. He already knows what humanity is capable of. He no longer fears death.

But Winter's words send a shockwave through him.

What's more unnerving, is that she notices it.

Her arms relax as she pushes forward. "The Craggs are your greatest threat. They're strong, and they're the largest faction. We can help you remove them from the Tournaments."

Before Raze can think of how to respond, there's the sound of hammering and banging from the direction of the Ring, making them both glance in that direction.

"Hurry up!" shouts a male voice. "We need to get this done before morning."

Winter turns wide startled eyes to Raze. "They're building something, aren't they? For the next fight?"

Answering her for the first time, Raze shrugs. He has as much idea as she does as to what tomorrow will bring. Evrest is determined that the People of Cy will win these Tournaments fairly. After this, the fighting will end.

Winter shuffles forward, resting her hand on his ankle. The sensation of her warm palm touching him, having her so close, has Raze drawing in a sharp breath. The light caress is…pleasant, and yet strangely painful at the same time. It makes his heart ache.

"Please," Winter says quietly. "We can help each other."

Heat creeps up Raze's leg, making him feel as if he's spent his whole life cold. Despite growing up in a sun-bleached land, it's like he's discovering the sensation of being hot for the first time.

Winter's fingers tighten as her lips part, almost as if she's just as shocked as him. Do they not touch in Fairbanks, either?

The clatter of timber snaps Raze out of the moment of weakness. He yanks his foot back and surges to his feet, watching as Winter scrabbles to do the same.

None of this matters. Raze won't be alive to see Lexis crowned as the Commander.

And neither will Winter.

"You could teach us to fight," she says quickly. "Or we could use a strategy like you did with Lexis. There are so many ways we'll be stronger if we work together."

Raze grips the knife and spins, slamming it into the wood behind him and making Winter leap back in fright. The blade impales deep into the wall of the hut, showing exactly how strong he is.

Alone.

Shoving his face close to Winter's, he shakes his head

sharply. Succinctly. Telling her unequivocally what the answer is.

No.

All she's doing is making this harder for him, not easier.

He grasps her hand, noting the way she flinches. She trusts him as much as he trusts her. He slaps the carving he just made into her palm. It was never a conscious decision to make it, but he did, and he no longer wants it.

Maybe it can be a reminder of what her people are named. Ghosts.

She unfurls her hand and gasps as she recognizes the dead boy she held in her arms that day in Fairbanks. The friend she cried over. The one she called Trakk.

Raze walks away, glad he could give her that.

Because he and Lexis have a Tournament to win tomorrow.

And Evrest has ordered they kill the Ghosts of Fairbanks.

GRAY

*G*ray hadn't meant to nap. He'd just thought if he lay down in the shade of Rusty's tent for a few minutes and rested, he'd be able to stay awake until nightfall.

But when he opens his eyes, he realizes far more than a few minutes have passed.

The sun is lower in the sky. Soon it will be dark.

And Winter is nowhere to be found.

He sits up and frowns. He knows she's his sister and he has no right to monitor her every move, but out here things feel different. He has to look after her. Just like he knows she's trying to look after him. And he really can't do that if she keeps disappearing. She should know it's not safe, especially after the way that Rusty guy was looking at her.

They were supposed to go and talk to Lexis and Raze together, but he'll bet everything he owns—which, admittedly, is only the clothes he's wearing right now—that she's gone without him.

Pushing to his feet, Gray leaves the tent and looks around. He draws in several deep breaths, trying to calm his nerves. Winter knows how to look after herself.

He hopes.

The Cragg are sitting in a circle, their animal hide clothing making them look like cattle at first glance. The Rust have completely vanished. A tumbleweed blows across the bare dirt of their segment as if on cue. The Never are lying on the dirt asleep, clearly not seeing the need to make any plans.

Winter isn't amongst any of them, which only confirms Gray's fear that she's sought out the twins without him. And as much as he'd love to leave her to it, he knows he can't do that. His sister could be in danger.

He glances left, then right, trying to decide whose segment he's going to pass through to get to the other side of the Ring to reach the People of Cy. Evrest had made it clear that nobody is to enter the Ring unless they're competing, and Gray most certainly doesn't want to give him any reason to start the next Tournament early.

Remembering the reception Winter had received from Slab when she'd approached him, Gray stalks across the empty segment of the Rust and walks quietly past the Never. They don't even bother to lift their heads to see who's passing. It seems impossible that a faction like the Never could have been declared victors at the first Tournament. But then again, that's good. Because if there's one thing Winter and Gray need right now it's for the impossible to come out on top.

The segment assigned to the People of Cy is different to the others, and as Gray steps over the line, he feels a shiver run down his spine. Whereas the other segments open out onto a world of neverending nothingness, the Cy segment spills onto a village of crudely constructed huts.

Gray has always known that people live like this, but seeing it at such close proximity is a shock. He'd grown up in luxury by comparison. Polaris may have creaked and groaned, but it had insulated its inhabitants—not just from Mother Nature, but from the rest of the world. In the short time Gray's been here, he's learned so much, not just about the other factions, but himself.

He's braver than he thought.

And so much more naïve...

He walks forward, part of him regretting not trying harder to talk Winter out of coming here, and the other part glad he didn't. Because no matter what road they took, they were going to die. At least this way they're going to leave this Earth understanding it a little better. And that's got to be worth something.

Gray approaches the closest hut and leans forward, trying to hear if there's any possibility Winter could be inside, but all he hears is snoring. He goes to another hut, not pausing for long when the wail of a baby escapes. The next hut he tries is completely silent.

It's with dread that he realizes it's not going to be possible to know if Winter is inside any of these huts if he doesn't check inside.

He goes to the door of the silent hut and raises a clenched fist, wondering if the savages in this faction have even heard of the notion of knocking. Manners don't seem to be their strong suit.

But before his knuckles can make contact with the rough timber, Gray is grabbed from behind and a hand is clamped over his mouth.

He struggles to break free, but whoever has him is stronger than he is.

"It's me," a deep voice hisses in his ear. "Stay quiet and I'll let go."

Having no idea who *me* might be, Gray stops fighting against his captor.

The firm grip is released and Gray spins around to find Rusty shaking his head at him.

"Are you mad?" Rusty asks in a whisper.

Gray's brows shoot up. "I thought you went home."

"Quiet, they'll hear you." Rusty grabs Gray by the arm and leads him through the small village.

It's only then that Gray notices long shadows beside the huts, swaying in the late afternoon sun.

They're being watched.

The People of Cy had heard Gray snooping through their village long before Rusty had taken hold of him. Pressing themselves to the outer walls of their huts, they're watching his every move. Biding their time. Looking for the excuse they need to kill him.

Do they even need an excuse?

As they step beyond the village, Gray turns back to see the shadows moving forward. A line of men forms, their eyes glued to Gray and Rusty, the spears clutched firmly in their hands doing the talking for them.

"Oh, fish shackles!" says Rusty. It takes Gray a few moments to realize he's cursing. "They saw us!"

They shuffle away from the village, trying not to look like they're running when they most definitely are.

"We were just passing through!" calls Rusty. "Nothing to see here. As you were."

The men lower their spears ever so slightly and Gray feels some pressure release in his lungs. Then he remembers why he'd entered the village in the first place.

"Where's Winter?" he asks Rusty, his steps coming to a stop. "I need to find her."

"She's fine." Rusty grabs his elbow and urges Gray in a different direction. "She was talking to Raze."

"I knew it!" Gray lets out a groan, refusing to move forward. "You have to take me there. Where is she?"

Rusty screws up his face like Gray just spoke another language. "She's not talking to him anymore, obviously."

Gray rolls his eyes. "How exactly is that obvious?"

. . .

Rusty points toward the Ring in the distance. "She's back at your tent. Well, my tent, technically."

Squinting into the distance, Gray sees a small figure beside what he thinks is the tent in the middle of the otherwise empty Fairbanks segment. It seems Rusty might just be speaking the truth. Relief washes through Gray and he lets out a deep breath.

Winter is safe.

"If she's over there," hisses Gray. "Then what are we doing here?"

Rusty points in the opposite direction this time.

Gray turns and blinks at an expanse of dirt stretching before them. Flat and barren like the rest of the Outlands, an area has been marked out to form a large square. Inside the square, lying in the center, is a small pile of weapons.

And standing beside it in a pose that could only be described as a fighter's stance, is Lexis.

At first, Gray thinks Rusty has brought him here to fight her. Then he realizes that Lexis is unaware they're even there. She's focused on an imaginary point in the air in front of her, her eyes boring into it like her worst enemy is staring her down.

She leaps into action, selecting a club from the pile of weapons in one continuous swift movement and swings it through the air. She brings it down with such force that Gray is certain he can feel the ground shake beneath his feet.

Had that enemy been real, he'd be very convincingly, absolutely dead. It's one of the most impressive things Gray's ever seen.

Without thinking, he claps.

Loudly.

Lexis doesn't startle. She doesn't even flinch. It's like she knew they were there, which perhaps she did.

She straightens her back and angles her body to face Gray and a stunned-looking Rusty. Still clutching the club with a murderous look in her eyes, Gray decides she's the most beautiful woman he's ever seen. Even more beautiful than Winter, and until today he'd thought that was impossible.

"Abort!" hisses Rusty. "Abort!"

"What?" Gray looks at him, confused.

"I brought you here to talk to her. To make an alliance." He hops on the spot nervously. "But now I think we should run."

Rusty takes off, making an arc around the village, leaving Gray standing there.

But Gray's not running. He's not going anywhere right now.

This is his chance to make an alliance. Maybe even to make a friend.

Gray steps over the line and enters the square.

"What are you doing?" Lexis shouts, swinging up the club so she's holding the other end in her palm. "This is our Training Ground. Make your own."

"Hi." Gray smiles at her, holding out his hands to show he isn't armed. "Have you got a sec?"

"Do I look like I have *a sec*?" She slaps the club on her palm and widens her stance.

"What is this place?" Gray asks, looking at the pile of weapons.

"Don't move another muscle." Lexis glares at him and he notices how piercing her blue eyes are. It's like she can see right into his soul. Or is that him looking directly into hers?

"Your name's Lexis," says Gray, realizing they've never been properly introduced. "I'm Gray. I like your...club. Is that what you call it?"

She shakes her head. "It's called a nockya."

"Oh." Gray nods, intrigued. "I haven't heard that word before."

She gives him a sly smile. "I call it that because I'm going to use it to nockya into tomorrow, do you understand?"

A laugh winds its way up Gray's throat. So, she's funny as well as fierce.

But before the laugh can find its way out, Lexis swings the club at the back of his knees. His legs buckle and he crashes to the ground.

"Hey!" he cries, holding up a hand. "That hurt."

"Are you for real?" Lexis paces before him. "You're seriously surprised? You're lucky I didn't kill you."

It never occurred to him that she would actually hurt him.

"You can hurt me again if you like, but I'm not going to lay as much as a finger on you." He pulls himself to his feet, wincing at the pain in his legs. "I just want to talk to you."

"I don't talk." Lexis throws her club back on the pile of weapons, which Gray decides to take as a very good sign, even though he's well aware she could kill him with her bare hands.

"I thought it was your brother who doesn't talk," he says.

She launches at him and he flinches as she grabs at his shirt, gathering it up at the neck. Her face is only inches from his.

"Do. Not. Mock. My. Brother," she spits out.

"I'm sorry!" he protests. "I wasn't mocking him. I like your brother! I like you."

She lets go of his shirt and throws him back to the ground. "You're a fool to like me."

"Why?" Gray shoots straight back to his feet, doing his best to show her he's a worthy opponent. Or even just an opponent. Because right now he knows that all she sees is a Ghost. "Why can't I like you?"

Lexis rolls her eyes. "Because I'm going to kill you. Not today. But maybe tomorrow. If not tomorrow, then maybe the day after that. But it's going to happen. You know it, and so do I."

Gray feels a stinging behind his eyes, and he steels himself. He is *not* going to cry in front of this girl made from sunbeams. He's here to make her his friend.

"It doesn't have to be like that," he says. "We can work as a team in the next Tournament. We can be an alliance. We can finish the job you started and take down Cragg."

"Cragg have more than two competitors," says Lexis. "Taking two down will win the Tournament, but it won't eliminate their faction."

Gray's eyes light up. She's talking strategy. This has to be a good sign. He waits for her to continue.

"But killing you and your sister will take out Fairbanks." Lexis smiles like she didn't just say those awful words. "It's the obvious choice."

"Obvious?" Gray laughs, wishing he could make it sound more genuine. "Doing the obvious isn't going to win you these games and you know it. That was why you went for Slab in the first Tournament. You were doing the unexpected."

"And look how far that got me," she snaps. "Why am I even having this conversation, anyway? Get back to your sister. I've got training to do."

Gray pulls his fists up to his chest and plants his feet on the ground. "Train me."

"Stop wasting my time." She sounds almost offended. "Get out of here before I decide to bring your death forward a day."

"Train me," he says again as he takes a step toward her. "Let's do the unexpected."

There's a flash of movement, then a kaleidoscope of colors blurs his vision. For the third time in as many minutes, Gray falls to the hard ground.

Putting his hand to his face, he feels warm sticky blood trailing from his nose.

"You punched me!" Gray looks up at Lexis as he pinches his nose. "What did you do that for?"

"I was training you," she says, brushing her hands on the leather of her tunic.

"For what?" Gray hauls himself to his feet and tries to steady himself. "You didn't teach me anything."

"Oh, but I did," she growls as she comes closer to him. He can feel her warm breath on his face. "I'm teaching you what it's going to feel like right before I kill you in the Tournaments."

Gray lets go of his nose and raises his fists. "Do it again. I wasn't ready last time."

"The Tournaments don't give second chances," she says, refusing to take his bait.

Deciding there's only one way to convince her, Gray throws out his fist in just the way Trakk taught him. Except instead of it landing on his target of Lexis's cheekbone, she catches his hand in her palm and twists.

Hard.

Gray is forced to spin around, and Lexis lands a kick in his lower spine, sending him down.

Again.

She takes a satisfied step back and scowls at him in such a way he's beginning to think that maybe she doesn't like him after all.

It's harder to stand this time, but somehow, Gray gets back on his feet and holds up his fists.

Lexis's eyes flare. She's either very shocked or very impressed.

He decides to believe the latter.

"You're a good teacher," he says, certain he'll be ready this time now that he knows what movements to watch out for. "Why don't we try that one more t—"

Blackness swallows Gray whole, robbing him of every one of his senses in quick succession.

As he falls to the ground, he decides to add one more word to his description of Lexis.

She's not only funny and fierce.

That girl is fantastic.

LEXIS

$\mathcal{L}$exis looks at the crumpled body at her feet. Is this how the Ghosts of Fairbanks have survived this long?

Simply by being tenacious?

Squatting, she notes he's still breathing, although she's not sure why she's bothering to check. She didn't punch to kill, just to get him to back off. Scanning his dark hair and unscarred skin, she admits he's handsome in a soft, I-smile-too-much kind of way. His loss will be a shame…

Shooting to her feet, she steps back. She can't afford to feel anything for this Gray guy. Not even a flicker of regret.

It's going to hurt too much to lose Raze, let alone if someone else were to creep beneath her armor.

Striding away, Lexis makes sure she doesn't look back. Gray's got the message. There will be no alliance.

He won't be alive long enough to uphold whatever his side of the bargain is.

Still, once she reaches the first hut, Lexis finds herself slowing. Tucking into the side, she peers at the Training Ground. Gray is still sprawled in the dirt, the trickle of blood under his nose drying in the evening heat. He needs to wake up. Lying there like that makes him a target. An easy one.

She should leave him alone and walk away. If one of the Cragg or Never find him and slit his throat, it means she won't have to be the one to kill him. It would be better for both of them that way.

She takes a step only to hesitate.

Although…there's no guarantee that the other factions will ensure his death is merciful. Lexis doesn't want that on her conscience. It's so crammed with guilt and heavy with loss, she can barely carry it as it is.

The decision made, Lexis picks up a pebble. She throws the small rock and it bounces off his cheek. Gray doesn't stir. Jaw tight, she throws another. This one glances off his nose, and those lips that are far too fascinating twitch. Lexis waits, breath held, as he jolts and swipes at his face as if a bug just annoyed him.

A second later, his eyes flutter open. Sitting up, he glances around. Lexis ducks back behind the hut and disappears from view. She waits for the space of a breath and then peeks again. Gray is pushing himself to his feet, apparently unaware she's here. He's grinning as he shakes his head and rubs his jaw. He dusts himself off and breaks into a lope, no doubt heading back to their lone, lame tent in the Fairbanks section.

Lexis watches him in amazement. What does it take to wipe that blinding smile off his face?

Frowning, she turns and makes her way back to her own hut, her stomach reminding her it's past evening meal time. Surely, he realizes she's not in a position to help him or his sister, twin or not.

If he doesn't, then he's more of a fool than she thought.

Weaving her way through the huts, Lexis hears a new sound peppering the darkening air. She cocks her head, recognizing it but instinctively knowing it's not good. Hammering and

128

banging have her wondering what's being built at this late hour.

Following the sporadic *thumps* and *cracks*, Lexis realizes she's heading back to the Ring. Tension tangles in her gut as she's reminded only the first Tournament has been completed. What has Evrest planned for them next…

Lexis approaches as cautiously as if it were the next Tournament, the scent of dirt thick around her. Scenes from earlier today flash through her mind. The Ghosts freezing as every body turned to them. The Craggs' eyes lighting up as they readied for an easy kill. Raze being pummeled by Slab's monstrous fists. The Never woman stealing her kill.

Lexis tightens her jaw, dust grinding between her clenched teeth.

Evrest's fury at their failure.

At least the Tournaments have meant he'd kept his clenched fists by his sides. Their father needs them in top physical condition to win these fights. They don't need more bruises and scars to add to their bodies.

Rounding the final hut, Lexis falters as the Ring comes into view. Her gaze roams the circular depression, trying to understand what she's seeing. A wooden structure rises from below ground level, jutting into the twilight sky.

A tower.

Why is a tower being built in the Ring?

Except there's no point asking the question, because she won't get an answer. Not until tomorrow morning when she and Raze jump in along with the other contestants. Ready for another fight to the death.

Consciously stacking vertebrae on vertebrae, Lexis straightens her spine. Ready to spill the blood that will ensure the lives of countless others won't be cut short.

Her stomach contracts painfully and she spins on her heel. The need to be back with Raze is so powerful that she doesn't immediately see her father only a few feet behind her. Jolting herself backward, she abruptly changes her momentum so they don't touch.

Her father narrows his eyes at her. "Lexis."

One word. Her name. And yet all the censure that she was taken by surprise has been infused into those five letters.

She turns sharply away so she's facing the Ring again, allowing the shame to burn at her insides but keeping her gaze impassive.

Her father comes to stand beside her, his hands behind his back, watching as another length of wood—little more than an uneven, barely straight branch—is hammered and strapped to the tower. Lexis waits, realizing he's here for a reason. Every move her father makes is calculated.

He angles his head to glance at the bare space the Rusts have vacated. "It's too bad they're gone. Their boats would've been useful."

"Once the Commander is chosen, they will swear allegiance," she says flatly. "Their boats will become ours."

Evrest grunts in approval. "Yes, they will." His body subtly changes angle, but Lexis notices. She learned at a young age to be highly vigilant around him. "The Never are sneaky. Watch your back."

"Yes, Evrest," Lexis replies dutifully.

"The Cragg are strong. And numerous. But stupid. Finishing them will be like destroying a boulder—you'll have to chip away at their faction, one by one."

Lexis nods. These are words she's heard before. She knows what needs to be done.

She tightens as her father's gaze falls on the Fairbanks area. Neither Winter nor Gray are visible, possibly off begging food or already asleep, for which Lexis is glad. The less she sees of them, the better.

Evrest cocks his head. "The Ghosts are what I assume the people of Askala must be like."

Lexis waits, a part of her not wanting to hear what he'll say next.

"They're softer. Harder to hate." He cocks his head. "Harder to kill."

Lexis's gaze flies to her father before she can stop it. She quickly yanks it away, focusing back on the growing tower, but she knows he saw it.

He knows he struck a chord.

His lip curls in a familiar look of disgust. "The people of Askala believe they're good. They act as if they're above killing." Evrest spits a thin stream of saliva into the dust. "And yet they leave us here to die."

Lexis's gut clenches. Once again, these are familiar words. But this time, they've taken on a new meaning.

Because she should've killed Gray with the first strike. And she should never have stopped to make sure he woke up and walked away.

She hesitated.

And somehow, her father knows it. She can sense the fury building in him.

"After seeing the first Tournament, I'm not sure you have what it takes, Lexis."

The fighter in her immediately steps up. Anger is far preferable to the humiliation scorching through her insides. "I've been preparing for this my whole life," she states emphatically.

She was born to do this.

But her father shakes his head. "Maybe the training wasn't enough. Maybe you have the same soft genes as your brother," he says. "Or maybe it's because you're female."

Lexis stiffens. "I'm strong enough," she hisses. Both she and Raze are.

They're both here, ready to die for this.

"Are you, daughter? Because the Commander can't just be strong of body." He grips his sinewy bicep as he flexes it. "They must be strong of mind, too. Maybe stronger in their conviction to end a life than just their ability to kill with their hands."

Lexis is wound so tight it feels like she might snap. "What do you want from me?"

Her father turns to her, his gaze so full of conviction it almost burns her. "I've already told you what I want. Every member of Cy was there to hear it."

The talk earlier. The one where Raze was as still as a statue beside her.

The one where Evrest stated the Ghosts of Fairbanks must be the next to die.

"The Ghosts are a blight on the Tournaments, Lexis. On everything we've worked toward. And they're dangerous. They'll seek to form alliances." He pins his scarred eyes on her. "They'll make people hesitate."

The irony that it's the same grueling training that Evrest called her childhood that prevents Lexis from reacting to those words—to the truth—isn't lost on her. As she stares impassively back at her father, she quells the sting of shame. The weak part of her that refuses to die.

She throws her shoulders back, mentally shaking off the smiling, handsome face that flashes through her mind. Her father's right. This was probably Gray's ploy all along. Find the foolish part of her that can still feel sympathy.

And use it to his advantage.

"I'll do what needs to be done," she states firmly. Grimly.

Evrest's gaze turns assessing. "We will see."

He turns away, looking back at the tower. Although free of his penetrating eyes, a heavy weight presses on Lexis's chest, making it hard to breathe. Remembering Raze's technique, she stares ahead, unseeing, as she counts silently.

One.

One night to come to terms with what she must do.

Two.

Two lives to end.

Three.

The number of days she would've known Gray…

Abruptly, her father steps away. "Your dinner is in your hut," he calls over his shoulder. "Ensure the double rations are not wasted."

Lexis startles. "Double rations?"

Her father turns and nods. "Of course. I need to keep you strong."

"And Raze?"

The moment the words are out, Lexis regrets it. Not only because her father's eyes flash with annoyance, but because she already knows the answer.

"Of course not," her father growls. "I'm not wasting something as essential as food on him."

On the freak. The one he expects to die.

Never mind it's his son.

"Of course not," Lexis murmurs. "Thank you, Evrest," she adds, her gaze averted.

The show of deference seems to mollify her father, because he walks away. She's glad she wasn't forced to promise she wouldn't share her rations. Some promises she can't keep.

The first one is going to be hard enough.

Because tomorrow, the Ghosts of Fairbanks cannot be alive by the end of the second Tournament.

WINTER

"May the Tournaments serve you well." Evrest's voice echoes across the harsh earth, each word reverberating against Winter's heart.

Everyone remains perfectly still as he leaps from the Ring and takes his place at the front of the crowd.

Winter's muscles coil, conscious of the stillness around her. The only part of the competitors' bodies that moves is their eyes as they track up and down the crude structure that's been built in the center of the Ring. There are three impossibly tall posts that join at the top like a teepee. An uneven branch juts out from the apex, and at the very end dangles a hessian bag.

"What's in there?" Gray whispers beside her.

"Something heavy," Winter murmurs, keeping one eye on the bag and the other on her competitors.

"It's a weapon," says Gray, his voice wavering. "We should get it."

"It could be a trap." Winter sees Slab take a step. Not toward the tower, but them. He's clearly decided whatever is in that bag isn't worth his interest.

Her stomach turns to stone. The Cy twins aren't making any

move to protect them. It seems the alliance they tried to forge is as worthless as she thought it was.

"I'm going to get the bag," says Gray, his face still covered in bruises from the negotiations he had with Lexis that he insisted went so well.

Winter looks back at the tower. "It doesn't look very stable."

"If you have a better plan, now would be the time to speak up," says Gray as Slab takes another step toward them, the other Cragg contracting around their leader. "Because right now, I wouldn't mind a weapon."

Winter swallows as she purses her lips and makes a decision she knows will determine whether they live or die.

She lets out a loud whistle. The exact same one Trakk would use when it was time to run in Fairbanks.

The sharp noise startles Slab and in the split second he hesitates, Winter and Gray run.

She throws herself at the closest post of the tower and Gray heads for the one just behind it. They climb, hauling themselves up with their arms while pushing with their bare feet. It feels almost like Trakk is right behind Winter, urging her on.

Pleased to find the pole is stable, she scrambles higher, aware that one slip could cost everything.

She. Cannot. Fall.

Gray is heavier, but stronger and despite her head start, he's making good progress. She's relieved. They're both safe. For now.

Kicking her foot sharply just in case someone is below her, Winter glances down, shocked to find nobody is following her up the post.

Instead, the other competitors are circling like a school of hungry leatherskins. Not attacking each other, but waiting patiently for their prey to fall.

Winter climbs a little higher as she draws in a harsh breath. Her muscles are used to this kind of punishment. She's scaled a thousand posts like this back in Fairbanks, even if they weren't quite so tall. However, right now, she's tired from the terrible sleep on the hard ground. Hungry, with the bread Rusty brought them not nearly enough to fill her stomach. And sore from the miles she and Gray had walked to get to these Tournaments.

But once the decision had been made to climb, there's only one way to go.

Up.

With each inch she covers as she heads toward the sky, she also gets a little closer to Gray. Soon, her post will meet his and she can draw the strength from him that she's going to need to finish this Tournament alive.

Glancing down, she sees that still, nobody is following them. This only confirms her suspicion that this was a trick. There's something about this tower that they all seem to have realized that Winter and Gray haven't seen. But it's too late to turn back now.

"Stop wasting our time!" one of the Cragg women calls up to them. "We haven't got all day. Git down here so we can kill you already."

"Maybe we're not the ones about to be killed," Gray shouts back. "I'd watch my back if I were you."

Winter winces as the woman shrieks with laughter. Does Gray not know how foolish he sounds? Of course, they're the target. Raze had agreed to nothing when Winter visited him in his hut. And there's no way Gray's meeting with Lexis went any better, no matter what he might think. Knocking someone unconscious isn't the usual way to sign an agreement.

Even for an Outlander.

With sweat staining her palms, climbing higher starts to get more difficult. Winter slips back down a foot, barely managing to stop herself before it would have become a deathly slide.

"You can do it!" says Gray, who's only a few feet away from her now as he waits at the top of his post.

"I know I can," Winter bites out, speaking only loud enough for Gray to hear. "But then what?"

"We get the weapon, climb down and kill ourselves a couple of Cragg." Gray grins at her. "Or if it's a crossbow, maybe we do the last bit the other way around."

Winter lets out a huff as she climbs her way to the top, not wanting to look at her brother's cheerful face when she knows the smile is only skin deep. He's not fooling her for a moment. Nor does she think there's a crossbow in that sack. The way it's hanging down from the branch, it's more likely to be full of dirt.

Gray reaches out as she gets to the apex and she grips harder with the soles of her feet, clinging to the thick twine that's binding the poles together.

She takes her brother's hand. His palms are sticky, and he's shaking. He knows just as well as she does that these could be their final moments.

"No regrets, Winter." His dark eyes blink at her. "I have no regrets and nor should you. This is the fault of the world we were born into. Not yours. Not mine."

She swallows as she squeezes his hand. "No regrets."

Looking away to hide her lie, she studies the sack they climbed up here for. It's the only thing that can save them now. There's no way they can reach it without one of them climbing across the uneven branch it's hanging from.

"I'll go," says Gray.

Winter shakes her head, releasing his hand to grip the post she's clinging to. "I'm lighter."

"No," Gray begs. "I already know what it's like to lose a sister. I am *not* losing another one."

"Then we have a problem," she says. "Because I can't hold onto this post for much longer."

She slips down a few inches as if proving her point. Her

muscles are shaking. It's simply not possible to remain here while Gray goes to get the bag.

He reaches over and grips her wrist, stopping her from sliding any further.

"Told you they were going to fall," floats up a snarl from below. "No point wasting precious energy finishing them off when they're stupid enough to do it themselves."

Winter looks down and catches the eye of the silent boy.

Raze.

The crystal blue of his irises flash up at her. If she didn't know any better, she'd think he was sad.

Please, she mouths at him. *Please.*

Please let him reconsider. Please let him turn on the Cragg and finish this Tournament without either Winter or Gray needing to climb out on that flimsy branch. It makes sense for them to work together. Can't he see that?

Yet, for some reason she can't explain, Raze stands alert but frozen by his sister's side as he waits for Winter and Gray to make a mistake.

Gray sees that Winter's distracted and makes a move over to the branch. But she's faster and she pushes hard with her legs, launching herself past him to grip the branch further along.

It bends with her weight as she swings by her arms, and she moves down a few more inches, threading one hand over the other.

"Get back!" she shouts. "It's going to break with both of us on here."

"Which was why you should have stayed where you were," he calls, as he retreats.

He's mad at her. She can hear it in his voice. But there's no way she was going to cling to that pole and watch this branch snap, sending him falling to his death. A death that would be guaranteed, because if the fall didn't kill him then those savages would be only too glad to finish the job.

Winter makes her way carefully to the end of the branch until she's within reach of the sack. With her arm muscles threatening to give up on her completely, she swings up her legs and loops them around to take some of her weight.

The branch groans and bends.

Glancing back, she sees Gray perched on top of the tower with his hands around the base of the branch, willing it to hold her. The faster she can do this, the better, before he falls off.

The sack is tied with twine and Winter gets to work undoing the knot, aware she needs to be on high alert. Once it comes undone, whatever's inside is going to fall and all this will have been for nothing if she doesn't catch it.

Each time her hand bumps the bag, she becomes more suspicious it's full of dirt. But she hasn't come this far not to make absolutely sure. Gray could be right. There might be a weapon inside.

After the risk they've taken, there'd better be a weapon inside! Their success or failure in this Tournament is riding on it.

"Hurry up!" a Cragg man with a bushy red beard calls up. "I've got things to do today."

"What?" the woman with the screechy voice asks. "You wanna wash your hair?"

There's laughter and Winter ignores the sick feeling building in her gut. They're treating this like a joke! What is wrong with these people? Death is many things, but a joke is not one of them.

"Let 'em try, will ya!" calls a man. "Leave 'em be."

Winter looks around as she continues working on the knot, trying to see who stood up for them. Because the only person to show them any kindness so far has been Rusty, and that definitely wasn't him.

"Shut up, Never!" calls the Cragg woman. "We're not saving you no easy kill. These two are ours."

The knot slips free in Winter's fingertips and she snaps out her hand as the hessian opens up.

Red dirt runs through her fingertips, raining down on the competitors below as it spills out in a constant stream.

Winter curses. She knew this was a trick! They've just sealed their fate. This bag of dirt was their last hope. And with every one of her numbered breaths, the hope drains from her soul along with the worthless contents of the sack.

The branch lifts higher into the air as the load it's supporting reduces. Unless the dirt fills her enemies' eyes and renders them blind, this Tournament is all but over.

She swings her legs down, preparing to return to Gray to see if he has any bright ideas, when a flash of something shiny inside the sack catches her eye.

"Winter!" cries Gray. "Look!"

With no time to respond, she lets go of the branch with one hand and reaches for the object just as it slips from the hessian, her eyes widening to see it's a small silver mace, the head of it covered in sharp spikes.

She swipes at it and misses, her breath hitching as one of the spikes catches on the hessian, leaving it dangling just out of her reach. The ruthless thugs below will be practically salivating at the sight, but Winter can't worry about them now. She has to get that weapon before it falls into their hands.

Gripping the branch with both hands, she swings out her legs and catches the mace between her knees. She winces as the spikes pierce her skin and a sharp flame of pain burns up her thighs.

The branch doesn't seem to like the sudden movement and it bends further.

"Winter!" cries Gray. "Get back here now! It's going to break!"

She threads her way along, putting one hand ahead of the other, but after covering only a couple of feet, she knows she's in trouble. Her muscles are shaking badly. The mace might be small but it's heavy and the searing pain of the spikes embedded in her legs isn't helping the situation one little bit.

"Gray!" she sobs as she bites down on her tongue for the words she knows she must say next. "I need help."

She hates asking this of him. It puts him in danger. But if she falls, then he's as dead as she is. There's no getting around the fact that she needs him.

And she sort of needs him right now.

Gray doesn't waste a moment. He climbs out on the branch with a series of determined movements and is hanging by her side in what feels like an instant.

The branch makes a loud creak and Winter tries not to look down. She's used to jumping and landing on her feet in her runs in Fairbanks and knows which distances are do-able and which are deadly. This branch has purposely been built too high and without the strength it needs to hold them.

Gray lets go with one hand and wraps it around her waist, unable to support her, but giving her a moment's relief.

"You can do this," he says. "You're doing an amazing job. Come on, I'm right here with you. No regrets, remember?"

"No regrets." The words feel like poison on her lips. She has so many regrets it's amazing the branch has lasted this long holding the weight of them all.

She inches toward safety, still clutching the mace as a trickle of blood runs down her shins.

"Oi!" calls the Cragg woman. "Your blood is drippin' into me eyes!"

"I told you to give it a rest!" calls the Never man from the sidelines.

Winter looks down, wondering where Rusty has gotten to. Is he urging the Never on? Is that why that man is being so nice to them? But she's distracted by the Cragg woman marching over to the base of the tower.

"I'll give you a bloody rest!" she shouts, throwing her weight against the post and causing the entire structure to shake.

The other Cragg seem to think this is a great idea and they join her, focusing on the other two posts. The golden twins watch on, not helping the Cragg but making no move to stop them either.

"Ignore them!" cries Gray, urging Winter another foot across the branch as the tower sways wildly.

She pushes back tears and bites down on her lip. "I can't—"

Before the words of defeat can form on her tongue, the branch snaps, still attached to the tower but pointing down now, instead of out.

Winter gasps as she slides down, the skin on her palms searing as gravity takes hold. Panic grips her tight around her middle. Somehow, the mace is still embedded in her skin, remaining firmly and painfully between her knees.

Gray is right behind her and they're almost at the end of the branch as the ground rushes up toward them. Winter desperately clings on harder, but just as she's about to slip right off, the entire tower breaks apart as the supporting posts snap the twine that was binding them.

Winter is flung into the air. As she's freefalling toward the hard ground, she grabs the mace by the handle and tears it from her skin. She holds it above her head, determined for her life to end as a victor, not a loser.

Bracing her legs for impact, she's thrown to the ground. The air is pushed from her lungs and every muscle in her body simultaneously jars as she prepares to die.

Except, the excruciating pain means she's not dead. She *should* be dead.

She tries to lift her head and a sharp pain throbs at her temples, telling her she's very alive right now. Relief pumps through her veins. Somehow, she's made it!

The slide down the branch must have partly spared her. As had this soft thing she seems to have landed on.

What is that?

And why is it screaming?

As her adrenaline surges and sweeps away the worst of the pain, she realizes the Cragg woman is beneath her. And she isn't very pleased about being used to break Winter's fall. Nor is she happy about the spiked mace embedded in the side of her head.

"You bitch!" the woman screams, her face contorted in agony.

Winter opens her mouth to apologize, then gives herself a mental slap. She steadies her feet and pulls the mace from the woman's head. Then squeezing her eyes closed, she brings it down.

Hard.

A warm splatter sprays Winter and she gags, knowing that the job is done.

"Winter!"

She opens her eyes to see Gray limp up beside her. She focuses on him instead of the woman she's certain she just killed.

He has a look of horror on his innocent face as he puts his shaking hands on hers. She lets go, giving him control of the mace.

That's one Cragg down.

One to go.

But as Winter stands and turns to her enemy, it's not the Cragg who are running toward them with a murderous look.

It's Lexis.

The golden killer.

The beautiful assassin.

"Gray!" Winter screams. "Look out!"

Gray turns to Lexis with the bloodied mace clutched in his hand.

"Kill her!" screams Winter, clenching her fists for a fight she's too exhausted to have.

But Gray doesn't raise the mace. He doesn't even flinch as Lexis grinds to a stop before them.

Instead, he holds out the weapon by the handle and…gives it to her.

He smiles proudly as Lexis takes the mace. "I knew you'd come to help us."

Winter collapses to her knees and buries her face in her hands.

Because *she knew* that one day her beautiful brother's trusting heart would be the thing that got them killed.

RAZE

*R*aze watches his sister stop as if someone just punched her in the gut. Lexis glances down at the mace she's now holding. The weapon that was gifted to her.

She falters, as if she's never held the weight of one before. As if she doesn't realize the damage it can inflict.

In that moment, Raze realizes she won't kill the Fairbanks boy.

And for some confusing reason, he's relieved. One blow from the mace and he would've been dead.

It would've been an easy kill. But also a heartless one.

Lexis spins around so her back is to the twins. She glances at Raze and he knows what she's communicating. One Cragg is dead. If they kill another, this Tournament is won.

"Kill them!" roars Slab, his hot gaze on the Ghosts of Fairbanks.

"Why would we?" taunts Lexis. "All we need to do is end one of you."

Slab's massive shoulders flex as his head drops menacingly. "Me daughter will be avenged."

Everything in Raze stills. The stakes just went up exponentially. The woman lying in a pool of blood was the Cragg leader's daughter.

Their need for blood is no longer only fueled by the desire to win the Tournaments. It's now powered by vengeance.

Slab points a thick finger at Winter. "She's dead." His arm swings to include her brother who just moved closer to her. "And then he is."

Raze's muscles coil as he clears his mind, shutting out the dull pain of the bruises he's already accumulated. The Ghosts of Fairbanks won't be dying today.

Which means someone else will.

The People of the Cragg come at them as one solid mass of fury, square faces twisted and snarling.

Lexis runs, just as Raze expected she would. Not only does it mean maintaining some distance between the Cragg and the Fairbanks twins, but she's letting them know she's not afraid.

That she'll meet them head on.

Raze joins her, glad she has the mace. There's no way they can stop this wall of hatred without it.

She swings it back, her arm stretching to gain the widest arc possible. Raze calculates the trajectories in the same way Lexis would be. She'll need to bring down the mace at just the right time to hit Slab in the side of the head. A one blow kill.

The mace sweeps in a diagonal curve, Lexis letting out a grunt with the exertion. Slab doesn't slow his furious pace, either too stupid to realize what's coming, or too stupid to care. Raze braces himself for it to hit flesh, wishing he didn't already know what it will sound like.

But Slab twists at the last moment, turning his head and angling his body. The mace slams into his shoulder, and instead of impaling in muscle, it glances off as if it just hit rock instead of man.

They have some sort of armor under their clothes!

Slab crashes through Lexis, knocking her out of the way like an annoying pebble, the mace flying out of her hand. She tucks herself in as she tumbles over the dirt, quickly regaining her footing the first opportunity she gets.

But by then Slab has moved on. His hot, stony gaze is locked on Winter.

And he now has the mace.

"We only have to kill one of them!" Lexis shouts.

Raze sets his sight on the man closest to him and raises his fists, never losing momentum. The Cragg tries to bowl him over in the same way Slab did Lexis—head down like a battering ram. But Raze was expecting that. He slams his elbows into either side of the man's neck as his head collides with Raze's chest.

Every molecule of air is knocked from his lungs, but it doesn't matter. Raze doesn't need oxygen right now. He needs to win.

And the Cragg just groaned as the double strike pulverized the tendons of his neck.

Raze's fist curves up, connecting with the man's chin and his forward momentum is instantly altered. His head snaps back as his spine arches and he's propelled backward. Raze follows him, fists pummeling without mercy.

The man collapses and Raze knows what he has to do next.
End this.

He kneels, ready to snap the man's neck when a body crashes into him. One that feels like a boulder. Raze slams into the dirt, finding another Cragg on top of him. Slab shoots past them, the way to Winter and Gray now unhampered.

"Take out the mute, Cairn," he calls.

The man's hands clamp around Raze's neck, his face twisted with victory above him. "When we end you Cy puppets, nothing will stop us from winning the Tournaments."

Raze grabs the man's forearms only to find they're forged

from cords of steel. He digs his fingers in, gripping the ropy muscles, and yanks.

The hold constricting his neck doesn't loosen.

Lexis grunts to his left somewhere, obviously in a fight of her own. And Raze isn't there to protect her.

Raze shoots his fists between the man's arms and powers them wide. The man's hands tear away from his neck, his thick fingernails gouging at the skin. Before the Cragg can make another move, Raze's fist smashes into his nose and blood gushes into his open mouth.

Raze bucks and knocks the man off. He stands, getting his bearings. There's no time to kill. They need to stop Slab before he reaches the Ghosts.

He's running as he registers where his sister is—sprinting toward Winter and Gray.

Just like Slab is, the spiked mace held high.

Raze injects everything he has into streaking at the man. Stopping him before he reaches either of his targets is his sole mission.

"Look out!" screams someone from behind Raze. Cairn. The Cragg he didn't finish.

Just as Raze is about to collide with Slab, the man turns, altering the trajectory of the mace. There's no chance for Raze to avoid it.

He twists, trying to protect himself. Pain explodes as the spikes impale into his thigh. Raze crumples, inhaling sharply as Slab yanks the mace out and the pain flames again. He clutches his leg, a scream lodged in his throat. Thick blood oozes over his fingers, agony clouding his vision.

"No!" screams Lexis.

But Slab is already moving again, his sights back on his targets.

Raze tries to stand, only to find his leg is little more than macerated meat. He groans silently as he stumbles and falls, dust sucking into his lungs with each pain-filled breath.

Lexis.

The others.

He's failed.

Cairn, the Cragg who tried to strangle Raze, joins Slab. They grin at each other before turning back to their victims. They're practically salivating in anticipation.

Raze blinks through the pain clouding his vision. Lexis is still, her feet planted firmly as she waits for the attack. Winter isn't far behind, her fists raised in a way that shows she has no idea what she's doing. Her twin, Gray, is glancing around frantically, as if he's sure there's a way out of this.

Except Lexis is facing two Cragg, and one with a weapon.

Raze drags himself along the ground, his leg nothing but a mass of pain. He'll die fighting for Lexis.

That's what he was born to do.

Suddenly, Gray is pointing at him.

Cairn clenches his fists. "We ain't fallin' for that trick, Ghost."

But Gray points with even more fervor, his face twisting with urgency.

Slab throws a disgusted look over his shoulder, barely glancing at Raze. "You fink he's gonna save you?" he jeers. "Once we're done with you, he's next."

Gray's gaze flickers beside Raze before Slab steps in his line of sight.

A scream that's desperate for sound echoes through Raze's throat as Slab and his friend launch at Lexis. She ducks the first swipe of the mace. Leaps over the second, even throwing out a kick that Slab deftly avoids.

And the whole time, the second Cragg is inching his way toward Winter and Gray.

Raze drags himself another inch, nausea climbing up his

throat as the world swims. He registers the hessian bag an arm's-length away, the one that was tied to the top of the tower, and he realizes that's what Gray was indicating to. Did the fool think Raze could use it as a weapon? That maybe he could use it to slap the Craggs into submission?

Raze is turning away when the glint of metal catches his eyes. He turns back, scrabbling through the brown material. Disbelief ricochets through him when his fingers wrap around something.

The smooth hilt of a blade.

Of course Evrest tucked a second weapon into the bag. It was sitting there, waiting for someone smart enough not to make assumptions.

Or desperate enough to check twice.

Raze rolls onto his side, seeing that Slab is still attacking Lexis. He's moving too fast to be a solid target.

Cairn, on the other hand, is now running at Winter, his roar of victory echoing through the Ring.

A roar that was shouted too soon.

A flick of the wrist and the knife is flying through the air. Cairn's roar is severed as the blade impales between his shoulder blades, becoming nothing more than a gurgle. Winter jumps back as his lifeless body falls to the dirt.

"No!" cries Slab. He spins around, his furious gaze on Raze. "You killed my son!"

But before he can move, someone leaps into the Ring. Evrest stalks through the bloody mayhem as everything falls silent. He claps once. Twice.

Slab bounces on the balls of his feet, the thirst for revenge thrumming through their bodies, but the need to win keeps them in place.

"The second Tournament has been won," Evrest says calmly. "Two Cragg are dead."

There's a pause and then a cry erupts from the crowd and

for long seconds, Raze can't think of what there is to celebrate. Everyone apart from the Cragg are still frozen with shock.

Evrest pauses as he strides past Raze. He barely glances at his son as he lies bloody and barely conscious in the dirt.

"And yet you both failed," he snarls under his breath.

As Evrest walks away, Raze drops his head, relieved it's over. Pain washes over him in greater and greater waves as the adrenaline recedes. He can feel the call of oblivion, and right now, he welcomes it.

Winter appears above him, her beautiful face twisted with worry.

Lexis appears beside her, her face hard. "He's going to be fine," she says as if her force of will is all that's needed to make that true.

"For that to happen, we'll have to stem the bleeding," says Winter.

Raze pants through the pain as Lexis quickly assesses his injury. His mind feels as decimated as his body.

Winter's face softens. "Thank you," she mouths.

Raze blinks, his eyes gritty with dust. They were supposed to kill this beautiful creature who is trying to give him comfort. They were supposed to end her and her twin, Gray.

And yet Lexis disobeyed Evrest.

"Hold on," Lexis says, steel laced through her voice.

A soft warm hand slips into his as Lexis presses firm pressure over his wound. Raze arches his back as pinpricks of black explode across his vision, clutching Winter's hand like a lifeline.

As the agony flares again, Raze loses consciousness. His last thoughts detonate through him with the same explosive power as the pain.

He knows why he helped his twin. Why he's glad she didn't follow orders.

He doesn't want Lexis becoming their cruel, cold-blooded father.

GRAY

*G*ray limps to the Fairbanks segment outside the Ring with his sister tucked under his arm. They're both injured. But, somehow, they're alive.

"I knew we could do it," he whispers.

"Shut up, Gray," Winter replies. "We got lucky, that's all."

They get to their tent and Winter crawls inside, wincing as she rolls up the legs of her pants to inspect the damage from the mace.

"How bad is it?" he crouches down beside her, grimacing as he sees the lines of blood that have stained her skin with streaks of crimson.

"They're only surface wounds." She pats the skin gently with her fingertips. "I'm nowhere near as injured as Raze. I'll live."

Gray smirks at her and she pokes out her tongue. She *will* live. But for how long? Forever, if it were up to him.

There's a rustle outside the tent and Gray spins around. It's no secret the Cragg want them dead, and he wouldn't be surprised if they took their chance outside the Tournaments where there are even fewer rules than within.

"You guys were awesome!" says Rusty, grinning as he squints in the beating sun.

"I didn't see you there." Gray makes no move to get out of the tent to greet him.

Winter leans forward. "You were with the Never, weren't you?"

"What makes you think that?" Rusty tilts his head as he squares his solid shoulders.

Winter narrows her eyes and Gray remembers the man from Never who'd shouted out in their defense. Except, he's not as sure as his sister seems that Rusty had anything to do with that.

"No reason," she says, cautiously.

"Yeah, I was with them," Rusty mumbles as he looks to his left.

Lie.

Everyone knows if someone looks to their left they're lying. But why? To seem like he was helping them, when clearly he wasn't? Rusty is certainly keen to impress when there's no danger to himself. He'd left Gray for dead in the Training Ground when they'd gone to talk to Lexis.

Except, there'd been no danger that time.

Lexis might have played a little rough, but she hadn't killed Gray when they all know she could have. And she'd made sure he was okay before she left him. Granted, throwing a pebble at someone's face isn't the usual way to express concern but that's what it was. She was *concerned* about him, whereas Rusty seems only to care about himself.

"What are you doing here, anyway?" Winter asks with a frown.

Rusty produces a thick, green stem of some kind of fleshy plant.

"Aloe vera," he says, proudly, like that's supposed to make any kind of sense. "Used for burns but also cuts. You should put it on your legs, so you don't get an infection."

He squats down and holds it out. Winter snatches it from his hands, making Gray think her wounds are bothering her more than she's letting on.

"Have you given any of this to Raze?" She tears off a piece of the plant and rubs it into her legs and sighs. The dampness wipes away the blood and she instantly looks so much better.

Rusty shakes his head. "Why would I give any to a Cy?"

"Why would you give any to Fairbanks?" Gray asks. "What are you up to, Rusty? What are you still doing here?"

Rusty eyes Gray cautiously. "There's no law against watching. I want to see what happens."

Winter continues to dab at her wounds. "Actually, I'm pretty sure the Rust were meant to go home when you lost the first Tournament."

"I did go home," he says. "But there's no rule about coming back."

"Is that where you got this?" Winter holds up the bloodied piece of plant. "Your home?"

Rusty makes a non-committal grunt as he stands. "The ocean isn't all that far from here."

Winter nods as she places the piece of aloe on the ground beside her.

"You can eat that." Rusty points at it. "It's gross, I know. But a bit of blood never killed anyone. Unless they're losing it, of course."

Winter screws up her face. "I think I'll pass."

"Can we eat the clean bit?" Gray asks.

"Do what you like with it." Rusty grins. "You can eat it for strength. You can use it on Winter's cuts. Or...you can give it to the Cy twins as a peace offering. Raze could sure use some of this stuff right now. It might be just the advantage you need."

Winter's brows shoot up.

Rusty turns to Gray. "By the way, your girlfriend's in the Training Ground if you want to talk to her."

"My girlfriend?" Gray feels a flush rise to his cheeks.

"You know who I mean." Rusty flashes him a smile and walks off.

Gray shakes his head, bewildered. "I don't get that guy."

Winter nods. "He's the most annoying guardian angel on the face of the earth."

A hot breeze floats through the tent and Gray stretches out his legs. He's going to be covered in bruises from when the tower was pushed over. It was only sheer luck that one of the poles had swept past him on its way to the ground and he'd been able to use it to break part of his fall.

"I think we should take the plant to Raze," says Winter. "Rusty's right. It's the option that makes best sense."

Gray's stomach groans in response. "Eating something also makes sense right now."

"Eating will keep us alive until the next Tournament." She reaches out to touch him on the arm. "Healing my cuts will do the same. But forging an alliance could keep us alive well past that."

He swallows, knowing she's right, but hating having to forego a meal.

"I tell you what." Winter takes the clean aloe from her pocket and snaps it in two. "This half is for Raze. And this half is for us."

She breaks the piece into half again and hands him a portion.

"Are you sure?" he asks as he takes it.

She nods and he rubs the moisture onto his dry lips, watching as his sister does the same.

"Cheers," she says, holding out her piece before taking a bite.

Gray puts a piece in his mouth, wincing at the bitterness but not caring in the slightest what it tastes like. It's both quenching his thirst and filling his empty stomach. The morsels of food that Rusty has brought them just haven't been enough.

"So, are you going to talk to her?" Winter asks as she chews.

"Who?" Gray licks a drop of moisture from his fingertips.

"Your *girlfriend*." His twin smirks playfully.

"I thought it was you who was going to talk to Raze," he points out, ignoring the way she's teasing him.

"I will," she says, as she lies down and pats her stomach. "But I need a catnap first. You know, sleep off this giant meal we just had."

"She saved our lives," he says, as the reality of Lexis's actions sinks in. "Raze did, too. They could have killed us, but they didn't."

"Handing Lexis that mace was probably the dumbest thing you've ever done." Winter closes her eyes as she tries to get comfortable. "And, also, the smartest."

Gray nods. He can see now what a risk he'd taken by doing that. It just hadn't occurred to him that Lexis might turn on them. And he'd been right. She'd turned on the Cragg instead.

"Are you sure you're okay?" he asks, the sudden need to thank Lexis burning inside him. "I won't be gone long."

"Go!" She waves a hand at him. "If she wanted to kill you, she'd have done that already. Although, I wouldn't rule out her punching you in the nose again. Be careful."

"How do I look?" he asks, smoothing down his dark tangle of hair.

"You want the truth?" His twin opens her eyes a crack. "You look good. Stupidly good for someone living out here."

He nods, happy with that answer and stalks to the outer edges of the camp so he can get to the Training Grounds without having to pass through any other faction's segment. Especially the Cragg. Lexis isn't easy to catch alone. This could be his only chance to thank her.

As he passes the outer edge of the Never's camp, he sets his eyes on the Training Ground in the distance and admits to

156

himself that thanking Lexis isn't the only reason he wants to see her.

He wants the chance to be near her. To find out more about the stories that lie beneath those haunted blue eyes. What experiences have made her so hard? And what's happened in her life that's meant she's been able to hold onto all the parts of her that he knows are still soft?

Because he's seen kindness in her. Loyalty to her brother. Compassion for Gray and Winter's plight. And a respect for human life. Those are qualities a person is born with, and he knows they still spark inside Lexis. If only life were different, and he could feed that spark and watch her shine bright.

But life isn't different, he reminds himself as Lexis comes into sight.

She's running through a routine of kicks and punches, sweeping her limbs through the air like she's punishing an invisible enemy. As he gets closer and sees the anguish on her face, he realizes that perhaps it's herself she's punishing.

He heard what her father said at the end of the Tournament. That Lexis and Raze had failed, when the fact they're still breathing is proof of their success.

Approaching quietly, he stands a few feet away from Lexis, waiting for her to notice him.

She finishes a series of roundhouse kicks then draws still, her back facing Gray.

"I know you're there," she says.

He smiles. Of course, she does. This girl is a trained warrior. Nobody can sneak up on her.

"Why don't you just leave me alone?" she asks.

"If you really want me to, then I will." His hands go to his hair and he stops himself from trying to fix it.

Lexis doesn't reply. Nor does she turn. Her back remains facing him.

"You're a good person," says Gray. "I know you are."

"I'm not." Her voice is a whisper.

"You are," he insists. "I've seen it."

"A good person wouldn't let their brother die for them." Her shoulders hunch just enough to tell Gray how upset she is.

"He didn't die," says Gray. "And nor did I. Thanks to you."

Lexis remains as quiet as her silent twin.

"You're a good person," he says again, wishing she'd believe him.

He stands still, concentrating on the hint of a breeze that's floating through the Training Ground. And for the first time, he thinks he might understand why Raze chooses not to speak—if in fact his silence is his choice. What words can be spoken to make any of this okay? They've been born into the cruelest of existences, with a future that none of them asked for, or any of them want.

He takes a step closer to Lexis. She must hear his footstep. She must be aware of the raggedness of his breathing. But she doesn't move.

He steps closer again.

And again.

And now he's right behind her with his heart beating fast.

"You're a good person, Lexis. I know you are. I see it. I see *you.*"

Slowly, she turns, and blinks at him, her lower lip trembling.

He remembers Winter's warning about Lexis punching him on the nose, but he doesn't flinch. Lexis won't hurt him. Just as he sees the truth in her soul, he knows she sees the truth in his.

"I see you, Lexis," he says, daring to lift his fingertips to her cheek. "I see you."

She leans into his touch and his stomach contracts as his breath hitches in his throat.

"I want to kiss you," he says. "Not because of how beautiful you are. Not because I want to take anything away from you. But because I want to be close to you."

He waits a few beats of his heart for her to pull away. To give him a sign that this isn't what she wants. This golden girl before him has grown up in a world where men take what they want from women. He has to know that she wants this, too.

She presses up on her toes, leveling the distance between their lips. This is what he was waiting for, and he wastes no time in kissing her.

Slowly. Gently. With far more restraint that he'd ideally like.

He wants to show Lexis how love can feel. How the power of touch doesn't always have to be deadly.

It can be...so good.

It's Lexis who deepens the kiss and Gray is right there with her. Kissing the girl who wants to be his enemy. Kissing the enemy he wants to be his girl.

"I see you," he murmurs against her lips, despite the fact his eyes are firmly closed.

Because what he sees is the only part of her that matters. He sees this warrior girl's beautiful, troubled soul.

And he likes it.

LEXIS

*L*exis can't breathe.

But she doesn't care. She doesn't want to.

She just found something else to fuel her.

Gray.

He's holding her in a way that she's never been held. He's touching her in a way she's never been touched.

And he's kissing her in a way that she never knew existed.

Gray's hands come up to cup her jaw, caressing her with a tenderness that makes her knees weak. And yet, his lips, his mouth, his tongue consume her. The sensations are heady. Intoxicating. She kisses him back as she falls, spirals, into the unknown. Into something she just discovered she desperately wants.

Lexis grips him as the desire for more explodes between them. She gasps. She had no idea there could be...more.

"Lexis," Gray breathes, sounding just as stunned as she is.

She draws away an inch, their breaths mingling. She wants to say it back. She wants to tell him this is rearranging every part of her existence, too.

There's a sound, a barely-there soft crunch of gravel, but it pierces the sweet haze that had been wrapping around her. She leaps back, desperately hoping it's not what she thought it was.

But her lifetime of training knows it is. Someone else is here.

And her lifetime of living with danger knows *who* it is.

Evrest.

He's standing at the edge of the Training Ground, which means he got far closer than he should've. Her stomach clenches, feeling like it's full of jagged shards. Lexis didn't hear him approach because she was kissing the enemy.

Stepping away from Gray as if he's suddenly poisonous, her gaze meets her father's. Even at this distance, she can feel the frozen fury that holds him still.

"We didn't do anything wrong, Lexis," Gray says quietly beside her.

She spins to face him, her face stamped with disbelief. How can he even say that? She just betrayed everything she's supposed to stand for. There's nothing right about that.

"You need to run, Gray. Now."

Most things are punishable by death in her world, including betrayal.

He frowns. "Because we kissed? That's just stupid." Something sparks in his dark eyes. "I'll run if you come with me."

Lexis blinks. How can she be drawn to someone who is so opposite to her? How can he think that's even an option?

Lexis turns back to her father and starts walking, doing the opposite of Gray's suggestion. She walks toward her father.

Evrest remains where he is at the edge of the Training Ground, watching her approach. He doesn't move a muscle, as still as the statue of Cy, the only thing in this world he loves.

The closer Lexis gets, the more details she sees. Evrest is barely breathing, barely blinking, not even a scar twitches on his face. And she has no idea what that means.

Fury she could've handled. Fury she can predict. Violence she's used to.

But the stillness terrifies her.

She stops a few feet away. "I was curious, nothing more."

"You wanted to see what scum tastes like?" Evrest asks quietly. Dispassionately.

It tasted like the sweetest mana Earth could create. Lexis doubts even Askala has anything that could compare.

But she keeps her gaze blank and steady as she regards her father. "And we now have a common enemy, the Cragg. An alliance with Fairbanks ensures we can remove our greatest threat from the Tournaments."

"That's quite the alliance, daughter," he sneers. "How far are you willing to go?"

Even though the jibe has bile crawling up her throat, Lexis ignores the way her father just demeaned the only moment in her life where she truly let go. "Killing my own twin isn't enough?" she spits back.

"There will be no alliance," her father promises, glancing over her shoulder and telling her that Gray is foolish enough to have remained. "Because I'm going to kill him."

He goes to step around her, his movements short and sharp, but she shifts to block him. "He's mine."

Evrest narrows his eyes at Lexis, the action small but infinitely dangerous.

"He's my kill," she says. "These Tournaments must be won fairly or the title of Commander could be contested."

Her father's eyes flare as he covers the distance between them. He stops so their feet are almost touching and his sour breath is brushing her face. His fury makes her blood run cold. "I need proof. You've been making too many mistakes. You're getting soft." He hisses the last word, as if he can barely even utter it.

Dread creeps up Lexis's spine. "What proof?"

"Your brother is injured. I just checked on him and the wound is a significant one. If he doesn't recover, give him this."

Evrest opens his hand to reveal a small pouch he must've been gripping the whole time.

It's why he came looking for her.

Lexis doesn't touch it. "What is it?"

Evrest's lips twist into a smile. "That depends on how much a person consumes. One pinch will help you sleep." His sick smile turns into a sadistic grin. "Double that and they're not waking up."

Evrest was always clear that if it came down to it, Lexis would have to kill Raze. But poison? Where is the honor in that? For her? Or for Raze...

Conscious Evrest is waiting, that she needs to pass this test, Lexis takes the pouch. It's not very big, maybe the size of a small rock. And yet carries the power of life or death.

"Raze is a dead man walking. You'd be doing him a favor and you'd be proving you can do what needs to be done." Her father lifts his hand a little higher. "I thought you realized how important this is. That sacrifices need to be made."

The five factions of the Outlands depend on the outcome of these Tournaments. Countless lives. Every soul who has died of disease or starvation or violence as humanity struggles to survive is a testament to what will happen if this fails.

Lexis tucks the pouch behind her belt, bitter bile staining her tongue. "Like I said, I'll do what it takes."

Evrest straightens. "If you fail, you might as well take it yourself," he snarls before turning and striding away.

Lexis watches her father leave, emotions crashing over each other so fast she feels light-headed. There's the relief that Gray wasn't killed just because she made the error of kissing him. There's the worry about Raze's injury.

And the horror at what she just agreed to.

She hears Gray approach and a part of her has to force herself to face him, but she does it anyway. She's never allowed herself to be a coward.

He stops, standing too close, and Lexis winces. Just as she suspected, looking at him hurts.

"I told you you're a good person," Gray says quietly. "You just saved my life, again."

Lexis swallows, wondering if this sick feeling burning in her stomach will ever go away. "How much did you hear?"

"Very little, but his intent was clear." Gray's lips twitch as if his smile is never far away. "He wanted to tear me limb from limb."

Standing there, so close to Gray, Lexis realizes why this soft, sweet Ghost slipped past her defenses. There's a light in Gray, one that nothing can extinguish. And in her bleak, dark world, she's like a moth to his eternal flame.

Except she can't afford to self-destruct like that. She tightens every muscle like she does each time she goes into battle. Each time she has to destroy, whether she likes it or not.

"So, you didn't hear that I told him that I wanted to kill you myself?" she growls. "That I intend on winning these Tournaments by being the last one standing?"

Gray reels back a little as each question is fired at him. He shakes his head. "You just said that so your father didn't kill me."

Lexis quickly closes the distance he just created, needing him to understand this. "I said it because I meant it. I will win these Tournaments. I will be the next Commander." Her gut twists as she says the next words. "The kiss changed nothing, Gray."

She steels herself for the hurt that will no doubt cross his face. A part of her hopes he'll get angry. Maybe hate her in the same way she hates herself right now.

Gray narrows his eyes. "From where I was standing, it changed everything."

Lexis blinks, bewildered. She should hit him, push him into the dirt. Show him who she really is.

Instead, she spins on her heel and strides away. Gray will

learn the truth about her in the Ring. They have five Tournaments to go. He won't be surviving one of them.

As she makes her way back to her hut, she realizes the sick feeling won't be going away. Not ever. Because all the parts that are wrong with Lexis are rotting her from the inside out.

Stepping through the door, Lexis discovers her father had been telling the truth—he's been here. Two cups of water sit in the middle of the hut, their rations beside it, Lexis's twice as much as Raze's.

But despite her forever-hungry stomach and permanent thirst, she's forgotten the rations the moment she looks at her brother. He's barely moved since she left him asleep on their mat, but Lexis can tell that in just the short amount of time she was gone, he's deteriorated. The shallow breathing, the pale skin painted in sweat, tell her that Evrest was right.

Raze's wound is a significant one.

She rushes over, falling to her knees. "Raze," she whispers. "It's bad. How bad?"

He turns his head slowly as his eyes open. His hand comes up to grasp hers and squeeze. He's trying to tell her he's okay.

Lexis's heart contracts painfully. Even if he could talk, Raze wouldn't tell her if he's in pain. He's the sacrificial lamb, and they don't get to complain.

Lexis reaches over to pick up one of the cups of water, being careful not to spill a drop. "Here," she says quietly. "You need to drink."

Something flickers in Raze's gaze but Lexis just frowns at him. This isn't a fight he's going to win. Grudgingly, he lifts his head, and she notes how his muscles tremble at the effort. Tipping the cup to his lips, she helps him drink.

Twice, he tries to pull away, but both times Lexis doesn't let him, knowing he's trying to save a larger proportion for her. She keeps tipping it up until the cup is empty. His head falls heavily once he's done, his eyes closing. The fact Raze didn't have the energy to throw his sister a scolding glare tells her how drained he is.

Next, she grabs a slice of the flatbread and brings it to his lips. "Here, just a bite."

Maybe she can get a little bit of energy into him before he rests. His body will need it to heal.

Except, Raze turns his head away. Frowning, Lexis shuffles closer and presses it against his mouth. "You need to have something."

But Raze's lips simply tighten, his head twisting back to face her. His blue gaze is hard with determination as he shakes his head.

Lexis sits back, hating the sense of helplessness that's growing within her. Raze will have the water, but not the food. No point wasting that on a wounded soldier.

Not when he's a dead man walking.

"Please," she whispers.

But Raze does what he always does when life becomes too painful. He closes his eyes and turns away. He shuts down, drawing his silent armor around him.

Lexis's shoulders sag. For brief seconds, she considers washing his wound with her own cup of water, only to quickly reject the idea. The water holds as much bacteria as the air. She'll probably be hastening the very scenario that's terrifying her right now.

Infection.

The pouch tucked into her belt feels like a jagged thorn in her side. When will she be expected to use it? When Raze is too weak to even drink? When he becomes feverish? When the wound is little more than festering flesh?

Lexis's eyes slam shut as she swallows down the bile that just rushed up. These were their roles since birth. If Raze is the sacrificial lamb, then she's the cold-blooded executioner.

Just like her father.

A quiet knock at the door has her shooting to her feet and reaching for her spear. The People of Cy don't knock, which means it's someone from the other factions.

Gray…

Lexis ignores the way her heart lurches, striding to the door as she stamps a ferocious frown on her face. This time, she will hit him.

Except it's not Gray standing there, it's Winter. She extends her hand, revealing something green sitting in her palm. "This is for you." She holds Lexis's gaze. "Slab wants us both dead. This is an alliance we both need."

Lexis barely glances at the peace offering as she sets down her spear. "What is it?"

"Aloe. You can eat it, or…" Winter glances over Lexis's shoulder to where Raze is lying on the ground. "You can use it to clean your twin's wound."

Every muscle in Lexis's body locks. If she lets Winter in, the alliance is cemented. They will owe the Ghosts of Fairbanks.

She steps back, creating space for Winter to enter. "Deal."

Winter looks startled for a second, as if she was expecting to have to convince Lexis more. But helping Raze is a given.

Lexis waves to her brother, hoping he sleeps through this. He'd approve of what she's doing as much as Evrest would. "Do what you can."

Winter nods, glancing around cautiously like she's expecting this to be a trap. When she sees they're alone, she moves to Raze and kneels beside him. Raze doesn't move when she lifts the scrap of material covering his wound.

Lexis looks away, not because of the sight of the macerated flesh, but because she knows their fates just became definitively interwoven. Maybe they were all along. Although, not because of the alliance. She was telling the truth when she told her father it would be advantageous.

No, it's the knowledge that by doing this, Lexis is inviting

Gray into her life. That now, the Tournaments have become even harder. More painful. A place where the only thing that defines victory is loss.

Her hand brushes her lips. Even though she's never experienced anything like their kiss, she knows it was special. Extraordinary. A once in a lifetime connection.

But she has that with Raze. A twin bond that doesn't need words, one that was forged in the womb.

And that won't be enough to stop her from killing him, too.

WINTER

W inter stares at the wound on Gray's leg and is transported back to a time when her older sister's body had been carried home after losing her newborn baby in the ruins of Fairbanks. Winter had only been young at the time and had hidden behind her mother's skirt. She remembers being frightened. Not by her sister's death, but by the grief vibrating off her mother.

Lexis has that same energy emanating from her. She's scared Raze is going to die. Which is kind of odd given that she must always have known he would. It's clear what his role is in life—to help Lexis win the Tournaments.

At any cost.

"Raze," Winter whispers. "Can you hear me?"

"He's asleep," says Lexis. "Do what you came here to do and leave."

Winter listens to the way Raze's breath picks up pace. He's not asleep. He's listening to every word.

"I'm just going to clean your wound with some aloe," she says. "I put some on my own legs earlier and they're feeling a lot better already. Not that my wounds are as bad as—"

She swallows, trying not to gag at the sight of his injury. When she'd offered Lexis the aloe to clean Raze's wounds, she hadn't expected to have to do it herself. But it's better this way. Now Lexis owes her just that little bit more.

Focusing on splitting the aloe down the middle to reveal its fleshy insides, she tries not to look at Raze. Or the piece of flatbread sitting beside him.

Her stomach groans loudly. Her eyes may not have fixed themselves on the bread, but it seems her stomach has. It protests again at the lack of attention she gives it.

"Get on with it," snaps Lexis, sensing her hesitation.

Winter takes one half of the aloe and presses it to the uppermost part of Raze's wound. If it hurts him, she has no way of knowing. This is a guy used to pain. He almost thrives on it.

As gently as she can, she gets to work, dabbing the aloe to clear away the dirt and small stones that have been caught in the wound and leaving behind a clear sticky film. She works methodically and quickly, doing her best not to cause any unnecessary pain.

Raze's legs are lined with muscled, altogether different to her brother's strong but lean frame. The hairs that coat his shins are dark blond, trailing up his thighs until they disappear before getting thicker again at the very top of his legs—where she is definitely not looking.

A flush spreads to her cheeks to think how close she is to all the parts of him that are most private, and she concentrates on what she's doing.

This guy is strong. This guy is handsome. She reluctantly admits, he's possibly even sexy. But he would kill her in less than a second if it meant advancing his sister in the Tournaments. She'd do well to remember that.

"My brother likes you," Winter says, putting aside the used aloe and reaching for the other half. Her cheeks cool now that she's deflected her attention to Lexis.

"That's unfortunate for him," Lexis replies.

"Why's that?" Winter squeezes some juice from the aloe and starts at the bottom of Raze's wound this time, preparing to go over it again.

"Let me be clear about what's happening here." Lexis crosses her arms. "I owe you. I realize that. But all that means is that instead of killing you and your brother first, we'll be killing you last."

Winter grimaces. She works a little faster, being less gentle than she was before as she absorbs the truth in what Lexis just said.

Raze tenses underneath her fingertips and she backs off.

"Sorry," she mumbles. It's not his fault his sister is so ruthless.

She finishes her work until all that remains of the aloe vera are two withered looking skins.

"I'm done," she tells Lexis as she stands and wipes her sticky hands on her shirt.

"Do you know what would help him heal even more?" Lexis asks.

"No?" Winter taps a foot as she waits for Lexis to explain.

"If he ate something." She points at the plate beside him. "Which he is currently refusing to do."

Winter's brows pull together as she accepts Lexis is talking more to Raze than she is to her. "And how exactly do you expect me to get him to eat?"

Lexis shrugs. "If he eats his piece, then I'll give you my extra piece. It will be his way of thanking you for helping him."

Winter takes a step back and shakes her head. "I'm not hungry, thank you." There's no way she's going to take a piece of bread from Lexis. Because if she does, then they'll be even again. And that is *not happening*.

"We can all hear your stomach groaning," says Lexis. "I think even the Cragg over in their camp can hear it. You're hungry.

And if Raze behaves himself and eats his portion, then you don't have to be hungry. It would be the right thing for my brother to do."

"I said I'm not hungry," Winter insists, almost whimpering at the sight of the meal she knows she must forego.

Raze props himself up on his elbows and looks at Winter with sad eyes. He knows what his sister is up to. They all do. But there's something in the way he's looking at her that seems to indicate something more. It's like he wants her to eat the bread for other reasons than just to make them even.

"You should eat your bread," she says to him. "But I don't need your sister to give me any of hers. We have an alliance now. You watch our backs. We'll watch yours."

Raze reaches for the bread and shoves the entire piece in his mouth, not removing his eyes from Winter once. He chews loudly as if proving a point, then points at the two pieces on Lexis's plate.

"I said *no thank you.*" Winter glares at him. "You can eat as much as you like. I'm not taking any of your bread. I came here to help you, not the other way around."

"Go on." Lexis picks it up and holds it out. "Take it. We'll still owe you. Helping my brother is worth more than a lousy piece of bread."

Winter almost trips over her feet in her haste to leave. Her mouth is watering badly and her hands are shaking. She wants that bread. She *needs* that bread. But under no circumstances is she going to take it.

She scurries back to the Fairbanks section to find Gray sitting inside their lonely tent. His knees are pulled up to his chest and he's staring directly at her approaching. And he's smiling.

No. He's grinning.

She shakes her head. Only her lunatic brother would be

smiling at a time like this. What on earth does he have to be happy about?

He shifts over to make room for her, and she flops down beside him.

"I took the aloe to Raze," she says. "We have an alliance now. They owe us."

Gray nods. "That's good, but you didn't need to do that, as it turns out."

She raises a brow, waiting for him to continue.

"Because things went well with Lexis." He grins even wider, which only makes her frown. "She's not going to hurt us."

"What does that mean?" Winter uses her stern voice. "What happened?"

He shakes his head. "Nothing."

"Something must have." She narrows her eyes at him. "What did you do? Or what did she do to make you think she won't hurt us?"

He looks away and a pink rash rises to his throat. "Nothing. Just trust me. They're on our side."

"Oh no, Gray, you didn't." She knows there's only one thing her gentleman brother would never tell her about in his dealings with Lexis. "Please, tell me you didn't kiss her."

Still avoiding her eye, he reaches behind him and retrieves something wrapped in a piece of cloth. "Look, I have bread."

Winter groans. This is even worse than him kissing Lexis. "She gave you bread! Gray! Why would you take bread from her?"

She lies down and covers her face with her hands, trying to accept the alliance has been blown. They owe the Cy twins now, with thanks to her idiotic brother and his trusting spirit.

"Rusty got it for us," he says, sounding a little offended. "It wasn't from Lexis."

"Oh." She uncovers her eyes and blinks up at him. "And where did he get it?"

"Same place he gets all his stuff." Gray shrugs. "Who knows."

Winter sits up and takes the bread, wasting no time in getting it into her mouth.

She groans again, although this time it's in sheer pleasure. She reminds herself to chew and savor when all she wants to do is gulp it down whole.

"I have water, too." Gray holds out a flask. "Hope you don't mind. I already had my half."

"Rusty is up to something," says Winter, taking a gulp. "But right now, I gotta say that I really don't care what it is."

"Me neither." Gray eats the last of his bread and laughs. "The annoying guardian angel strikes again!"

"So annoying," she agrees.

Something catches Gray's eye and he leans out of the tent. "What are they doing?"

Winter joins him and sees Evrest instructing two of his men who are carrying a timber box into the center of the Ring. They place it down carefully and take a few steps back. It seems the next Tournament is going to begin sooner than any of them thought. Evrest really is keen to get this over with.

"What's in the box?" Gray asks, as if Winter has any idea. "Another weapon?"

She shrugs. "I don't have a good feeling about this."

"We need to get that weapon first again," he says, ignoring her negativity. "Or at least shield Lexis and Raze while they get it."

"Competitors!" Evrest's voice booms. "The third Tournament begins on the morrow when the sun hits the highest point in the sky. I suggest you sleep well."

The sound of his voice echoes across the Ring and Winter has to fight not to bring up the bread she just ate.

She hopes their alliance hasn't been blown.

She hopes Raze is well enough to fight.

She hopes that whatever's in that box won't spell the end of the Tournaments for either her or Gray.

Because there's no doubt the energy she sensed in Lexis earlier is currently seeping from her own very frightened pores.

RAZE

*E*ven the weight of the heat feels too much as Raze stands in the Ring, Lexis beside him. Pain radiates from his wound, shooting up his leg and multiplying along every nerve, trying to steal his focus. He blinks, concentrating on the enemies he's now surrounded by.

The Cragg are opposite them, flexing their powerful muscles as they spew hate from their eyes. The Never are to Raze's left, contracted together as they wait to see what this next Tournament will involve.

Winter and Gray are to his right, keeping to their segment of the Ring. Raze's glance flickers to Winter's fingers as they twitch by her side. Those same hands tended to him yesterday. They were careful. Gentle. Almost soothing.

Like she cared whether she was hurting him.

He frowns, looking away. She was just doing that because she and her twin need the alliance so badly.

He can't afford to entertain the idea that there's something special about him. That he's more than a stepping stone in the vital mission of uniting the Outlands. These Tournaments are the only way they can end the same miserable existence every person here has to endure. He'll honor the alliance, just like he and Lexis said they would.

Then he'll fulfil his destiny.

Straightening his shoulders, Raze takes stock of the moving parts of this Tournament.

Four quadrants. Four factions.

A wooden box sitting in the center of the Ring.

He's already studied it carefully, just as every other contestant would have. It's not very big, so unlikely to hold a weapon as large as a mace. Maybe a knife. Maybe a cup of water or some flatbread, both something many in the Outlands would kill for.

The wood it's made of looks flimsy, the joints holding it together roughly carved. Whatever is in there will be easy to access. What does their father have planned for them this time?

As if that thought was his cue, Evrest leaps into the Ring.

"Welcome remaining contestants," he says in his cold monotone. "The third Tournament is about to begin."

There's a murmur of excitement from the spectators a few feet above them, several moving in closer. Arc jostles with another Cy warrior, excitement painting their features.

Raze looks away in disgust. He never considered the Tournaments would turn killing into a sport. He saw them as a means to an end. A necessary tool to select the strongest in both mind and body.

Evrest steps around the box, chest puffed and Raze realizes this was his father's intent all along. That this is little more than a game for the man who sired him, one where people are the pawns and the price of losing is fatal.

"As always," his father says. "The rules are simple. One death using what's contained in that box and the Tournament is over. May they serve you well."

He strides to the edge of the Ring and leaps out. Raze is about to look away, knowing everyone else in the Ring is contemplating whether they want to find out what's in the box, when Evrest leans down and picks up a rock. Raze stills, subtly moving in front of Lexis. There's no way of knowing what their father is planning to do with that stone.

Evrest lifts his arm and throws it directly into the center of the Ring. The rock propels through the air, a missile unerringly shooting towards its target.

The box.

The wood splinters as the rock shatters it, shards of timber exploding outward from the impact. There's a collective gasp as everyone in the Ring leaps back when they see what's inside.

A snake.

A black viper.

A deadly reptile whose venom has evolved to kill a person in minutes, as if it, too, learned that death must be quick here in the Outlands.

The viper rears, furious that its dark haven has been violently destroyed. The snake shoots forward, its glossy black body glinting in the bright sunlight. It slithers in lightning fast movements, the heat of the sun having warmed its blood, aiming straight toward the Never people.

The Never instantly divide and run, the black viper cleaving their group into halves. Two run toward the Cragg, three toward Raze and Lexis. The moment they're close enough, Slab and another Cragg shove them away as if the snake has a target on their back.

Raze watches with his breath held. If a Never is bitten, then this Tournament is over, an outcome his leg is already begging for. Just standing here is agony.

But the two Never scramble in an effort to not get any closer to the viper, quickly changing direction and joining their three teammates.

Who are now crowded behind Lexis and Raze.

The snake turns suddenly and moves quickly until it hits the wall of the Ring. It tries to slither up the side, reaching about a foot before the weight of its body has it tumbling back into the dust. It tries again and again, wanting out of here just as much as the humans watching it. But it never gains traction, its thick serpentine body thumping to the ground each time.

Everyone in the Ring knows when the viper gives up. The snake curls back around, facing the center. Taking in the semicircle of people who are watching its every move.

"Is one of us supposed to sacrifice ourselves?" one of the Never asks incredulously.

Raze tears his gaze away from the viper to glance at his father. Evrest is standing beside the statue of Cy, smiling slightly. Is this what he had planned for Raze? To throw himself at the snake so this Tournament can be won?

Does he really think so little of his son that he's looking forward to watching him die in such a painful, senseless way? Raze swallows, already knowing the answer to that question.

"No," Lexis growls beside him. "The snake *is* the weapon."

Raze stiffens with shock. Lexis is right. One wrong move and it's a weapon that can kill the hunter before the hunted.

The viper raises its obsidian head, its forked tongue tasting the air. A drop of sweat trickles down Raze's temple as the merciless sun watches on with the same intensity as Evrest and the spectators. Who will the viper choose for its victim?

The snake twists around again, slithering back to the wall and one of the Never lets out a breath. The viper slips through the sliver of shade the wall has provided, stopping for long seconds, only to twitch with agitation. Raze realizes it's looking for shelter from the oppressive heat.

It turns around, tongue sampling the dusty air again as its onyx eyes scan the Ring. Suddenly, it's on the move again, and this time it's not meandering aimlessly. The viper has an objective. Its black body needs shade.

And the humans in this Ring are the only ones who can provide that.

The Cragg are talking in muted voices, gesturing heatedly toward the snake. Raze looks at them long enough to decide they're not planning to attack him or those he's bound to protect, then focuses back on the viper. They need a strategy.

The Never huddle together, only a few feet away. "We need to stand still," one of them instructs.

Except they just created the largest shaded area in the Ring.

Raze turns to Lexis, indicating with his hands that they need to split up. It's the only way to ensure they're not a target for the snake while they try to figure out how to end this.

She frowns. "I don't know what you're saying."

Raze moves his hands faster, trying to show her that they need to spread out. The snake is doing exactly what he expected it to—it's moving toward the Never.

Lexis shakes her head. "No way. We're sticking together for this. You're not throwing yourself on some snake."

Raze clenches his jaw in frustration. There's no time to try and communicate why he's suggesting this. Not without words.

Which means he has no choice but to approach the snake before it reaches them. To try to take the weapon for himself. To do exactly what Lexis just said she doesn't want him to.

Raze drags his gaze away from his twin, locking his muscles. If he dies doing this, he dies protecting her, just like he's supposed to. He tells himself that's enough.

On his other side, he notes Winter has moved further away, Gray with her. Maybe she's realized they need to spread out as well. He's glad. She'll live to see the end of this Tournament, too.

For some reason, that makes what he's about to do twice as worth it.

But before Raze can move, a Cragg breaks away from their faction, running straight for the viper. The snake rears as the boulder of man cannonballs at him, the top half of its body rising like ink-colored smoke.

The Cragg roars, making the viper jerk in response. A

second later, its body flicks like black lightning, shooting for the man's thigh. Everyone knows black vipers aim for the thigh. It's the height their raised bodies can reach, but Raze has always wondered if they evolved to hit that area because the thick blood vessels in the thigh means their venom will be pumped through their victim faster.

The snake's mouth opens, exposing its pink fleshy gums and thick ivory fangs. The Cragg sweeps his arm down as if to knock the viper away and the jaws clamp around his forearm.

The man roars as the viper takes hold and doesn't let go and Raze hides his wince. This man's death was going to be his own.

Except the Cragg doesn't collapse. He raises his arm, the snake's body writhing and twisting as it hangs from him. He roars again and Raze realizes what that sound was meant to be.

The call of victory.

The Cragg grabs the viper's head, pressing on either side of its jaw. The snake releases his arm, exposing two tears in the man's shirt where the viper's fangs pierced. Below it isn't vulnerable flesh, but a sheet of thick red plastic.

The Cragg's armor.

"Finish her!" Slab shouts.

Raze spins right, seeing what no one else did while they were watching the Cragg's feat of speed and stupidity. Winter's eyes are wide with terror as Slab holds her against his chest, two other Craggs holding her arms out wide.

"No!" screams Gray.

He runs toward his twin. The moment he reaches her, the nearest Cragg slams his foot into Gray's torso.

Gray crumples, groaning as he holds his stomach. "No, Winter," he moans.

The Cragg with the viper steadily approaches her, his eyes alive with sick excitement. Winter tries to struggle; except she's held tight. Her face pales as she has no choice but to watch the lethal reptile come closer.

Raze takes a step forward only for Lexis's arm to whip across his chest. "No, you're injured," Lexis says loudly. "They'll kill you."

Raze clenches his sister's arm. *But what about the alliance? What about Winter?*

"There's no one to save you now," Slab growls as he jerks Winter's head back against his chest. "This is for Nell."

"No," moans Gray, trying to push himself up on all fours only to be shoved back into the dirt by the Cragg's boot.

"It's too risky to save her," Lexis states flatly.

She draws her hand away, her gaze never leaving Winter. Raze's stomach is a writhing knot of revulsion and denial.

How can he stand by and watch this happen?

He realizes what is even harder to accept.

Lexis is going to stand by and watch this happen. Just like their father would.

Her hand brushes his as it returns to her side, the fingers flicking ever so slightly. Raze freezes. He knows what that signal means.

In the code they developed to communicate during battle, she just instructed him to do the opposite of what she just said.

It means attack.

The Cragg with the viper stops in front of Winter and the two men tighten their hold on her arms. The Cragg squeezes the snake's jaws so they open wide, exposing the deadly fangs. Winter moans softly as venom drips down the snake's mouth.

Raze and Lexis snap into action simultaneously. Agony jolts up his leg as they launch at the men holding Winter, but he just uses the pain to fuel him. To power his role as protector.

Slab's eyes widen as he realizes they're approaching, but he never has a chance to warn his teammate. Raze and Lexis split at the last second. Lexis ploughs into the man's arm while Raze slams into his back.

The man cries out as the viper he's holding changes course.

It's now on a direct trajectory for his throat. Lexis punches out, shoving his arm so it only moves faster. Raze shoves him so he can't retreat.

The viper latches onto the man's neck, right over his jugular.

"Bastards!" Slab screams as he pushes Winter away. She stumbles and Raze springs around the Cragg to catch her, pain scorching up his leg. The Cragg drops to the ground, writhing as he tries to yank the viper off his throat.

Winter falls into Raze's arms, and for an impossible moment, he's struck by how soft she is. Lexis is the only other female he's ever held, and she's nothing but honed muscle. He draws Winter in tighter as Slab surges past to get to his man, and something tightens in his chest when she clings to him.

Slab stops, standing over his fellow Cragg, registering what everyone else already has. Pink stained foam froths at the man's mouth as his glassy eyes stare at the sky. Although his body twitches spasmodically it's obvious the man is dead. The venom injected straight into his artery worked fast.

Slab grabs the viper's thick serpentine body, its mouth still wide open and clamped on the man's throat and snaps it. The snake goes limp, doubling the death toll in the Ring.

Three claps echo through the space and they all turn around to see Evrest approaching them. He stops in the center.

"Well done. The third Tournament is complete."

A round of applause rises from the onlookers and Raze suddenly realizes he's still holding Winter. His arms drop and he quickly steps away.

Gray appears by her side. "Well, that was the easiest one so far," he says quietly, a hint of humor in his voice.

Even as Raze tries to understand how Gray can be so light-hearted, relief courses through him. He made it through this round, despite his injury. It's not an outcome he expected. Gray's right, this was the easiest one so far.

Evrest raises his arms and the crowd falls silent. Raze tenses again, wondering if the next Tournament is about to be announced. Right now, even tomorrow feels too soon.

"And I have more good news."

Lexis steps toward Raze at the same moment he moves closer to her. They both know this announcement is going to be the opposite of good.

Two men appear at the edge of the Ring, carrying another box. This one is the same size as the first, looking just as flimsy. They place it gingerly next to Evrest before scooting away as if it contains an explosive.

Evrest turns to the competitors, his scars twisting as he smiles. "The third Tournament was merely a warmup for the fourth."

GRAY

*G*ray stares at the box in horror.

Not. Another. Snake!

Winter is breathing heavily beside him, the ordeal she endured still fresh.

"We'll be okay." He puts a hand on her back, ignoring the pain in his chest after the Cragg immobilized him in the last Tournament. He's certain he has at least one broken rib. Maybe two. "Our alliance will protect us."

Winter bites down on her bottom lip. "I can't… Not so soon. I can't."

"You don't have to." Gray moves a little closer to his twin, vowing to do better at keeping her safe. If Lexis and Raze hadn't intervened, all that would be beside him right now would be hot stifling air. When the snake is let out of the box this time, it's not going anywhere near Winter.

Evrest marches over to Slab who's still holding the lifeless viper, staring at his dead friend like he expects him to wipe the froth from his mouth and stand up to fight.

"The Cragg will eat snake for dinner tonight," Evrest announces. "Their loss is also their win."

Seeming to forget about his friend, Slab holds the snake above his head in victory and smirks at the Cy twins. Gray hadn't even realized the guy was capable of tipping his lips in an upward direction.

"That is if the Cragg live to have another meal," Evrest adds dryly.

That erases the glee from Slab's face. He throws the dead reptile to a Cragg spectator and stomps to the box in the center of the Ring, staking an early claim on the second snake. The other remaining competitor from their faction joins him and stands at the opposite corner, rubbing his filthy red beard like it's going to bring him good luck.

The Never stay well back, their fear of snakes clear to all.

Winter remains rooted to the spot, Gray steadfast by her side.

Not to be outplayed by the Cragg, Lexis and Raze approach the box, separating to position themselves at the vacant corners.

"Easy, Red," Slab says to his teammate.

"That snake is ours," Red growls.

With the box surrounded, the outcome of this next Tournament is going to depend entirely on which way the snake decides to flee when it's released from the confines of its flimsy prison. And how successful its captor is at taking hold of it without being bitten first.

Gray watches Lexis. This is the hard version of the beautiful girl he maybe-possibly-almost-definitely is falling for, not the soft version who'd melted under his touch when he'd kissed her. He feels a tug on his heart. How can he stay where he is and watch Lexis put herself in mortal danger?

Because she's the most capable person he's ever met, that's how. She doesn't need Gray to protect her. She's a warrior. She's trained her whole life for moments like these.

Evrest climbs out of the Ring and stands beside the glittering statue of Cy. "This Tournament will conclude when you've killed the contents of the box. It may result in no deaths, or every last one of you may die."

Before Gray has a chance to wonder what that means, Evrest sweeps out his hands.

"May the Tournament serve you well. Let it begin!"

The competitors wait for Evrest to throw a stone at the box like he did last time, but instead he crosses his arms, looking almost bored.

"He wants us to open it," says Winter at the exact moment Lexis pounces. Her movements are fast and she has the box clutched awkwardly to her chest in split seconds.

Raze leaps, but with one leg so badly injured, he's not fast enough to stop both Slab and Red. Slab slips past him, making a grab for Lexis just as she pushes to her feet and takes off toward an empty section of the Ring.

Slab chases after her and Gray jiggles his legs, the urge to help her burning like lava inside him. But he knows he can't leave Winter.

He soon realizes this doesn't mean she can't leave him.

"Go and help Lexis!" Winter turns her back and rushes to Raze, who's struggling to keep Red pinned to the ground.

Hoping she knows what she's doing, Gray runs after Slab, desperate to distract him from his target.

Lexis may have the box, but it's not going to remain intact for long. She needs time to extract the snake and get hold of the head to use as her weapon, not a vehicle to her own death.

"Slab!" Gray shouts.

But this mountain of a man isn't listening. He powers toward Lexis who's having a difficult time getting a proper grasp on the awkwardly shaped box. If she's not careful, it's going to break in her hands.

"Nell!" Gray shouts the name of Slab's daughter whose death he's hellbent on avenging, hoping this tactic might just work. "Nell! Nell!"

Slab pauses—only for a second, but his confusion is enough for Lexis to plant her feet and raise the box above her head.

Both Slab and Gray come to a halt, knowing the chase is over. Lexis has full control of the box and it's clear she's going to make the most of it. Gray just hopes it doesn't break before she has a chance to make her next move or that snake is going to fall right on her head.

"Get back," she growls at Slab. "Now!"

He makes no move.

"You, too, Gray," she says, not taking her eyes off Slab. "Do it."

Gray takes two steps back without hesitation.

"Put it down," snarls Slab. "I'll kill it and we'll both live. You heard ya father. Nobody has to die this time."

"He also said we could all die," she adds. "And I'd rather die than make any kind of deal with scum like you."

Slab lets out a roar and rushes forward. But Lexis is ready for him. She throws the box hard at his chest and leaps back as it splits open.

"What the—" Gray's eyes widen as the contents of the box reveal themselves.

It's not a black viper.

It's *many* black vipers.

Twenty or more angry juvenile snakes about as long as his arm burst from the box. Several land on Slab and he flicks them onto the ground to join their slivering siblings, somehow managing not to be bitten.

Some snakes cluster together, and others spread out, wanting to get as far from the commotion as possible.

Gray takes a few more steps back, deciding these snakes are not just frightened.

They're furious!

No wonder Evrest said they might all die. There's enough venom in these small but lethal fangs to kill every last person in the Ring. That must've been the mother snake killed in the last Tournament. There's no way Evrest could've caught more than one of these rare species for his precious games.

"Gray!" cries Winter.

Looking down, he sees one of the snakes heading directly for him.

He runs to his sister who's let go of Red now there's no reason to help Raze keep him pinned. But there are snakes everywhere, their black bodies glistening as they streak around the Ring, even more frightened than the competitors they've been set upon.

Winter reaches him just as the sound of one of the Never screaming echoes around the Ring.

Pressing his back to his sister, they slowly turn in a circle, seeing nothing but panic and fear swirling around them.

The golden twins have picked up the broken pieces of the box and Raze is using the sharp ends to deter anyone from approaching, while Lexis darts around trying to grab herself a snake.

The Cragg are using their boots to kill the vipers, which Gray isn't going to complain about. The fewer deadly reptiles in this Ring of death, the better. The Cragg can eat the whole lot for dinner as far as he cares.

The Never are huddled together, seeming unsure what to do with their friend who is on the ground, convulsing. There's a reason there are still five of them left in the Tournaments. They stole a kill in the first round, sat out the second one, then did absolutely nothing in the third. Is their strategy to get to the end by simply being the last ones standing, while everyone else takes each other out?

"Gray!" Winter cries, forcing him to the left.

Determined not to be as impassive as these spineless competitors, Gray rushes toward the dying man and takes hold of the viper that still has a mouthful of Never flesh. He rips it away and holds it the same way he saw the Cragg thug do earlier when he'd held the mother snake to Winter's throat.

Except Gray isn't going to let this snake turn on him.

It's stronger than he thought and thrashes in the tight grip of his hand. He had no idea a snake could pack so much power, especially one so young. He understands now how the mother got the better of the Cragg. She must've had ten times the force at least.

He holds up the snake at the Never, unsure what he's supposed to do next.

They scream as they clutch each other, backing away.

"Evrest said nobody had to die!" a woman shouts. "Get that thing away from us!"

Gray nods, ashamed. Killing the Never has no purpose in this Tournament. It's obvious now how it will end.

They have to end the life of every last one of these deadly but innocent creatures.

Human versus reptile.

It's time to kill or be killed.

At least they'll be well fed tonight...

Gray breaks the neck of the viper, wincing as he feels its life escape. When he's certain it's dead, he tucks it into his waistband by the tail.

The Never woman who'd just spoken gasps as she looks behind Gray and the man beside her shakes his head, telling her to be quiet. Her gasp is cut short and she looks away.

Gray spins around, seeing two more snakes slithering toward him. Anger boils inside him. These people whose lives he'd just spared weren't going to warn him, taking their chance that the snakes would attack him first.

With the Never behind him and two snakes intent on his death, Gray braces himself.

The snakes take only milliseconds to reach him. Just as they're about to rear up, Gray dives forward, a move Trakk taught him when they were only boys. He sails over the snakes, landing on the hard ground on his palms. Agony ricochets through his chest as he springboards himself into the air, twisting his body so he's propelled further forward until his feet slam back onto the earth.

That was one helluva somersault, if he does say so himself!

Turning back, he sees the snakes went right under him and have set themselves on the Never who are running for their lives.

Winter appears by his side, a dead viper in her hands and he's reminded of the way they used to hunt rats in Fairbanks, back when they had no idea how cruel this world could be.

"We should help them," he says, watching the Never dodge and scream.

"They didn't help you," she reminds him. "They didn't even warn you."

"We can't just watch them die." Gray jogs forward, knowing he has to try to help. These Tournaments may have changed him forever as a person, but they haven't blackened his heart. Evrest said nobody had to die. And the Never aren't his enemy right now.

The vipers are.

The only way he can move forward in these games is to put those frightened creatures out of their misery and end this Tournament.

Now.

He closes the gap on the four surviving Never, shocked to see them hit the wall of the Ring and climb right out.

"Stop!" Gray calls, knowing the consequences of such an act won't be good. "Stop!"

The two snakes use the Never like a human ladder and are out of the Ring in no time. There's more screaming as the spectators disperse and run about with their hands in the air. They'd come to watch people be killed, not become part of the entertainment themselves.

Gray stops at the edge of the Ring with Winter panting beside him. The Cy twins approach, Raze limply badly. They stand with them to watch the mayhem unfold.

Raze points to the north and Gray sees the Never running into the distance. Evrest's guards are following with spears clutched in their hands.

There's no way they're going to let them get away.

A snake is thrown back into the Ring and Lexis reaches out, catching it mid-air and snapping it in half like it's a twig. She tucks it into her belt to dangle beside four of its siblings.

Gray swallows down a cocktail of emotions.

Disgust.

Admiration.

Awe.

Lust.

He blinks as that last word settles in his mind, but he can't deny it. He does lust after Lexis. What guy wouldn't. Now that he looks at her with the muscle that lines her curves, he decides that lusting after her isn't likely to be something exclusive to guys.

That girl is hot! And he was the one who got to kiss her. He can hardly believe it.

"They're all dead," says Winter.

"Sadly, yes," says Gray, watching as the Never disappear into the distance.

"I meant the snakes," she clarifies, as the remaining viper is tossed back into the Ring, only to be immediately crushed by a Cragg.

A hush falls over the crowd as Evrest claps four times.

"Tournament four has concluded," he calls out. "Remain where you are until further notice."

Raze looks at his sister, puzzled, and she shrugs.

"What are we waiting for?" Winter asks, like Gray has any better idea. "Please don't tell me there's another Tournament."

"I don't know," he replies. Although, he's fairly certain that's not what it is.

They're waiting for the Never to be brought back.

The faction who will no longer be impassive players in Evrest's brutal games.

It seems Gray and Winter are about to find out exactly what would have happened to them if they hadn't fought the persistent urge to run.

LEXIS

*I*t's not long before her father's men return. Lexis wipes the sweat trickling along the line of her jaw, glad it will be over sooner rather than later. Raze needs to take the strain off his injured leg.

The warriors first appear as a row of silhouettes on the horizon, the same five men who left, each walking with their spear pointed to the sky. They're alive, which means no one died retrieving the Never, but they also aren't dragging any captives along with them.

"They didn't catch them," Gray says beside her.

Except no Cy warrior would return empty handed. Something has happened.

Winter shakes her head. "They probably killed them and left them to rot."

Raze and Lexis exchange a glance. They both know Evrest would never do anything so subtle. Their father likes to make a statement.

Death in the Tournaments is public. It's used to show strength. To dominate.

The men trudge over the bleached and baked land, coming

steadily closer. Lexis narrows her eyes, seeing that Arc is carrying something tucked under his arm.

She stifles an involuntary gasp when she realizes what it is. She knows when Raze sees it too, because he stills, his breathing slowing considerably as he focuses on regulating it.

The warriors stop and huddle in together, their spears coming down as if they're inspecting them.

"What are they doing?" Gray asks, nervousness creeping into his voice. He senses that something's not right.

Arc hoists his spoil of war and jams it on the tip of his comrade's spear.

"No…" Winter breathes. "They couldn't be that heartless."

The sound of retching has Lexis spinning around and grabbing Gray's arm. "You can't lose what little food you've eaten."

Gray is as pale as the ghosts he's been named after. "But they…"

He retches again and Lexis grips his arm tighter. "Yes, it's cruel and barbaric. But the only way to face it is by being strong."

Gray swallows as he nods. He squeezes the hand that's still holding him. "Thanks." He angles his head, the harsh sun gliding through his dark hair. "I think you could be my hero."

Lexis yanks her hand away, her face flushing. She scowls at him, trying to pretend the heat is anger. She should never have let Gray kiss her.

"How can they be smiling like that?" Winter whispers, dismay and disgust painted across her features.

The warriors of Cy continue their approach now that their preparations are complete. Their spears are back to pointing at the sky. Four of them have been proudly crowned.

With the heads of the murdered Never.

There's a cry from somewhere behind Lexis, and she's sure it's one of the women from their faction. Her father or brother or partner could be one of the heads up on those spikes. The rest of the spectators are silent, no doubt as shocked and sickened as Winter and Gray.

Lexis wishes she could shift closer to Raze, maybe brush her hand over his. Although what Evrest has ordered wouldn't be a surprise, the gruesome sight is still hard to stomach. Even as he stands there stoic and silent, she knows this is as hard for him as any of the others. Seeing such brutality never stopped impacting him, he just learned at a young age to never show weakness.

As the Cy warriors reach the village, their comrades let out a resounding cheer. They come to stand beside Evrest and the statue, slamming their spears into the soil with great pride. Another round of celebratory roars only makes them grin harder.

Evrest raises his arms and his men fall silent. "This is what happens to those who run. To cowards." His hard gaze sweeps the contestants, hovering a split second longer on his two children. "To the weak."

The pouch of poison is suddenly like a burning piece of coal tucked in Lexis's belt. Surely he's not talking about Raze...

Evrest drops his arms. "The fifth Tournament begins at dawn."

He turns and walks away, indicating for his warriors to follow. They leave the heads of the Never with their sightless eyes and mouths trapped in a forever-scream by the statue of Cy. Lexis has no doubt they'll remain there for the rest of the Tournaments. Serving as an example.

Ignoring the bile that stains her tongue Lexis leaps out of the Ring, finding Winter and Gray right behind her. They probably want to get away from the awful sight as quickly as she does. She turns to see Raze drawing in a breath as he prepares to jump out, too. With his injured leg, the Tournament has taken its toll on him. Lexis reaches out a hand to him, wanting to help, but Raze ignores it. He leaps high enough to get over the dirt wall, only barely making it. The moment he lands, his wounded leg gives out.

Lexis has to stop herself from going to him as self-loathing coils its way through her chest. Their father could be watching, and it won't look good for either of them if she helps her weakened brother.

Winter stumbles into Raze, tucking herself into his side and becoming a human crutch. "Sorry," she says, glancing up at him with an apologetic smile. "I tripped."

Raze looks just as stunned as Lexis feels. His arm has instinctively wrapped around Winter as she props him up and he seems to have lost the ability to move. A thought strikes Lexis. Maybe he doesn't really want to.

Suddenly, his spine stiffens and he pulls away. He glances at Winter, scowling as he taps his chin with his fingertips.

Lexis comes to stand beside him. "He just said thank you."

Winter squints up at Raze. "You're welcome."

"Let's get out of here," Gray mutters. "I can't stomach the sight of what happened to those poor people."

Winter nods. "The next Tournament is less than twenty-four hours away. We need to eat and rest."

Lexis glances at the single snake hanging from Gray's belt, conscious she has five hanging from hers. She hesitates. Should they share their food? Winter and Gray honored their part of the alliance during the last Tournament. But at the same time, this is far more food than Lexis and Raze have seen in a long time. It could feed them for two or three days, at least.

Gray seems to be looking at Lexis as if he expects her to say something.

Winter grabs his hand. "Come on, they're not going to share."

Gray allows his twin to tug him away, disappointment clear on his face. Lexis doesn't know if she feels guilty or angry. What did he expect from her? These are Tournaments. She was born Cy. He's the enemy.

The Fairbanks twins have just reached the edge of their segment when someone rushes over to them, their arms full. Raze taps Lexis's arm.

"Yeah, I see it, too."

She narrows her eyes. It's the boy from Rust, the one who's been hanging around even though his faction was eliminated. And he's holding an armful of firewood as he smiles at Winter and Gray.

Lexis is moving before she realizes it. She storms over to stand beside Gray, glaring at the Rust. "What do you want?"

Lexis watches with satisfaction as the guy's eyes widen imperceptibly. "Ah, I thought these two would need something to cook their snake."

"No one helps in the Tournaments without a reason."

Gray shifts his weight. "Some might," he points out quietly.

Lexis's heart clenches. Why does it feel like Gray would help her, expecting nothing in return? She scowls at the Rust boy. "He wouldn't. What do you want?"

The pale-haired boy takes a step back, dropping the wood as he raises his hands. "Nothing. I've been helping them." He slides a glance at Winter. "They'd probably be dead without me."

Raze steps closer to her, his hands clenched as he stares at Rust-boy. The weakling seems to wilt under his gaze.

Lexis spins on her heel. "They don't need any firewood from you. We're eating in our hut."

There's a pause. "Yes, we are," Gray announces as he jolts into action. A moment later he's by Lexis's side, Winter right behind him.

Lexis glances over her shoulder, what she's done sinking in. Raze must think she's a fool. That she's grown soft, just like their father does.

Except Raze is quickly picking up some of the firewood

the Rust-boy dropped. He scowls at him, and Rust shrinks back even more, before limping away. Lexis and the others slow so he can catch up. Her brother is willing to share their food, too.

A sidelong glance at Gray shows him smiling. Lexis quickly looks away but it's too late, the impact of those upturned lips spreads through her chest, making her feel light and warm. Inexplicably, it feels like she just did the right thing.

Lexis leads them back to their hut, noticing that everyone from her faction has retired to their own homes, leaving their village quiet and empty. It seems the deaths of the Never have made an impact, even amongst those familiar with violence and death. Lexis is glad, she doesn't want to have to answer to her father about sharing their food with the Ghosts.

Back at their hut, Raze begins to make a fire but Lexis quickly takes the wood from him. "You go lay down. You need to rest."

Raze frowns then shakes his head.

Winter comes to stand beside Raze, her hands hiking onto her hips. "How are you going to protect your twin if your leg doesn't get a chance to heal?"

Raze scowls as he spins around and limps to his mat. Lexis's jaw almost drops open. Normally, Raze would've continued to make the fire, despite her protests. She looks at Winter, suddenly curious about this young woman who has had such an impact on her reclusive, stubborn brother. Is it just her beauty, or is it more than that?

But Winter is already arranging the wood on the embers of last night's fire. She blows on it and flames quickly spark to life, as if even Mother Nature is at her bidding.

Gray appears beside Lexis, his hand extended. "I can cook them if you like?"

His eyes are warm with gratitude...and something else. There's the memory of their kiss is his dark gaze. The knowledge that they share a secret. She nods, passing him the vipers, feeling off kilter and not liking it.

Gray makes short work of weaving them through some sticks and placing them amongst the coals at the edge of the fire. That done, he comes to sit beside Lexis, his shoulder brushing hers. Lexis tenses but he doesn't say anything, doesn't move. Gray seems content to just sit there, watching their meal cook.

Lexis stares at the flames, conflicting emotions rushing through her. She wants to push Gray away and end these strange sensations. She wants to draw him closer and show him what his nearness is doing to her.

The snakes cook quickly, in part because they're only small, but also because Lexis takes them off the fire the moment it looks like the flesh has turned white. She's not sure if she's relieved or disappointed that her time beside Gray is over, but the chorus of grumbling stomachs tells her everyone else is as hungry as she is.

She lays them on a piece of wood. Five snakes. Four of them. A veritable feast.

Winter's hand whips out and grabs two, making Lexis frown. Although she understands hunger, she hadn't expected Winter to be so...rude. Except Winter shuffles to the back of the hut, passing one of the snakes to Raze.

She sits beside him. "For every mouthful that I have and you don't, I'm going to poke your wound," she says sternly.

Gray stifles a chuckle as Raze scowls the deepest Lexis has seen so far. He snaps the head off the snake and takes a bite. Winter smiles, her body relaxing as she has a mouthful of her own.

Lexis turns to Gray. "Your sister is a witch," she says under her breath.

He leans over, picking up a snake and passing it to her. "Actually, I wouldn't mind her powers of persuasion," he murmurs.

Lexis takes the snake, finding her fingers brushing his as he doesn't let go. She tugs but he doesn't release it, his full lips tipping up at the edges.

He's teasing her.

Lexis blinks, unsure what to do with the delightful glint in his eye. She could simply yank the snake away. Or…she could meet his challenge.

She leans forward, liking the way his eyes widen. "What would you have me do, Gray?" she asks quietly, a husky tone in her voice she's never heard before.

His gaze darkens as it slides to her lips. "It would start with a kiss…"

Lexis's breath disintegrates. She knows what happens after kissing, but imposing herself and Gray into those images changes the flashes of what she's seen. She doesn't feel repulsed or fearful or degraded.

She feels hot and impatient and excited.

"Another one." Winter's voice, cajoling yet laced with steel, has Lexis jumping back. She finds she's panting as if she just jogged here.

Gray slips closer, pressing his fingers to his lips in a gesture to keep quiet. He tears away a piece of snake and passes it to her. Lexis takes it and places it into her mouth, conscious that Gray watches her every move. She grabs a snake of her own and does the same, fascinated by the firelight playing over his lips as the meat disappears into his mouth.

Despite their hunger, they share their snakes slowly, Lexis never checking that their portions are equal. She's not fighting to make sure Raze eats enough. She's not fighting to make sure she doesn't miss out.

She's watching Gray eat and enjoying the sight, wanting his body to have nourishment. She's having morsels of meat passed to her by a guy who looks like he wants to eat her instead.

For just this period of time, Lexis allows herself to forget.

She tells herself there's no pouch of poison tucked in her belt. She isn't sharing a meal with her enemies.

She pushes away the images of the dead Never, choosing the fragile, beautiful emotion coming to life inside of her.

Just for tonight, she pretends tomorrow isn't the next Tournament.

That not everything good in her life is destined to die.

WINTER

*I*t's early morning and Winter can feel Gray watching her as she sleeps.

It's disconcerting.

She opens her eyes to tell him to stop being so irritating.

"Do you know what I just realized?" he asks the moment he sees she's awake.

"Do you know what *I* just realized?" she asks him straight back.

"What?" Gray pulls his knees up to his chest, then winces and stays as he was.

"That I just woke up and this nightmare is still going," she says, having little interest in what optimism he was going to spout.

"Well." He shuffles a little closer in their small tent, clearly deciding to tell her anyway. "I realized that we've survived four Tournaments and there are only three more to go. We're past the halfway mark!"

"How do I break this to you?" Winter sits up and glares at him. "All that means, is that we're even closer to dying now than we were before."

He opens his mouth, but no words come out.

Because he knows she's right.

These games are designed to have only one person left alive at the end. Now that the Never are out, there are only two competitors each from Cragg, Cy and Fairbanks. The chances of one of them dying today have never been higher.

"Who do you think will win?" she asks. "Surely, it's got to be Lexis."

"Maybe it will be you," says Gray. "You've been doing so well."

Her brows shoot up at his interesting definition of the word *well*.

"Maybe it will be you," she replies, even though she doesn't believe that's even a remote possibility.

"It will be Lexis," he says. "Which to be honest, is my second choice after you."

"You'd choose her over yourself?" Winter purses her lips and nods. "Interesting."

"Oh." Gray blushes. "I didn't realize that's what I was saying. But, yeah, maybe I would. She's a good person, Winter. She's different to her father. She'd be a good leader."

Winter lets out a long sigh. She hasn't seen her brother like this before. When she'd suggested they enter these games, she'd never thought this would be the place he'd find love.

"Be careful," she warns. "You don't really know her. We can't trust anyone out here, except each other."

He nods. "Winter, I've seen the way you and Raze look at each other. I'm not the only one to let someone get under their skin."

Now it's Winter's turn to blush. She hadn't thought anyone had noticed. She's not even sure she understands what's going on between her and Raze just yet. Something seems to have shifted between them since she tended to him. It was like she'd not only helped to soothe his injured leg, but somehow she'd also healed something in his damaged heart.

She pats her pocket where she carries the figurine of Trakk that he carved for her. She thought it might bring her luck to have him with her. But has it brought her something else? An unwanted affection for the golden boy who carved it for her?

"There's nothing between us," she tells Gray. "I'm just grateful he hasn't killed us yet."

Gray gives her a smile that tells her he doesn't believe her, but he'll let it slide for now.

"Do you think they're still out there?" Gray nods in the direction of the Ring.

Winter swallows down a sick feeling, knowing exactly what he's talking about.

"I'll check." She climbs out of the tent and looks toward the silver statue of Cy. The three heads of the Never remain exactly where they are, a swarm of flies around them visible even from a distance. The stench of rotting flesh floats on the breeze and Winter goes back inside, not needing to give Gray an update. The look on her face will be an answer enough.

"The Never weren't so bad," says Gray. "They didn't deserve that."

"Nobody deserves that." She grimaces. "Not even Slab."

"Well, maybe Slab..." He gives her a sly smile and she slaps him on the arm.

"Careful!" He winces as he holds his ribs. "I think one or two of these might be broken."

She doesn't like the sound of that. It will make him vulnerable in the next Tournament. Thankfully it's Winter who Slab has a score to settle with first.

"I'm fine," he says, seeing her concern. "We have full stomachs and an alliance to see us through today. The Cragg are toast."

"What even is toast?" she asks.

He shrugs. "No idea, but it sounds good."

"So, we take out the Cragg today, and then what?" she asks. "It will be the four of us. How's that going to play out?"

A sadness crosses Gray's dark eyes. He doesn't like the idea of having to kill the Cy twins any more than she does. Although, it's a better option than being killed by them, he supposes.

Gray lies down carefully on the compacted dirt floor of their tent and Winter stretches out beside him.

"Do you remember what Mom said?" she asks. "About living the life our sister couldn't."

He nods. "That's what we're doing, Winter. She didn't have the chance to fight for her life. We do."

"Even if the fight is useless?" She goes to rest her head on his chest then remembers he's injured, so pulls up her arm to act as a pillow. "Even if we have to kill to do that?"

"It's not useless," he tells her. "Rest now. We have a big day ahead."

"You were the one who woke me up staring at me," she reminds him.

"Don't make me laugh," he says. "It hurts."

She decides to do what he suggests and rest while she can.

She closes her eyes and thinks of her mom. She thinks of her sister. She thinks of the baby nephew she never got to meet. She thinks of her father who's been dead so long she can't remember his face. Soon, she and Gray will be joining them and their whole family will be gone, as if they never existed.

Drifting off into a deep sleep borne of sheer exhaustion, Winter dreams of sitting on a cloud and seeing her family again one day. Although, knowing their luck, it would probably be a storm cloud...

"Winter!" Gray calls gently. "It's time."

She groans. "Tell Evrest to wait."

"Very funny." He leaves the tent, almost like he's excited,

which she knows for a fact he isn't. Perhaps he's looking forward to seeing Lexis again.

She takes her time getting up, then slips her hand into Gray's as she stands beside him. There's no point pretending they don't care about each other. The Cragg figured them out long ago.

Slab and Red are already in the Ring, keeping their distance from Evrest who's standing in the center, looking impatient. At least there's no box there this time. No climbing frame or mystery bags of weapons. But, surely, he must be up to something.

The Cy twins appear at the opposite side and climb down into the Ring. Raze's injury doesn't look like it's getting any better and he's limping badly. But it hasn't killed him yet, which has to be a good sign.

She gives him a small smile, which he catches and returns, before they both look quickly away.

Winter and Gray lower themselves into the Ring, making no move to join Lexis and Raze. It's better to keep the Cragg surrounded.

The spectators gather, although without the Rust or the Never, some of the frenzied atmosphere of the first Tournament is lost. Rusty is standing alone in his empty segment. He nods at Winter like he's her coach. She ignores him, unable to spare an ounce of her energy to care about him right now. Around ten Cragg supporters remain in their segment, all just as uncouth and disheveled as their two remaining fighters. Then there's the People of Cy. Dozens of them crowd at the front of their section beside the spears that Winter refuses to look at.

"Welcome to our fifth Tournament," Evrest calls over the crowd who immediately hush. "Six competitors remain. The one who's still standing at the end of these Tournaments will lead the Outlands to a victory so sweet that nobody here will ever go hungry again. Askala will be ours!"

A ripple of excitement washes over the people.

"To lead us to such a victory, our Commander will need to be tough," Evrest continues. "Hard decisions will need to be made. Decisions that are necessary but not always palatable. A true leader will keep the bigger picture in mind. They won't hesitate. They will do what needs to be done."

Winter squeezes Gray's hand tighter. She's not sure where this is heading but it's not going anywhere good.

"Today, we have a prize." Evrest removes a small knife with a carved wooden handle from his belt and waves it in the air. "The winner of today's Tournament will be allowed to use this weapon in the sixth Tournament. Some of you may call that an unfair advantage. But I call it life. Because we all know that life isn't fair. Some have more than others. It's what you do with what you have that decides if you're a true leader."

"We need that knife," Gray whispers.

"Shh," Winter hushes as she nods. Evrest hasn't told them yet exactly what they have to do to win it.

"May I remind you that nobody leaves the Tournaments without permission." Evrest walks to the edge of the Ring and stands beneath the severed heads of the Never, then looks to the crowd of onlookers. "And that includes all of you."

The spectators shrug, wondering why they'd want to miss out on watching whatever brutal show Evrest has planned. Entertainment like this doesn't come along very often in the Outlands.

"The winner of the fifth Tournament is the first competitor to make a kill," says Evrest, turning back to face the six who remain.

Winter sees Lexis clenching her fists as she looks at Slab. She can't wait to get her hands on him, and Winter will do everything she can to help.

This should be simple enough.

Kill Slab.

Claim the knife.

Live to see another day.

"Oh, and just one more thing," Evrest adds. "This time, the competitors must all stay alive. Anyone who kills a fellow competitor will be added to my collection of heads."

"Then how do we win?" shouts Slab. "You said first kill wins."

Evrest waves his hands toward the gathered crowd. "First competitor to kill a spectator wins."

A collective gasp explodes from outside the Ring as the people realize they're the entertainment now. This doesn't seem such an attractive option.

Winter looks at Gray, her jaw falling open in disbelief. They'll live to see another day, that's a certainty now.

But at what price?

Can she live with the guilt of taking an innocent life? If what Evrest says is true, perhaps she wouldn't make a good leader after all.

"We need that knife," Gray says, not sounding as confident as he did the last time he said that.

"May the Tournaments serve you well." Evrest steps back as his guards close in around him, making sure he's not the spectator whose life will be extinguished

"I don't know what to do." Winter is frozen to the spot, her eyes scanning the Cragg and Cy spectators, trying to find one life she could feel comfortable about ending. Even though she doesn't especially like any of these people, she doesn't want to see them dead.

"Kill a Cragg."

Winter spins around to see Rusty behind her.

"Kill a Cragg," he says again. "It's your best move. They already hate you. You don't want to get the People of Cy offside. Well, any more than they already are."

She looks at her brother to see his thoughts on this suggestion, only to find him staring at Rusty with a strange look on his face. Tilting her head to study him, it dawns on her.

Rusty is a spectator.

Winter looks back at Rusty and narrows her eyes, trying to decide if she could possibly go through with killing this most annoying guardian angel.

"What?" He glances between them, oblivious.

Gray lunges at Rusty before he has a chance to figure out what's going on. He wraps his hands around his neck and squeezes hard.

"Help me, Winter!" Gray cries out, his voice laced with anguish at what he's attempting to do.

Rusty's eyes are popping out of his head, both from shock and lack of oxygen, as he tries desperately to prize Gray's fingers off his neck.

Winter slams her full body weight into her twin, aiming directly for his injured ribs, knowing that's what will have the most impact.

He falls to the ground and groans.

Rusty sucks in a deep breath and wastes no time in turning to run.

Except, Gray has hold of his ankle and Rusty crashes to the ground beside him.

"Gray, let go!" screams Winter. "Don't do this."

She knows they need to win the knife. But she also knows that whether or not they win it, they're going to die soon anyway. And she can't possibly see her brother's sweet innocence taken away before that happens. He's a good person. The best person she's ever met and she wants him to stay that way.

"Don't do it, Gray," she sobs. "Please, don't."

Gray lets go of Rusty's ankle, and like a bird being released from a cage, he flies off into the mayhem.

"Thank you." Winter turns to her brother.

Gray shakes his head at her. "That was our chance, Winter. Our only chance."

"Then I don't want the chance," she says. "Not that chance. This isn't right. None of this is. You know it and I know it. I'd rather die being the person I am than win having become one of them."

Her twin's head hangs as he works to control the emotions wracking his body.

She scans the crowd, waiting to see who's going to win the advantage. She wants it to be Lexis or Raze, of course. But there's a part of her that doesn't. Because that makes them the savages she was hoping they weren't. It would prove her right when she told Gray the only people they should trust is each other.

"Gray, look." She puts out her hand to help her brother to his feet then indicates the line that separates the Cragg segment from the Cy.

Lexis and Raze stand on their side, eyeing off the Cragg spectators.

Slab and Red are on the other, snarling at anyone from Cy who dares to look their way.

Someone has to make the first move eventually.

And for the first time since Winter and Gray arrived at these cursed Tournaments, she feels safe. For this one blissful moment, nobody is trying to hurt her. She's protected by Evrest's vicious threat.

Before she has a chance to voice this feeling of lightness to her brother, Lexis steps over the line, charging at the frightened Cragg.

Winter glances at Gray, his expression twisted into yet another version of the confusion and pain he's experienced in the only Tournament where he's been perfectly safe.

"Look!" he breathes as he points.

Shifting her gaze just in time, she sees Slab make his move.

Not toward the Cy competitors as she'd have expected but toward his own people who are in much closer reach.

With three giant steps Slab plucks a girl from the crowd. She must be fifteen at most.

He snaps her neck before Lexis has even had the chance to land a flying kick.

The girl falls to the ground like a puddle, and Slab raises his hands over his head in victory.

Except the crowd doesn't roar or cheer. They watch on in stunned silence, as another Cragg woman steps forward to cradle the dead girl in her arms and weep.

Lexis withdraws back to Raze's side and Red goes to Slab, slapping him on the back and grinning maniacally.

Winter feels sick. The Cragg have the advantage now, which is officially their worst case scenario.

"We can still do it," says Gray. "There's four of us and only two of them."

"Three if you count the knife," she murmurs.

Evrest emerges from his wall of guards and claps five times. He marches over to Slab and presses the knife into his hand.

"The fifth Tournament goes to Cragg," he announces. "The next Tournament—the penultimate Tournament—will take place on the morrow."

Slab slaps the flat side of the blade on his palm as he sneers at Lexis, letting her know exactly what he intends to do with his prize.

"The Cragg have just proved they're good at killing their own," says Evrest. "The next Tournament will test just how good they are at this. The winner will be the first to kill a competitor from their own faction."

"But…" Red shouts, realizing that the prize he thought his faction won is no prize at all. Well, maybe to Slab, but most definitely not to him. "Why would we do that? We want numbers for the final fight."

Evrest smiles. "Because the winner of the next Tournament will receive an even bigger prize. An advantage far better than having a teammate by their side."

A guard steps forward, holding something Winter's only ever heard about, but recognizes immediately.

It's a flamethrower.

The greatest prize of all.

RAZE

*B*ack in their hut, Raze gingerly lowers himself to the sleeping mat. The constant pain in his leg feels like it's progressively taking over his body, making it hard to think.

Which is probably a saving grace.

Tomorrow is the moment he and Lexis have worked toward. Tomorrow is the reason he was born.

Tomorrow is the day he dies.

Although Raze knows there are two other factions who could lose a member, he's already decided he'll be the one to go. There's little point in fighting to continue, his wound is too severe.

His twin sits beside him, chewing on her lip as she stares at the ground. Lexis goes to check his wound but he gently pushes her hand away. What's the point? Tomorrow he'll be free of all the myriad of pain this world has brought him.

Lexis doesn't put up a fight, instead tucking her hand back into her lap, her eyes averted. Raze nudges her, trying to catch her gaze. She's been as silent as he is since the next Tournament was announced.

Lexis lifts her troubled blue eyes to his. "I don't think—"

But Raze swipes his hand through the air, cutting her off. He grabs her wrist, squeezing tightly. He tries to communicate what he has so many times before.

I'm ready.

"Are you?" she asks softly.

Raze releases her as if she just burned him. He scowls at her. Of course he's ready.

Even if he wanted to, he can't fight the inevitable. Has Lexis ever considered what it would look like if he wasn't prepared to do this? He always knew this would be hard for his twin. How could it not be? Going willingly is the last gift he can give her. A little less guilt for her to live with.

He thumps his chest. He's ready.

Lexis's shoulders drop. "Except I'm not," she whispers. "You're my twin, Raze. How can I be expected to do this?"

Raze shakes his arm as he flexes his muscles. *You can do this.*

Lexis's blue eyes flash. "If the tables were turned, would you be able to? Could you kill me?"

Raze snaps his mouth shut, even though there was no response waiting to be said. He wishes this isn't what needs to happen. He wishes there was another way.

But there's not.

He points to the two cups of water sitting in the hut, waiting for their return. He points to the flatbread sitting beside it. He waves his arm to encompass the desiccated walls and floor.

This is all their world can provide them. Constant thirst. Permanent hunger. A never ending battle to survive.

They need a Commander. They need hope.

And that person isn't Raze.

He points at his twin, then forms a fist. *You're strong.* He points at himself, and shakes his head. *I'm weak.* He grips his throat, opening his mouth to show no sound will come out.

He can't even speak.

Lexis shoots to her feet, pacing the small hut. "I'm learning there's more than one way to be strong, Raze."

He waits, unsure what that means. He needs to know Lexis is going to do what it takes.

"And I think our father's definition is wrong."

Raze nods. These Tournaments have been far more violent and brutal than even he expected. Is that what the Outlands wants to stand for?

Once again, he points at Lexis. She's the one who can lead them to a new future.

Lexis stops in the center of the hut. "You're right," she says, her features hardening with resolve. "This is what I need to fight for."

Raze lays back on the mat, those words a balm to his aching soul. That is something worth dying for.

The sounds of shouting reach through their open doorway, angry and barbed.

"Stay there," Lexis commands as she peers outside. Raze considers refusing, but decides to save his energy. If danger is coming, he'll protect Lexis. But if it's just some Cy warriors fighting over a piece of bread, then he's going to forgo the pain of movement.

More shouts batter the air, and Raze realizes they're from further away. Whoever that is, it's not Cy.

Lexis takes another step out, frowning. "It's the Cragg. They're fighting."

Probably because Slab callously killed one of their own, a young woman who was here to champion her leader. And all so he could secure himself a knife. Raze wouldn't be surprised if Red might have tried to steal it from him.

A woman shrieks and a man screams back. Their words are too distorted by fury to be understood, but the message is clear.

Their faction is divided about what happened. What Slab was willing to do to win.

Lexis's frown deepens. "A couple of them are walking away."

Raze isn't sure why that's significant until he realizes why Lexis is concerned—she's worried about the Fairbanks twins. They both know that anger can spill over, wanting to hurt anyone or anything nearby. With the Rusts and the Never gone, their tent is alone and vulnerable.

And Gray has brought out something in Lexis that Raze was scared had died long ago.

He points to the door. *Go.*

She hesitates. "I just want to quickly check."

Raze makes a shooing motion with his hands. There's another shout and Lexis practically breaks into a run. The urgency stamped on her face is unmistakable.

Raze lays back down, glad their discussion is over. Although whatever has bloomed between those two is doomed, it's reinforced what he always hoped.

That Evrest hasn't destroyed Lexis's heart. That she won't be molded into the cruel Commander he believes the Outlands needs.

He draws in a breath, pulling the dusty air deep into his lungs. Without the distraction of his sister or the Tournaments, the pain in his leg once more infects his mind. The agony is becoming a palpable weight he can't shake.

He drops his arm over his face, letting out a sigh. It will all be over soon. His pain will end, which also means he won't have to be around to see either of the Fairbanks twins die. Those two should never have been part of the Tournaments. They're too...good.

There's a shuffle at the door and Raze sits up, alert and ready to fight.

Winter offers him a small smile from the doorway. "I think Gray and Lexis wanted to talk."

Raze freezes, unsure of what to do. She can't come in here.

Winter glances over her shoulder. "Maybe just for a

moment? Rusty is heading this way." She wrinkles her nose. "He probably wants to thank me for saving his life at the Tournament."

Raze scowls, indicating for her to enter. He doesn't like the way that boy looks at Winter. She's not some pawn or piece of meat.

Relieved, she enters and closes the door. She walks past the water and food in the center of the room, her gaze flickering to it and then quickly away. Sitting down on the other side, she smiles thinly. "Hopefully my brother and your sister won't be too long."

Raze indicates toward the water and bread. He saw her hungry glance, and there's no point in him having any.

Winter hesitates, but then quickly shuffles over. She picks up the cup and looks at him, challenge sparking in her dark eyes. "You drink half first. Then I'll have mine."

Raze reinstates his scowl. What is it with this girl and making sure he's looked after? Doesn't she realize what his role is in these Tournaments?

Even though he shouldn't care whether Winter drinks or not, Raze takes the cup. His fingers brush hers and for a moment he pauses. Her skin is soft. Warm. Everything his heart aches for.

She withdraws her hand, flushing. It's the most fascinating thing Raze has ever seen. Confusing. Confounding. But fascinating. He takes a quick gulp, finding his mouth is far drier than it was a moment ago, and passes it back.

Winter simply raises an eyebrow. "In Fairbanks, half means equal portions."

Letting out a frustrated breath, Raze takes another gulp, bringing the water down to the halfway mark. He passes the cup back, already anticipating the touch of her hand. His whole body is in suspended animation, waiting for it.

Winter takes it, and this time, the motion is much slower. As if she's curious, too. As if she also wants to feel it for longer.

A delicate warmth sparks where their fingers touch, blooming to a delicious heat as her hand brushes over his. Raze loses the ability to breathe. He never knew touch had such layers.

Winter brings the cup to her lips. The flush is back, this time a dusky rose that reaches down her neck.

Raze isn't sure he wants to draw air again. This is a moment he doesn't want to end.

The sound of more shouts filters from beyond the walls, reminding Raze of what's waiting for them.

The sixth Tournament.

The promise of death.

Winter sighs, as if the knowledge is weighing on her, too. She reaches over and takes two slices of flatbread, holding one out for him. "Here, we're going to need it."

Raze finds himself chewing it before he realizes what he's doing. He wants Winter to eat. He wants her to be strong.

"Do you think…" She swallows, her eyes becoming bottomless pools that Raze is steadily drowning in. "Do you think I could rest here until Lexis comes back?"

Raze nods, not ready for her to go.

Something sparks in her midnight eyes, a flash that lights something in Raze, too, and she quickly scoots forward.

She tilts her head. "You should also rest."

Once more confounded and confused, Raze lies down. He freezes in shocked disbelief as she lies down, too, turning her back and tucking into his side. He's held Lexis, but it was never like this.

He's never felt so…alive.

"Is this okay?" she asks quietly.

His answer is to shift his arm down. Winter lifts her head

and he slips it under. Their bodies seem to intuitively mold together.

"Raze."

Just the whisper of his name is enough to jolt his heart.

"I want you to know. Maybe, if things were different…"

If things were different.

Raze hasn't allowed himself that thought for a very long time. Now, his mind is drawn down that impossible path like a moth to a flame.

He'd touch her. See if her skin feels as exquisite as it looks. He'd carve for her. Create the very images his mind is suddenly full of.

He'd talk. He'd tell Winter that she's beautiful. That she touches him in places no one else has.

Raze yanks himself away from the foolish, useless images. He can't afford to think like this. It hurts too much.

But that doesn't mean he can't hold this beguiling, determined woman for just a little while. In fact, he's glad he got to taste what beauty could be like.

This is the world Lexis will fight for.

Winter's soft breathing fills the hut, a sweet, rhythmic cadence that counts the seconds until tomorrow's Tournament. But as the moments stretch out, as Raze's body sings along every place they touch, he realizes he made a mistake.

He should've sent Winter away. He shouldn't have touched her.

He certainly shouldn't be lying here with her.

Because, suddenly, he's not as ready to die as he thought.

GRAY

*G*ray watches Lexis across from him in the tent. She sits with one leg folded underneath herself and the other foot planted on the ground with her knee bent up. It's the pose of someone who's on alert for imminent attack. She could push up to her feet in no time and be ready to fight.

Except, he's not going to fight this beautiful, complicated girl.

The only fight he's having is the one taking place in his heart.

One part of him wants to take her in his arms. And the other knows he can't.

He doesn't want to make her job any harder than it already is. Eventually, she's going to have to watch him die. Because even if they make it to the final two, only one of them can live. And he can't imagine any circumstance where he'd be able to go through with taking Lexis's life. It had been hard enough trying to kill Rusty, and he doesn't even like him.

Which means Lexis will witness his final breath. He knows that with the same certainty he knows that he's in love with her. It's just the way it is.

The Cragg are still brawling at their camp, which is why Lexis is on high alert. But Gray doesn't think Slab will bother them tonight. They have enough of their own problems to sort out first.

"Would you really have killed a spectator if Slab hadn't done it first?" he asks, even though he knows she wouldn't have.

"Of course." She looks at him strangely and it takes him a moment to realize what she just said.

"You mean, *of course not?*" he clarifies. "That poor innocent girl never saw it coming."

"Gray." She leans forward to make sure he's listening. "I said, *of course.* It would have won me the Tournament and nothing's more important than that."

"Nothing?" he asks, wondering why she's lying to herself like this.

"Nothing." She lets out a sigh. "Except, now the joke's on the man who calls himself Red."

"Do you think that's what the fighting's about?" Gray indicates his head toward the Cragg camp.

Lexis nods. "Slab's people are unhappy with him."

"Which is interesting," says Gray. "Because let's just say Slab wins these Tournaments, what happens next? Not only does every other faction hate him, but now his own people hate him, too. How does that make him a good Commander?"

Lexis curls a little into herself as she takes this in. These Tournaments aren't the honorable tests she's been raised to believe they are. If only she could step back for a moment, she'd see that.

"A leader needs to be tough," she says, repeating her father's words. "They do what needs to be done."

"But why did that need to be done?" he asks gently. "Especially when the result has been to lose respect, rather than gain it."

"A leader doesn't hesitate." She blinks, uncomfortably. "A true leader always has the bigger picture in mind."

"Lexis." Gray dares to shuffle closer, pleased that his ribs seem to be more bruised than they are broken. "You're smart. I know you are. Think about what you're saying. It's okay to challenge what you've been told. That's a true sign of a good leader."

"I do think," she snaps. "And I think you're trying to confuse me."

"I'm sorry." He folds his hands on his lap to show he poses no threat.

"We need to figure out how to beat a flamethrower." Her voice is back to business. "Because we already know how the next Tournament will play out."

"Do we?" Gray tilts his head.

She huffs. "Slab will use his knife in the first minute to kill Red and win the flamethrower. It's the only possible outcome."

Gray hesitates, unsure if he should say what he's thinking. Lexis can kill a man with her bare hands. She's a trained fighter with little use for something like a knife. Which means that Slab killing Red is not the only possible outcome...

"Go on then." She crosses her arms. A dangerous move for a warrior on high alert... "Say it."

"What?" He throws out his hands.

"Say that there's another option." She uncrosses her arms to point a finger into his chest. "Say that I could kill my brother in less than a minute. Say that I could win the flamethrower before Slab's even had the chance to raise the knife in his hand."

"I..." Gray looks at this girl in awe, marveling at how accurately she just read his mind. "I..."

"You what?" She glares at him, her finger still pressed against his chest, sending sparks radiating through his body.

"I love you," he says, shaking his head. "I love you, Lexis."

Her jaw drops as her eyes widen. Perhaps she's not such a great mind reader after all.

"I don't understand," she murmurs.

"What don't you understand?" He wraps his hand around her finger, and when she doesn't resist he presses his palm against hers. To hell with making her job easier. It's already impossible for them both.

"I don't understand love," she says. "I don't understand you. And I don't understand why you just said that."

"You told me there's nothing more important than the Tournaments. Then you told me how easily you could win the next one." He smiles, unable to remove his eyes from those lips he's desperate to kiss one more time. "And you're choosing not to win?"

She shakes her head, dipping her gaze to the ground. "I never said that."

"You may as well have." He reaches for her face and tips it up to him. "You want to keep Raze alive more than you want to win the Tournaments. Don't tell me you don't understand love."

A single tear falls from her eye, proving just how human this warrior girl is.

"If I don't kill Raze," she whispers. "And I don't kill you. Or Winter. Then...Evrest will kill us all. These Tournaments will have been for nothing."

"Maybe they always were." He brings her hand to his lips and kisses her fingertips. "But I'm still glad I entered."

"How can you be glad?" She removes her hand from his grasp and strokes his cheek.

"Because I met you." He reaches out and pulls her against his chest, his need to hold her far outweighing the aching pain in his ribs. He might die tomorrow. The way things are going, who knows, he might die tonight. He literally has nothing left to lose.

Lexis makes a sudden move, and he thinks she's going to pull away.

But, instead, she climbs onto his lap, straddling him to press her torso against his.

And she holds him tight, like a mother reunited with a lost child.

"If wanting to keep someone alive means you love them, then, I love you, too," she says, her breath hot on his ear.

He turns his face to take the kiss he's been yearning for.

Her lips find his and time ceases to exist. There's no yesterday or tomorrow. No Tournaments or factions or twin siblings to look out for.

It's just Gray and Lexis.

The ghost and the savage.

Two people supposed to hate each other who somehow, accidentally, fell in love.

The heat of their kiss trails from their lips right down into Gray's chest as the taste of Lexis silences any logical thought.

He's lost in this moment with no care for anything that isn't related to what's happening right now. He can't even hear the Cragg fighting anymore.

Lexis moans as she presses herself impossibly closer and lights his whole body on fire. She reaches for the bottom of his shirt and pulls it over his head. He feels the warmth of her soft leather bodice against his bare skin.

It's too much.

And yet it's also not nearly enough.

"Lexis," he breathes as he draws back for air. "Slow down."

"We don't have time." She undoes the string of her bodice and it falls apart, revealing the most vulnerable side of her he's seen yet. "We could be dead tomorrow. We can't slow down."

He loses himself in her kiss, both agreeing with her and screaming his protest.

They *could* be dead tomorrow. Which is why he doesn't want to rush this. He once told Winter that no matter how bad things are, one day always turns out to be the best of your life.

And for Gray, that day is today.

Which means he wants it to last forever. Because it might also be his last.

But Lexis refuses to listen, having clear wants of her own.

"We have no future," she says, her voice breathless. "We only have right now."

"Stop." He presses his finger against her soft lips. "I want to show you what love is."

He tilts up his face and kisses her jawline, working his way slowly upward. He presses his mouth to each of her closed eyes then trails down the other side of her face, kissing every part of her face except her lips.

"I love you, Lexis," he says, wanting her to really hear his words this time.

Caressing her back, then daring to edge his hands further forward, he takes in the feel of her underneath his palms, wanting to touch her in all the ways he's never touched anyone before.

He presses his mouth to her neck, feeling her pulse underneath his lips. She tips back her head and makes a small noise to let him know she's feeling this as much as he is, and he very slowly moves along the underside of her jaw.

She tastes of salt and sweetness and all things Lexis, and he drinks her in, reveling in the feeling of closeness between them.

When the heat gets too much, she lifts her face and he pulls back to look deep into her eyes.

She drops her gaze first, focusing on his mouth as she bites down on her lip.

She wants the kiss that's coming just as much as he does. But this time it won't be an action born purely of lust or attraction. This time, she's going to feel his love.

He leans forward and claims her parted lips with his own.

The kiss is everything he thought it would be. And a whole lot more.

It isn't just hot.

It's electric.

"Don't make me wait any longer," she says, removing what remains of any clothes that separate them.

And now it's skin on skin.

"Lexis," he gasps as she eliminates any space between them, her hands clawing at his back.

As all his senses unravel, he focuses his energy on the most fascinating, wondrous, incredible human he's ever met.

He does love her. He feels like he always has…

Lexis is the reason he's always been so optimistic. She's why he was able to believe so strongly that there was something beautiful waiting for him in this life.

Because there was.

His warrior girl takes him to a place he never dreamed possible and when she cries out, he joins her, and together they make this moment last forever.

It might be the only moment they ever get.

And it's not nearly enough.

LEXIS

*L*exis stands in the Ring, willing the cold, numb feeling to flow through her veins once more. It's the only way she'll be able to get through this Tournament. It's what has allowed her to do everything she's ever had to do.

Hurt.

Steal.

Kill.

But it doesn't come. She grits her teeth, trying to shut down her mind. Her heart.

And fails.

She glances left, seeing Slab and Red clenching their hands over and over again, the knife Slab's holding glinting in the morning sun. Their faces are full of the cold, hard determination Lexis is supposed to be feeling.

They're ready to do what it takes.

But Lexis has lost that feeling, and it's because of the boy who's standing in the other tripoint of the Ring. Gray is standing close to Winter, his gaze full of the incredible words and soft touches of last night.

I love you, Lexis.

As Lexis had returned to her hut afterward, those words had echoed through her mind. They'd been both a healing balm and had shattered everything she believed to be true. She'd stopped in the door of their hut, shocked, as mute as her brother at the sight that greeted her.

Raze was asleep on his back, Winter curled into his side, her head on his chest. Raze's arm was wrapped around her in a protective way that had the breath leaving Lexis's body.

After everything she experienced with Gray, she knew what she was bearing witness to.

The fragile, beautiful, blossoming of love.

Winter had stirred and Lexis had slipped around the side of the hut. A moment later, Gray's twin had slipped away, returning to their tent. Lexis had gone back in and curled up beside Raze. Silently, achingly, he'd drawn her into his side.

Until these Tournaments, that was the only love Lexis had ever known. A twin bond that existed before she even had a memory of loving Raze. But that touch, that hold, was so different to the moments with Gray. Lexis realized they're both love, but each its own sweet flavor that stirs the soul.

She never knew there could be more than one. That her heart would hold both and be stronger for it.

Evrest leaps into the Ring, strutting to the center where he raises his arms and turns in a slow circle. The crowd cheers, although with far more caution than past Tournaments. They've learned nothing is sacred with Evrest. Their lives hold just as much value as those within the Ring.

Her father drops his arms and the crowd hushes. He glares at the contestants, continuing his slow revolutions. "Everyone will remain in their own section of the Ring for the sixth Tournament. One contestant from a single faction must die for this round to be won."

He reaches Lexis and pauses, his gaze hard and icy. The same ice she's supposed to be feeling, that should be building a fortress around her, from the inside out. The same ice that has thawed in Lexis as surely as the icecaps did hundreds of years ago, creating the deadly world they now live in.

Evrest is reminding her of what she's expected to do. That she is going to have to kill Raze. That their bond, that any bond or connection or love, will never be enough to claim victory and free the Outlands.

For most of her life, Lexis believed he was right.

Their father doesn't even look at Raze as he strides out of the Ring, coming to stand beside the statue of Cy, flanked by the severed heads on spikes. It's like his son no longer exists.

Lexis suspects he was never really alive in Evrest's eyes. Maybe that's what makes it so easy to wish him dead.

Raze turns to Lexis, nodding once as he raises his fists. *It's time.*

Lexis's responding stance is automatic, honed through years of training. If someone is ready to fight, she must be, too. Her own fists appear before her face, all her weight shifting to her toes. Raze looks relieved, as if he wasn't sure she'd do this. He steps to the side, beginning their usual dance when they train.

Except the movement is stilted because of his wound. Except his eyes are blank in a way she's never seen before.

Except Lexis is no longer living by reflex or acting without thought.

She's about to drop her fists when there's a roar of rage from the Cragg. Lexis instantly turns around, the need to protect Raze or Gray or Winter, all of them at once if necessary, humming through her muscles. But Slab is launching himself at Red, the dagger in his hand aiming for Red's heart.

Red leaps back, and the tip slashes nothing but air, eddies of dust exploding in its wake. In one swift movement, he changes direction and launches at Slab, trying to shoulder the knife out of his hand. Slab twists as if he was expecting it, ramming an elbow into his teammate's torso as he brings the knife back around. Red crouches and leaps away before the knife can slice his flesh.

The crowd roars as the fight continues to unfold. These men are equally matched, just like Raze and Lexis. They've trained together. Even though Slab has the knife, they know each other's moves, their strengths and weaknesses.

This is going to be a fight drenched with blood, one dripping with entertainment.

The thought makes Lexis sick as she realizes this is what the crowd would be doing if she and Raze were fighting. It might even be more exciting, the stakes higher, because they're brother and sister.

Slab screams another battle cry as he launches at Red once again, knowing he has the advantage. Red leaps back, the same dance playing out. This time, the moment his feet touch soil and he launches forward, he powers his fist toward Slab's face. There's a sickening crunch as they connect, the impact sending shockwaves through Slab's body. The blow would send anyone else reeling, stumbling backward.

But not those who have prepared for the Tournaments. Not those who have spent their lives fighting. Desperate to win.

Slab knows pain doesn't stop you from doing what needs to be done.

Impossibly, he absorbs the impact and as the ripples course through him, he drives forward, the knife on a deadly trajectory toward Red's breastbone.

Red blocks Slab's arm but it's too late. The knife impales his chest, just not straight through the heart like Slab was intending. All Red did was sacrifice his chance at a quick death. He arches as the blade embeds itself, crimson instantly gushing down his torso.

There's a gasp from Lexis's right and she knows it was Winter. This is gruesome to watch, even by Cy standards.

Slab steps back, breathing hard as he watches a member of

his faction's life drain away. He glances at Evrest, trying to school his features into the triumph of victory, but Lexis can see he's struggling. Even someone as callous as Slab knows what he just did is tainted.

Lexis stills as Red lurches forward, yanking the blade out of his chest at the same time. Slab opens his mouth in shock, but never has a chance to utter a cry of surprise.

He never blocks Red as he falls onto him. Never alters the trajectory of the knife. He never saw this coming.

The dagger impales his chest, puncturing his heart, a fresh flow of oxygen-rich blood joining Red's.

It's impossible to tell who dies first as the two men crumple onto the bloodied soil.

Silence rises along with the heat, suffocating and sickly. The contestants glance at each other, unsure of what just happened. Winter and Gray are holding hands, the united front they've always been as they, too, try to comprehend this unexpected outcome.

Lexis almost buckles under the wave of relief that floods her. One Cragg killed another. The sixth Tournament is complete. She has another reprieve, even if it's only for a day. That's more time to decide what to do.

Maybe another night spent with Gray, discovering everything that takes life from existence to living. A part of life she couldn't discover until he came into her life.

Evrest leaps back into the Ring and Lexis straightens, waiting for the six claps that will announce the end of this round. He walks over and stands beside Slab and Red as the soil beneath them turns to thick, rust-colored mud.

"Both Cragg are dead, which means this Tournament is not complete. The sixth round will play on." He glares at Lexis. "One must kill someone from their own faction. The other must remain standing."

The silence is absolute as he leaves again. The spectators are the first to break its oppressive weight, their feet shuffling as they move in a little closer. They're curious about what will happen next. Who will pick up this sick, macabre gauntlet.

And Lexis knows it has to be her.

She glances at Gray, seeing the subtle shake of his head. He's telling her not to do this. Except someone must die for this Tournament to end. For a Commander to be chosen.

Lexis doesn't have a choice.

As that realization hits her, so does the solution. The only choice she can live with.

She glances at her father, hatred so deep it burns her very marrow scorching her from the inside out. He's the one who's given her no alternative.

Ironically, he's the one who also gave her the means to do this.

She turns away, not wanting such a vile, virulent emotion to be a part of her anymore. Slowly, she spins to face Raze. Her twin. Her first lesson in love.

On the way, her gaze catches Gray's. He shakes his head again, even though his dark eyes are telling her that no matter what happens next, it changes nothing.

Gray. The future she never could've had. The love that changed everything.

Continuing her slow spiral, Lexis surreptitiously reaches into her belt. The pouch is there, like it has been from the moment her father gave it to her. She digs her fingers in.

One pinch will help you sleep.

The powder is bitter and gritty on her tongue, her chest twisting in the way she won't let show on her features.

Double that and they're not waking up.

She quickly takes the second pinch, grinding it between her teeth with determination.

When she straightens to face Raze, she pulls her shoulders

back. She can already feel the poison working as it dulls her senses. Good. She wants this to be quick.

Raze swallows as he nods. *I'm ready.*

Except his gaze flickers to Winter, the dreams he never let himself have flashing through his blue eyes. When they return to her, Lexis watches her brother push them away, just like everything he has in his life.

The words that he wanted to say.

The future he didn't know was possible.

The chance at more than a taste of happiness.

Lexis raises her fists, stomach lurching as the world tilts one way then another. "Fight me," she growls. "You owe me that, Raze."

He nods, trying to stop the pain drenching his eyes from distorting his sweet face.

He swings, beginning the sequence she knew he would. Just like Slab and Red, she knows her twin's moves. Knows he'll throw a punch to her chest, another to her gut, before swiping his powerful fist at her temple.

Lexis lets the first land, locking her legs so she doesn't stumble. Through the foggy haze that's steadily shrouding her brain, she sees Raze's eyes flare with confusion as he lands the second. Lexis lifts her fist to block the third, knowing he'd expect her to do that. Relief relaxes his features. He believes she wants it to look like he went down fighting. That she didn't just beat her brother to death.

Even now, he's doing what he can to put her first.

Except she lowers her hand, withdrawing the block that would've protected her at the last moment. In truth, her arms suddenly feel like lead. She's not sure she could've kept them up. As Raze's fist connects with her temple, Lexis's legs give out.

She barely feels it as she hits the ground, her body bouncing like a doll's.

"No!"

Gray's voice reaches her, his face flashing above as Lexis's eyes close. She wishes she had the strength to say his name one last time.

Gray. Even Winter. The Ghosts of Fairbanks who arrived with nothing, the two with no appetite for death, were the ones who had it right all along.

She will always be grateful that Gray had the courage to show her this.

The cold she was seeking so desperately at the beginning of the Tournament creeps through her limbs. Her heart rate slows and fades. She no longer has the energy to draw breath.

As blackness claims her, Lexis is enveloped by three final waves that even the poison can't dull.

Aching regret for all the hurt she's caused.

A bone-deep wish things could've been different.

And peace.

WINTER

*W*inter's hands fly to her mouth.

Lexis can't be dead!

She's so strong. And brave. The best fighter Winter's ever seen.

Which means this is impossible.

She must be faking it.

But...Gray is crumpled beside Lexis with his shoulders shaking. Raze is standing frozen, a picture of distress. And Evrest is marching toward his daughter, his face the color of the snowflakes that fell upon this land in generations gone by.

Winter fights the whirlpool of emotions that overtake her. She doesn't want Lexis to be dead. But...her death means that Raze is still alive. And Gray. And even Winter herself.

She pushes down the relief that threatens to bubble up underneath her distress, refusing to allow even the smallest part of her to be okay with this.

Lexis was a good person. According to Gray, she was *the best* person. The Tournaments were not supposed to go like this.

Evrest takes a wide arc around the bodies of Slab and Red, and Winter darts forward to take Gray's arm.

"Get back," she hisses. "Quickly!"

Because Evrest's face is no longer the color of snow. It's the color of the ocean—a deep rusty red. His daughter is dead and he's furious. Gray doesn't need to be caught in the middle of that.

"Get back," she urges. "Gray!"

Her brother reluctantly allows her to pull him to his feet and they shuffle back a couple of yards.

But it turns out Lexis isn't Evrest's target. He reaches Raze and grabs him by the throat.

Winter lets go of Gray, and now it's him pleading with her to keep out of harm's way.

Raze's injured leg gives way, and he hangs like a puppet in Evrest's hands, not making any effort to fight back. Maybe he knows there's no point. Or maybe a quick death is what he wants.

"No, Raze," Winter sobs. "Don't give up."

He turns his eyes and holds her gaze. She swallows as she loses herself in the sky blue depths, trying to read all the things he's trying to say.

He's sorry. He's hurting. He's tired. But most of all...he's broken.

So strong all his life, this incredible guy who'd lost his voice has now lost his will to live.

Evrest's fist lands in the middle of Raze's face, breaking the moment almost as certainly as he breaks his nose. He pulls back his arm and slams his knuckles into Raze's jaw before letting go of his throat to release a volley of punches into his stomach.

Raze tolerates it for several excruciating seconds before falling to the ground beside his sister.

The crowd erupts into wild cheers at the spectacle before them.

Gray pulls Winter to his side and presses her face to his

chest, trying to block her vision as the brutal attack continues, this time with Evrest's feet instead of his hands.

Through her brother's fingers, Winter sees Raze curl himself into Lexis's body and she's reminded of the way she'd fallen asleep beside him only the night before.

"He's not going to kill him," Gray says into her hair.

"How do you know that?" Winter pulls herself free of her brother and takes a few steps forward. She doesn't want to see what's happening to Raze, but she owes it to him to watch. She can't abandon him now or he really will have nothing left in this world.

"If he kills him, Fairbanks will be the last faction standing!" shouts Gray.

These words echo around the Ring and the crowd falls silent as the truth hits home.

He's right.

If Evrest doesn't stop then either Winter or Gray will rule the Outlands, which is an outcome nobody could have predicted. It's also an outcome that nobody wants.

Was this why Winter had been driven to enter these Tournaments? Is it her destiny to lead these people to victory over Askala?

But then she looks at the guy she's fallen for lying on the hard ground next to his dead twin as his father continues to torture him with his boot, and Winter knows she doesn't want to win.

The price is far too great.

Evrest's tirade draws to a close and he spins around as he registers that the Ring is cloaked in silence.

His face works through the full spectrum of emotions as he pulls himself together. Smoothing down his tunic, he flexes his knuckles then claps six times.

The Tournament is complete.

More unwanted relief washes over Winter. Part of her had

wondered if they were going to be made to continue until one person from each faction had been killed. And neither she nor Gray would ever go down that path. Evrest would need to kill one of them himself.

"The Cragg have been eliminated," says Evrest. "And my gutless daughter is dead, proving to us that she was never destined to be your Commander. She chose love over leadership and I have never been more ashamed."

He grabs Raze roughly under the arms and drags him to his feet. He has blood running from his nose and is unable to stand straight as he clutches at his middle. But he's alive and for that Winter is grateful.

"My son is a mute," says Evrest. "But it seems that unlike his sister, he is no coward. He will fight in the final Tournament, and we'll see what he's made of. Perhaps I've underestimated him all these years."

The People of Cy murmur as they speculate over Raze's chances.

Winter and Gray remain silent. Raze may be the better fighter, but it's clear to everyone here that Fairbanks is in far better shape. It's doubtful with Raze's injuries he'd be able to kill a cockroach running over his chest at night, let alone the pair of them. Although, he will have a flamethrower as his prize for his twin's death...

Is that what Evrest is banking on here? Is that why he ended the Tournament without forcing them to continue until one of them is dead? In some ways, it makes sense. If Raze can kill two people with the injuries he has, he might just be able to win the Outlanders' respect as well as the title of Commander.

Has this whole thing just been an elaborate act to bring them to this moment?

She tries to catch Raze's eye again, but he keeps his gaze on the ground, his head slumped as he stands limply by his father who's still supporting most of his weight.

"The final Tournament will take place on the morrow," Evrest announces. "Lexis's body will remain in the Ring as a reminder to all of how cowards are treated in the Outlands. When the Tournament starts, we'll have a new offering for the almighty Cy."

Winter glances at the statue with the decaying remains of the People of the Never still on spears beside it. She blanches at the barbarity.

Evrest lets out a growl. "My lily-livered daughter's head will look quite pretty on a stick, don't you think?"

Gray whimpers and Winter rushes back to him just as Evrest lets go of Raze. He collapses back to the ground beside Lexis, and Evrest strides over to Winter and Gray.

"Prepare to die," he hisses quietly. "Because over my dead body will either of you rule the Outlands."

"You mean over your daughter's dead body," Gray corrects, his voice etched with pain.

Winter grimaces as she puts a hand on her brother's back, trying to silence him.

"You're a fool if you think she loved you." Evrest's voice is as icy as his heart.

Gray's body tenses and Winter steps in front of him before he can make this any worse.

"It seems you're the smart one." Evrest sneers at her. "Although, I thought Lexis was the smart one, too, and look what happened to her."

Winter clenches both her jaw and her fists as she wills herself not to react.

Evrest gives her a sly smile and walks away.

She turns immediately to face Gray. He has tears streaking down his cheeks, leaving trails in the fine layer of dust that coats his skin.

"You're not a fool," says Winter. "And she did love you. I know she did."

"How could he have killed her?" Gray asks with a hard edge to his voice. "He was supposed to protect her."

Winter's eyes flare at the unfamiliar animosity in his voice. "Raze would never have done that on purpose," she says. "Never. You know people can die from one punch. It was an accident."

Gray shakes his head. "They were trained fighters. He did it on purpose. He must ha—"

"No!" She jams her hands on her hips refusing to believe that. Of all the times for her brother to lose his optimism, please let it not be now. "Something else must've happened. There was so much going on out there. We don't really know how it played out. But he didn't mean to kill her. He loved Lexis. He wouldn't do that."

"I should have helped her." Gray shakes his head slowly. "Why didn't I help her?"

Winter reaches for his hands. "It was an accident. You couldn't have predicted that outcome. None of us could."

"She didn't deserve to die." Gray blinks back his tears and looks away.

Winter follows his gaze. Raze has pulled himself closer to Lexis and is sitting up, cradling her head in his lap. He's staring down at her as if he can't believe what he did.

Winter's heart both hardens and cracks wide open. How can the world be this cruel? Hasn't Mother Nature punished them enough already? Do humans really have to treat each other like this in order to survive? Maybe the people of Askala have got the right idea isolating themselves from this violence.

"None of us deserve this." She squeezes her brother's arm before going to Raze.

He's so wrapped up in his grief, he doesn't hear her approach.

She squats beside him and puts a hand gently on his back. "I'm here, Raze. You still have me."

He moves her hand away, keeping his eyes on his sister. She

looks as beautiful in death as she had when she was alive. Actually, no. She's more beautiful. Because now she looks at peace.

"Raze." She tries again. "It's me. It's Winter. I'm here."

He shoves her hand away more roughly this time, still refusing to look at her.

She swallows down her shock at this rebuke. A thousand words swirl in her mind as she tries to settle on which ones to say.

But then she realizes that Raze has taught her far more than just how to open her heart to love. He's taught her what little value words hold. Out here, people tell lies, they give false promises, they twist and deceive, and stab each other in the back. It's their actions that speak the truth.

So, she doesn't tell him that she knows he didn't mean to kill Lexis.

Nor does she tell him that she knows he pushed her away because he can't stand to live with the pain of letting her in only to have to watch her get taken away.

She doesn't even tell him that everything's going to be okay.

Because it isn't.

Instead, she reaches out to take his hand and holds it to her heart, relieved to find that although he doesn't look up, he doesn't move away.

With her other hand, she presses her fingertips to the left side of Raze's chest.

They stay there like that for countless moments.

Friend to friend.

Heart to hammering heart.

No words, just the rhythmic beating of their lifeforce connecting them in ways that words will never be able.

Slowly, he lifts his eyes.

But instead of seeing love and grief etched into his soulful depths, she sees...

Nothing.

Raze looks at her like he's the one who died in the Tournament.

Winter's jaw falls open as she takes in the hopeless sight before her.

Pushing to her feet, she runs to the only place she can right now.

Her tent.

A shelter built for her by a stranger that can shield her from the elements but has no hope at protecting her from the pain her heart has endured.

There's no point in competing in the final Tournament.

Because the three of them who remain have already lost.

RAZE

*R*aze has been slowly dying all his life.

First, his voice died.

Then, his wish that his destiny was anything but what his father had planned.

Then, his desire to keep living in this brutal world.

So, the fact that he's still alive while Lexis isn't, is a cruel twist he's struggling to comprehend.

Lexis was supposed to win.

She was supposed to live.

Raze sits beside her lifeless body in the middle of the Ring, knowing he's still breathing while she's not. He should be feeling that his body is macerated, pulverized by their father. He should be feeling the loss of the harsh heat as the sun sinks into the horizon. He should be feeling thirst or hunger or...something. But he doesn't.

The final part of him is gone.

His soul has died.

Raze hears movement behind him and leaps to his feet. If Evrest has come to take Lexis's body and do what he promised, then Raze is about to finish what was started so long ago. He'll die stopping his monstrous father.

But it's not Evrest.

Winter and Gray stand in the twilight. Raze sways, his battered body doesn't even have the energy to stand. Winter quickly slips under his arm. The usual warmth that he feels at her touch doesn't spark. He's glad. If he feels that, then he'll feel the pain.

"Raze," Winter breathes. "We want to help."

He glances from her to Gray. Both their faces are tear-streaked in a way Raze's isn't. That's because their hearts had a chance to thrive. To hope. To see the world so differently.

Lexis realized that. It was one of the reasons she was so drawn to Gray.

Raze turns away, folding down beside his sister again. It's too late for him.

Winter kneels next to him. "We need to take Lexis away. Before Evrest comes." Her gaze flickers to the heads of the Never on the spikes before quickly darting away.

Raze realizes they're right. He can barely stand, let alone fight. One strike from Evrest and he'd be useless. Gently, Raze slips his arms under Lexis's armpits. Her body is still warm. As if blood is still pumping through her body and she could wake any moment. But he knows it's just from the relentless sun that beat down on her all day.

Something twinges in Raze's chest but he ignores it. He doesn't want a heart anymore. He prefers being soulless. It's easier.

But Winter presses a hand to his arm, stopping him. "No, Gray will do it."

Her brother steps forward, fresh tears already tracking their way down his cheeks. "I'll take her to the ocean. The way it's supposed to be done."

Raze blinks. A warrior's goodbye. It's what Lexis deserves.

But he shakes his head, making a motion of a knife across his throat. Don't they realize Evrest will kill them if they're caught?

Gray's hands clench. "We have nothing to lose."

"That's right," says Winter. "We were too scared before but now...it's far more dangerous to stay here than it is to leave."

And they've now seen the devastation of one twin killing another.

"I'll wait until it's dark," Gray reassures him. "I've been watching the guards. I think I know how to avoid them."

Raze swallows, hating that he can't do it himself. Even his limbs feel too heavy to move right now.

Gray glances at Lexis, his face crumpling with sorrow. "I love her. Please, let me do this for her."

Raze's chest tightens as if it's being assaulted all over again. He swallows, then nods. Evrest will be unable to exact his revenge. Lexis will be able to escape his last act of brutality. Raze would do anything to make that happen.

Winter steps in closer. "And before sunrise tomorrow, when you've rested, we'll join Gray."

Raze snaps his head toward her, their dusky surroundings taking a second to catch up. He sways again but Winter presses herself more tightly against him.

"We'll leave these cruel, awful Tournaments and never come back," she whispers fiercely.

Leave?

Run away?

It feels like these Fairbanks twins have started talking in a different language.

"We stay, and only one of us survives, Raze," says Gray. "Possibly none of us. If we leave, we can all live."

"It's what Lexis would've wanted for you," Winter adds.

Raze's brain is working in slow motion. Images of Lexis dropping her arm and failing to block his strike slide through his mind. Although his blow wasn't at full power, it was enough to kill her.

She sacrificed herself for him.

Except Lexis didn't realize he wasn't worth sacrificing herself for. Not the mute who isn't supposed to be alive. Not the mute who killed his twin.

He shakes his head, pointing at them and then at the horizon. *You go.*

Gray sighs. "Winter said you'd say that. She also told me she won't leave without you." His gaze turns pleading. "Please, you have to come. I've lost Lexis, I can't lose her, too."

Raze looks down at Winter. Her dark eyes are fathomless pools in the half-light, but she doesn't break his gaze. She's as unflinching as her determination.

Raze frowns, confused and unsure. Why is this beautiful woman so intent on seeing him live? Did she not see what he just did?

Still holding his gaze, she pulls something out of her pocket. The carving of the boy he made her. She's kept it…

"I want you to make me more of these," she says softly.

Raze can't imagine ever carving again, but he nods anyway. He'll run. But he'll run because it means Winter can escape this hell in a way Lexis was never able to. He'll run because it means his father will lose his chance at winning these Tournaments.

Winter's body unwinds with relief. She tightens her arm around his waist. "Come. There can't be anyone around while Gray does this."

Her brother needs to get away with Lexis's body as silently and unobtrusively as possible. Evrest will be furious when he discovers what's happened.

Raze allows Winter to lead him away, surprised when Gray slips under his other arm.

Somehow, he manages to pull up a ghost of a smile as he glances at Raze. "Think of this as weight training." His face hardens in a way Raze has never seen before. "I'll come back shortly when it's a little darker."

Raze allows the twins to lead him to his hut. The few people they pass avert their eyes and Raze imagines their disgust. He's supposed to be their last hope in winning the Tournaments. He could be their Commander.

It seems it's a good thing he'll be leaving. Raze was never meant to be Commander. That was supposed to be Lexis's destiny. Or if not her, anyone else but him.

Inside the hut, Raze lowers himself to his mat, drawing his numbness back around him like armor. He doesn't want to feel anything ever again.

Winter and Gray hug, making promises to meet by the ocean the following morning before Gray slips back out, making sure no one sees him. If Raze could speak, he'd tell him to take care of his sister. He'd thank him for doing this. He'd tell him to be careful.

If Evrest catches them, there will be more than one extra head on a spike.

But Raze doesn't, so he simply lays on his back with his arm over his eyes. He wants to think about as much as he wants to feel.

Winter hesitates where she's standing, then softly pads over. Carefully, she lays beside him, shuffling in closer. "Does this hurt?"

Raze doesn't move. Nothing hurts. Nothing feels.

She slips in a little closer, gently resting her head on his shoulder. "Is this okay?"

Once again, Raze doesn't respond. Nothing is okay.

Winter pauses again, then slips a tender arm over his chest as she presses the length of her against his side. "I know there's nothing I can say that will make this better," she says quietly.

Raze blinks beneath his arm over his face. Winter is probably one of the few people who would have some idea of what he's going through. She's a twin. She has a half to her whole.

He mentally shakes himself. He doesn't want to hear this.

"But I want you to know, it wasn't your fault, Raze," she says, her voice now thick with tears.

A flash of pain slices through Raze, taking his breath away. He focuses on his breathing.

One.

"Lexis wanted you to have the chance to live."

Two.

"I think she chose this. She was determined it would end like this, no matter what you did."

Raze never reaches three. Grief explodes through his mind. Loss presses its choking weight on his chest. Anguish fills every cell in his body.

He does the only thing he can. The only thing he knows.

He fights it.

He tries to push Winter away, desperately clutching at the numbness that protected him. But Winter is faster than his muted, painful movements. Her shoulders slip out of his grip, her hands slide through his grasp. She repeatedly, determinedly, keeps a hold of him.

"You're not pushing me away, Raze," she says fiercely. She clasps his face and then tenderly presses her lips to one cheek, then the other. "I'm not leaving you alone."

And then he's holding Winter. Drawing her close. Curling around her, trying to climb in. Her arms wrap around him as she strokes his hair, his face, his torso.

"I know," she murmurs over and over. "I know. I'm here."

Raze chokes on the emotion welling up, but he doesn't stop it. He realizes he can't let Winter in without opening himself to the pain, too. He can't have a sliver of hope, the chance to escape like they've planned, unless he chooses to live.

As silent sobs wrack through Raze, he discovers why that was a choice he didn't want to make.

His body is a twisted mess of pain.

But that agony is nothing compared to the heart he just discovered still throbbing in his chest.

GRAY

Gray creeps into the Ring using the darkness as his cloak.

He hates that he left Winter. If only they could take Lexis to the ocean together, they could run straight to Fairbanks and pretend this nightmare never happened.

But it's safer this way.

Less chance of the guards noticing only one person running into the night. Which means less chance of Evrest noticing his daughter's body missing until morning and they're all far away.

He approaches Lexis, still unable to believe she's really dead.

She'd been so alive when she visited him in his tent.

So warm.

So vulnerable.

So strong...

If the circumstances were different, the memory would make him smile. Instead, it makes his eyes sting with grief.

Crouching down, he reaches out to touch her soft cheek. And he realizes he doesn't want to pretend this nightmare never happened. Because that would be pretending Lexis never happened. And knowing her changed everything. He could never wish away the crossing of their paths.

A noise outside the Ring startles him, and Gray scoops up Lexis before he misses his chance. If he's caught, it won't just be Lexis who loses her head.

What he's doing is incredibly dangerous, but there's a reason Winter didn't try to stop him. It's also incredibly necessary. He can't stand by and watch Lexis's remains be disrespected in the way Evrest has threatened.

That last Tournament had been the catalyst Gray and Winter had needed to get themselves out of here. Lexis's death made everything so real. It had also made the risk of being killed for trying to escape seem like not such a bad option. Far better than being killed at the unwilling hand of your twin while a crowd of bloodthirsty spectators cheer them on.

"I'm sorry," he whispers to Lexis as he holds her close to his chest and places a kiss on her forehead. "I wish I could have kept you safe. But I'm going to make sure you have a proper goodbye."

That is if Gray can even find the ocean. It wasn't until after he'd left Winter and Raze that he realized he has no idea where the ocean actually is. Although, if he can't find it, then burying Lexis in the desert will be better than what her father has planned. No matter what happens, he's going to make sure he does her proud.

For someone so slight, she feels heavy in his arms, his bruised ribs protesting at the extra weight he's holding. He walks through the Ring, being careful to tread lightly so his footsteps can't be heard.

If only the four of them had made a run for it the night before, they might just have made it. The risk would have been worth it. Especially for Lexis, as it turns out.

"I'm sorry," he says again, even though he knows it wasn't his fault. He doesn't even blame Raze for what happened.

It's Evrest he'll always hold responsible.

The man who sired the most beautiful girl in the world is the same man who murdered her.

Gray hates him in the same way he hates the monster who stabbed Trakk.

Reaching the edge of the Ring, he carefully places Lexis's body on the ledge, climbs out, and lies flat on the ground beside her while he waits for his moment. He feels his pocket to check it's still filled with rocks as he wonders if the oldest trick in the book might actually work.

It had better. He really doesn't have any other ideas for how to distract the guards.

There's a small fire burning in the Cy village, casting eerie shadows on the falling down huts and sending the scent of baked flatbread floating in the still night air. Gray had decided to exit the Ring right into the lion's den. There are too many eyes on the Fairbanks camp. And too much trouble anywhere near the Cragg, who seem to have decided to stick around to watch the final Tournament. Either that or they're not quite sure what to do without their leader.

Evrest's guards won't expect trouble so close to home. Nobody is on high alert when they're on their own turf. Escaping from under their noses is his best shot.

After saying goodbye to Winter and pretending to return to his tent, Gray had crept back to watch the two guards patrolling the perimeter of the Cy camp, studying the route they took. Which means that now as he holds his breath in the dim light, he knows which way they're about to walk.

The guards walk up to the edge of the Ring a few yards away from Gray, and he keeps himself flat on the warm earth.

"Can you see her?" one guard asks. "I can't see her."

"I can't see nuttin' in the dark," the other replies. "Not like she could get up and walk away."

The first guard grunts and their silhouettes turn and walk back to the village to finish their circuit.

Removing a stone from his pocket, Gray throws it as far as he can, hearing it land against the timber wall of a hut. Quickly following this with another stone, he keeps it going, sending one after the other pelting into the Village of Cy.

The guards take the bait, shouting to each other as they deviate off course and run toward the haphazardly erected homes of their people.

Gray scrambles to his feet and lifts Lexis's body, draping her over his shoulder this time so he can move faster.

"Sorry," he says to her again as her head bumps against his spine.

He takes off through a different section of the village, knowing he doesn't have much time to get away.

"Hey, you!" one of the guards shouts. "I see you! Stop right there."

Gray's heart turns to lead as tries to decide what to do. How can he outrun these men with Lexis slung over his shoulder and a set of bruised ribs?

It's impossible!

He comes to a slow stop, deciding his chances are better if he faces these thugs right here and now.

"Oh, fish shackles!" comes Rusty's voice from nowhere. "It's only me. Didn't mean to startle you."

"What the hell are you doing here?" the guard growls.

"I was just passing through." Rusty's voice is shaking. He's clearly petrified. "I tripped over. Didn't mean to make so much noise."

Gray swallows as he steps into the shadow of a hut. The annoying guardian angel strikes again! He's clearly covering for Gray.

"Git out of here before we kill you," says the guard. "I'm sick of you creeping around. Go back where you came from, you piece of washed-up Rust scum."

"I'm going," says Rusty, speaking far louder than necessary. "In fact, I'm going to go straight home to the ocean. Which is right over that mountain you can see in the distance. Except it's quicker to curve left around it, of course."

Gray shakes his head. Rusty knows he's here. And he's telling him where he needs to go. Why is he helping him like this? Especially after he tried to kill the guy in the fifth Tournament. It makes no sense.

"We can let him go," the other guard says. "But I say we teach him a lesson first. You know, make sure he never comes back."

Rusty gasps and there's the sound of a scuffle.

Gray decides not to wait. He's of no help to Rusty right now. And if he ever had a chance to get Lexis away unnoticed, it's right now.

Darting through the outskirts of the village, he moves quickly and quietly, reaching the Training Ground and trying not to think about that incredible first kiss he shared with Lexis. It was the first kiss he'd shared with anyone and he doubts he'll kiss anyone ever again. Partly because it's possible he's about to die. But mostly because there will never be anyone else like Lexis.

He presses on, trying not to stumble as he runs into the pitch dark. He knows the mountain is behind the Training Ground and there's a bright star in that exact direction. Gray's certain it's Polaris. Not the building that was once his home, but the north star it was named after. His older sister once told him that following it will take you in a purposeful direction. And he's never needed a more purposeful direction than he does right now.

Ignoring the pain, Gray walks further into the night.

He follows the star.

He holds on tight to Lexis.

And he talks to her the entire time.

He tells her what he thought the moment he first saw her. He tells her how his heart grew during the Tournaments to accommodate her exact shape. He tells her about the future he wishes they could have had. And when he runs out of words to express how he feels about her, he tells her about his sister, his mother, and the nephew he never met. He speaks of his home, his hopes, and every one of his heartbreaks. He tells her everything he wished he could have before it was too late.

And perhaps instead of having an annoying guardian angel here on Earth, he also has one now in the stars. Because, somehow, he feels like she hears him.

As he reaches the mountain, the moon rises in the sky and lights the worn path that Rusty told him to take.

"Was that you, Lexis?" he asks, glancing up. "Because that sure makes it easier to walk."

As he winds his way down the path, he falls into silence, surprised to see the occasional shrub or tree swaying in the moonlight. He even thinks he sees an aloe vera plant. So, this is where Rusty gathered the supplies he brought them. It must also be where Evrest's men come to look for food. Which means he must be careful. Despite the distance he's covered, he's still far from safe.

The change from hard ground below his worn shoes to sand is so gradual over the hours that he barely notices until he's walking on soft sand.

"Can you hear that, Lexis?" he asks. "It's the waves breaking on the shore. We're close now. You'll get the warrior's sendoff you deserve. It's too late for Evrest to get his hands on you now. I've got you."

His feet dig into the sand as he stumbles forward. When the soft sand turns to wet, he comes to a stop and gently lifts Lexis from his shoulder to cradle her at his chest.

"I'm sorry I had to carry you like that. It was faster. And to be honest, my ribs are killing m—" He freezes at what he just said. "Sorry, I meant to say my ribs are really sore. I'm okay, though."

A wave laps at his feet and he winces at the sting of acid. He's never been to the beach before and this really wasn't how he imagined it would go. The moon is behind him, casting shadows across the water that he knows is the color of rust. But right now, it looks black.

"We need to do this quickly," he tells Lexis, hating the idea of what he knows he must do. "I'll take you out as far as I can."

He steps into the water. It's warm, and if it weren't for the acid, it might even feel nice.

Wading out, he ignores the stinging pain on his skin, until he's waist deep with waves lapping at his torso. He's ready to lower Lexis into the water so her body can dissolve as she's sent back to the Earth from where she was born.

Except…

He can't do it.

How can he possibly let her go?

Salty tears run down his cheeks to join the acid of the ocean and he tries to force himself to say goodbye.

"Lexis," he says. "I love you. I hope wherever you are, you can hear that. I love you so much."

As his legs scream in pain for relief, he leans forward and reluctantly lowers her into the water.

"Goodbye, my beautiful girl," he says, desperately reminding himself that this is merely her shell. "Travel well, my angel."

Lexis submerges, still cradled in his arms with only her head above the surface. He winces as very slowly, she slides away.

But just as her face is about to slip under, her eyes open wide, and she looks at him in terror.

"Lexis!" Gray shouts as he scrambles to get hold of her, his heart racing. "Lexis!"

She blinks wildly, not seeming to be able to move any other part of her body, and he scoops her out of the water.

Unsure if this is just some kind of weird physical reaction in death, he clutches her to his chest and wades back through the water, hurrying to shore. Please, let this be the miracle he hadn't dared to hope for.

Lying Lexis down on the sand, he leans over to see if she's breathing.

Her eyes are still open, but other than that there's no sign she's alive.

"Lexis, can you hear me?" He presses his ear to her mouth, trying to pick up on the slightest of sounds. "Please, Lexis. Can you hear me?"

She draws in a sudden deep breath, and he pulls back. Her eyes lock on his in the moonlight and she reaches up a hand to stroke his face.

Gray begins to sob. It *is* a miracle.

Lexis is alive.

LEXIS

*L*exis spends the night on the beach, doing something she's done very little of in her life. Something that was always a luxury she couldn't afford in the dangerous world she was born into. Something that only the foolish or weak or naïve do.

She sleeps.

And she does it curled up in Gray's arms, feeling safe in a way she didn't fathom existed.

It means when she wakes up, she's disorientated at first. For brief seconds, she wonders if she did die when she swallowed the poison. Her body is rested. Almost pain free. There's a warmth in her chest that was never more than an ember that was tired of trying to stay alive.

Surely, this is the heaven she refused to believe in.

But then she feels Gray's chest beneath her cheek, gently rising and falling with his steady breathing. She feels the weight of his arm around her waist as if he's not planning on letting her go anytime soon. She feels the gentle thud of his heart under her palm as it rests on his chest.

Lexis is alive.

And she's never been happier to know that.

Gray stirs, his dark eyes fluttering open to find her looking at him. His lips lift in a slow, lazy smile. It has Lexis's pulse tripping with an entirely different type of warmth. "Good morning," he murmurs.

Lexis pushes up, enjoying the sensation of her body grazing his. "I've never thought that was an accurate saying." Hot morning. Nice not to be dead morning. But never good morning. "But today, it is an understatement." She presses her lips to Gray's. "It's a great morning."

Gray's eyes flash with their own heat as his hand cups her head. "Well said, beautiful girl."

And then he presses his lips to hers.

Just the endearment is enough to take Lexis's breath away. But the depth of passion and emotion in that one kiss ensures Lexis doesn't get it back. She climbs higher up his body, instinctively wanting more. Air is no longer necessary to survival. To wanting to live.

Gray is.

She owes him her life, in more ways than one. Not only did he stop her father from doing to her what he did to the Never people, Gray has given Lexis a reason to breathe.

He gasps as she deepens the kiss, his fingers tightening. She shifts so she's laying completely on top of him, and gasps herself. She goes from breathless to panting in a flash, desire throbbing through her body.

Gray draws back, his thumb stroking her cheek. "Do you feel okay?"

"I feel as great as this morning," she murmurs, trying to kiss him again.

With a quick press of lips, Gray holds her still. "Everyone thought you were dead yesterday," the hitch in his voice echoes the pain in his eyes. "You're lucky to be here, Lexis."

"It seems I didn't take enough poison to die," she says softly. "But obviously it was enough to look like I was…"

She can't finish the sentence. Regret fills her at the decision she made. She chose to leave Gray after everything he's given her. And yet, she would make the same choice. When she chose to die, she was choosing for Raze to live.

Gray's other hand comes up and he cups her face. "I know why you did it, Lexis. It was the only way you knew how to turn your back on these awful Tournaments and what was expected of you."

To kill her twin.

Lexis melts into the warm body she's resting on. How could so much compassion be living in one person? And how is that beautiful soul looking at her with such…tenderness?

"I don't deserv—"

"Few people would have the courage or strength to do what you did, warrior girl of mine. And you did it because you love Raze more than anything."

Lexis raises her hands and cups Gray's face, mirroring the way he's holding her. "I love you more than anything."

Another impossible feat of this gentle, handsome, sweet man.

Gray's smile lights up his face. Simultaneously, they draw in closer. This kiss is soft and brief, but one that holds everything they've found together. Love. Passion. A future.

They pull back, now both smiling.

"And Winter and Raze will be joining us soon," says Gray, his face full of anticipation. Having their twins here will take today from being great to perfect. "Raze needed to rest, but they planned to leave before dawn."

Lexis plants her elbow in the sand and hooks her chin on her palm. When Gray told her all this last night, it had felt too good to be true.

But the fact that she's lying here with him, alive, well rested and smiling shows the miracles Gray has worked.

"I suspect it will be slow going, though," Gray continues. "Raze was pretty banged up."

Because of the beating from Evrest, their father. For the first time, anger simmers through Lexis's veins. Evrest's never loved Raze. To do that, to beat him because he won, shows their father hates him.

And soon, her brother will be free of him.

They all will be.

Lexis wriggles a little, loving the way Gray's eyes flare. "So, we have some time to spare?" she asks huskily.

Gray chuckles. "We have our whole lives ahead of us." With a sharp movement, he flips them over so his body is covering hers. Lexis's skin flames in every place they touch. "Which is why you're going to rest. The moment our twins get here, we're heading to Fairbanks."

Lexis's passion cools. Gray told her this last night, but her brain was too cloudy from the poison to realize that this plan won't work.

She shakes her head. "Fairbanks is the first place they'll look for you. For all of you. Evrest will tear the city apart looking for any signs of…" Of those who defied him. Betrayed him. "At a chance for retribution."

Gray rolls off and sits up. "Then where do we go?"

"I'm not sure," Lexis says heavily, also sitting up. They may need to be as nomadic as the Never for a little while. "Let's wait until Raze and Winter arrive and discuss it then."

Gray nods. "Hopefully, it won't be long."

They shuffle closer together, the sand shifting beneath them as they shelter under a scraggly bush. Once Raze and Winter join them, then they can disappear. They'll search for a place Evrest will never find them.

The sun steadily climbs higher, bringing the heat with it.

Gray periodically stands and walks to the top of the sand dune they're on and scans the horizon. The first couple of times he convinces Lexis to remain where she is. After that, he doesn't stand a chance at keeping her still.

She wants to be there when he sees them.

She wants to be there when they're finally all back together.

But each time, the horizon is empty. As the morning progresses, heat shimmers and obscures the distance. The skyline becomes little more than a hazy, empty vista.

"Where are they?" Lexis says through gritted teeth.

"They'll be here," Gray promises. "The only way Winter and Raze would stand us up is if they were—"

Gray stops even though Lexis hasn't said a thing, but it's too late. The final word hangs between them.

If they were *dead*.

Lexis turns back to the horizon, feeling sick. If Evrest found out what happened, he would...

She gasps, narrowing her eyes. "Look!"

Gray straightens as his gaze follows where her finger is pointing. "Yes!"

A hazy shape has taken form on the horizon, one that is steadily gaining substance.

"It has to be them!" Gray says with excitement.

Instinctively, Lexis grabs Gray and drags him down into a crouch as she does the same. Years of training remind her it could be anyone of the others—the Rust, the Never. Evrest himself.

The outline progressively gains shape and Lexis realizes what they're looking at. A single body.

Gray frowns. "There's only one."

Lexis slowly pushes to her feet, no longer caring that she'll be seen. Raze was badly beaten. What if he didn't make it...

Long moments pass before Lexis can make out any features. The first thing she sees is pale hair and her heart leaps into her throat. But she quickly registers that the shoulders are too slight to be Raze, and that whoever it is, he isn't quite as tall as her brother.

In fact, she isn't sure whether she's relieved or worried when she realizes it's the boy from Rust.

Gray hikes his hands on his hips. "Rusty," he mutters darkly.

They watch and wait in silence as the Rust boy trudges down the track. He limps slightly, one arm cradled against his chest.

"I don't like him," growls Lexis.

"Me neither. But he gave Winter and me food and water, even a tent." Gray sighs. "And when I was sneaking you out, I would've been caught if he hadn't distracted the guards. I think he's walking like that because they beat him."

Given the chance, that's exactly what any guard of Cy would do. Especially Arc.

It's apparent when Rusty sees them, because his shoulders straighten and his shuffling pace picks up. There are long minutes where Lexis doesn't allow herself to think, to wonder what Rusty approaching means.

She'll find out soon enough.

Rusty stops several feet away. His face is puffy and bruised, his arm still clutched to his chest.

Lexis steps forward. "What brings you here, Rust?"

"Holy fish shackles!" Rusty stares at her like he's seeing a ghost. "I thought you were dead."

"So did I for a little while," she says. "But it appears not."

Rusty shakes his head, trying to regain his focus. "I come with news."

Except Lexis doesn't want news. She wants her brother. She wants Gray reunited with his sister.

"What is it?" Gray asks sharply.

It's the first time Lexis has heard an edge in Gray's voice. It has the dread she was trying to control exploding through her chest.

"I don't know how to tell you this." Rusty shuffles, his swollen lips working as if he's trying to find the words. "It's Raze and Winter. Evrest found them together in Raze's hut."

"You told the Cy warriors?" Gray gasps.

"No! Do you think I would be stupid enough to come here if I did? Do you think I would've taken that beating if I wasn't on your side?" Rusty shouts. He draws in a shuddering breath. "Evrest went into a rage."

Lexis takes an involuntary step back, pain replacing the dread. It erupts with a force that makes her light headed. She already knows how this ends.

Evrest's fury would've been unstoppable. A blaze that could only be quenched with one thing.

Death.

Rusty's shoulders start heaving. "He killed them both."

Lexis blinks. Then blinks again. But Rusty is still there. This is all still painfully real. She shakes her head, unwilling to accept it. "You lie!"

Rusty steps forward and opens his palm, showing them what he's holding. "I wish I was."

"No," moans Gray.

Lexis's knees go weak. Although she doesn't recognize the boy the carved figurine represents, she knows the craftsmanship. Raze made whatever is resting in Rusty's palm.

"That's Winter's," says Gray hoarsely. "She kept it with her always. What are you doing with it?"

Rusty's face crumples. "It fell out of her hand when they were taking her body away. I quickly grabbed it before anyone saw." He holds it out to Gray, who takes it. "I thought you'd want it."

Gray stares at the figurine, his hand trembling. "This can't be all I have left of her..."

Seeing his pain only compounds Lexis's own. She's never felt anything so virulent and yet so helpless all at once.

She grips her hands so hard her nails dig into her palms. Her father caused this. Her father not only took Raze from her, he took Winter from Gray. This is not how it ends.

"I'm going to kill him."

Lexis takes two steps before Gray's hand grabs her. She stops, fury thumping through her veins, powered by years of pain and resentment and disappointment. Evrest took everything from her. Her peace. Her belief that good is possible. Her future. Gray had just returned them and now her father has killed Raze. How can she live in a world where she has those but not her brother? How can this have been the price she and Gray paid?

"What?" she snaps, tugging on her hand.

She's going to take the only thing she can from Evrest—his tomorrows. He won't live to see a Commander crowned. His Tournaments would've been for nothing.

Gray's eyes are bleeding with the same pain carving through Lexis's heart. "What would Raze want you to do?"

Lexis stills. Of all the questions that Gray could've asked, that's the only one that could stop her. "He'd want..." She chokes as the truth climbs up her throat. A single tear trickles down her cheek, fracturing the agony that's screaming to be heard.

Gray nods, knowing how she's feeling because he's experiencing it, too. "He'd want the same thing Winter would."

"For us to live," Lexis whispers hoarsely.

That's all Raze ever wanted for her.

Gray steps in, his thumb wiping away the tear in a gentle caress. "We'll do what we planned. We'll run away. We'll live the life that was taken away from them." He smiles for the briefest of seconds. "Evrest would hate that."

Suddenly Lexis doesn't want to hear about her father. When

he took Raze, he severed her ties to him. In some ways, he's already dead to her.

She wraps her arms around Gray's waist, drawing strength from knowing that no matter how impossible it seems, something beautiful has survived all this destruction. "That's exactly what we'll do." They'll disappear. "Together."

"Where will you go?" Rusty asks.

Lexis almost jolts. She'd forgotten he was there. She holds Gray's gaze. "Nowhere," she says.

"Everywhere," adds Gray.

They clasp each other's hands, the bittersweet pain of this moment clamping around Lexis's heart and squeezing hard.

They'll walk away. Find somewhere to call their own.

They'll live, they'll grieve.

And through it all, they'll love.

WINTER

*W*inter runs through the sky, just like she used to in Fairbanks. The clouds are her stepping-stones. The stars are her hand-holds. The moon is her compass.

She's free.

Free of hunger and pain.

Free of heartbreak and longing.

Free of Evrest's cruel games.

And Gray is beside her like he has been her entire life.

There's a thought nagging at her and she pushes it away, desperately trying to hold onto this feeling of intense happiness. But it nips at her consciousness, demanding her attention, and eventually she realizes what it is.

Gray's not beside her.

It's Raze.

And now she's no longer running. She's turning to Raze, eyes closed, breath held, heart beating faster than it's ever done before.

Warmth spreads through her chest as her mouth finds his, and she reaches up to entangle her fingers in his hair, almost like she thinks he's going to try to escape. But the way he presses himself closer as he takes control, parting her lips with his own, tells her he's right here with her.

The kiss goes from gentle to desperate in a matter of seconds, and they cling to each other as energy sparks from every cell in her body. Everything in the world right now is made up from this one kiss. Nobody else exists. Nothing else matters. It's just Winter and Raze in a sky of glittering diamonds.

He moans and for one crazy second, she thinks he's going to talk to her. But, instead, he pulls back.

Her eyes spring open.

She's not in the sky. Or Fairbanks.

She's in Raze's hut in the Outlands.

And it's well past sunrise.

"We slept in," she gasps. "We're supposed to be on our way to meet Gray by now."

Raze nods and focuses on her. His jaw is covered in purple bruises and the bridge of his nose is swollen. She knows his torso will be in even worse shape. There's no way he could have run away last night. She can only hope he's well enough to go now. Because there's no way she's going to leave him.

"Can you sit up?" She reaches out her hands wishing she was as good as Lexis at speaking to him without words. "We have to leave now."

He slips his hands into hers and she pulls him to a seated position, hoping it's still early enough that the rest of the Cy camp is fast asleep.

"Good job." She gives Raze an encouraging smile. "Now, try to stand up."

He lets go of one of her hands to hold up his palm.

"You need a moment?" she asks,

Raze shakes his head as he reaches out and touches her cheek, looking deep into her eyes.

I'm okay.

She hears his words as if he spoke them out loud, his meaning is so clear.

They've held each other through the night. They've drawn close and taken comfort from their touch. They experienced a kiss like Winter could never have imagined was possible. But this look he's giving her is…next level. Did Lexis look at Gray like this? If so, she can see why her brother fell so desperately in love.

She stands and helps Raze to his feet. His leg is still badly injured. Maybe once they get to the ocean, they can rest for a few days. The way he looks, they might not have a whole lot of choice. One night's rest has made a small difference, but he needs plenty more.

Opening the door a crack, she peers out, only for it to swing toward her. She jumps back before the timber hits her in the face.

"What the—" Her eyes widen in the early morning light to see Rusty standing outside the hut panting heavily, his legs coated in a layer of fine sand. He's almost as badly beaten as Raze. "Rusty? What happened?"

"Thank goodness I caught you in time," he says, between heavy breaths. "I thought I missed you."

"What do you mean?" she asks, wondering exactly what he knows about their planned escape. "Where do you think I'm going?"

"I saw Gray leave with Lexis's body." He lowers his voice, and he urges her back in the hut so they can speak. "I followed him. I know you plan to meet him."

Winter glances at Raze who seems just as puzzled as she is about how he knows all this.

"We really don't have time," Winter hisses at Rusty. "I need you to get to the point, like now."

"You can't go to Gray." Rusty twists at the hem of his shirt. "It's a trap."

Winter frowns. "Talk faster. Please!"

"Gray took Lexis to the ocean, and released her body deep into the water," he says. "Then, when he turned around to head back, Evrest's men were waiting for him. They lined the shoreline and wouldn't let him out of the water. He knew they were going to kill him as soon as he set foot on sand, so he…"

"He what?" A sick feeling burns at the back of Winter's throat. "He what, Rusty? Tell me!"

"He dove under the water and joined Lexis." Rusty swallows as he looks to the ground. "He's dead, Winter. There's no point joining him. He's gone."

"No." Winter takes a step back, almost like she can escape this terrible news by getting further away from it. "No, he can't be dead. We're meeting him today."

"I'm sorry, Winter." Rusty looks at her through swollen eyes. "But it's true. Evrest's men are waiting for you. If you try to leave, they'll kill you. Your best chance is to stay right where you are. You can win the next Tournament. I know you can."

Raze's hands land on Winter's shoulders and she turns to bury her face in his chest, her need for comfort overriding the need to be gentle with him. He shows no sign of pain, and pulls her in close.

Tears explode down her face and she wishes she were back asleep with Gray running beside her in the sky. This can't be true.

Gray's gone! Lexis is gone! Both their twins are dead. This is the worst possible news she could imagine.

"You need to win the next Tournament, Winter," says Rusty, not giving up. "Maybe Raze will even let you. You know, do for you what he was supposed to do for his sister."

Her head snaps up so she can glare at him. "Don't ever talk about Raze like he's not standing right here. Just because he can't talk, doesn't mean he can't hear you."

Raze grips her tighter at these words and she holds onto

him, wincing as pain radiates out from her heart. Her hand slips to her pocket as she seeks the familiar comfort of the carved figure of Trakk, only to realize it's missing.

"It's gone?" She breaks away and checks her pocket more carefully.

Raze tilts his head.

"The figure you made me," she explains. "I keep it on me always. It must've fallen out of my pocket last night when Gray and I helped you back here. Rusty, did you see it out there?"

Rusty shrugs. "It could be anywhere."

Raze mimes carving. *I'll make you a new one.*

"Thanks," she says, knowing it won't be the same. But then again, nothing will ever be the same now that Gray's dead. Just like Trakk. Just like her mom and her sister and her little baby nephew. If it weren't for Raze standing before her, she'd have nobody left in the world to care about.

"We need to talk about the next Tournament," says Rusty, making no move to leave them in peace to either run away or grieve.

"There is no next Tournament." Winter steps toward the door. "Raze and I are leaving. And we're going right now."

"But I told you." Rusty positions himself between Winter and the exit. "Gray's dead. There's no point in leaving."

Raze works his way forward to block Winter from Rusty, and glares at him.

"Then we'll go somewhere else," says Winter. "It doesn't have to be the ocean."

"I can't let you go." Rusty folds his arms across his broad chest. "You need to fight in the final Tournament."

"Why do you care so much about that?" She narrows her eyes at him from behind Raze. "In fact, why do you care so much about me? What are you up to, Rusty?"

"I'm just…" A small line of blood runs from the corner of his busted up eye and down his face. "I'm just...you just...You just need to compete, okay? You need to kill him."

Raze shoves Rusty at the door so hard, it swings open the other way and he flies out, landing on his butt outside the hut.

He cries out in pain before crawling away.

Winter turns to give Raze a quick embrace. "Now let's get out of h—"

Evrest fills the vacant space outside the hut. "Am I interrupting something?"

Raze lets go of Winter immediately, and she knows it's to protect her, rather than himself. But she also knows it's too late. The look of fury in Evrest's eyes is unmistakable. They're not running away this morning.

Or ever.

"Where is she?" Evrest asks, fixing his gaze on Raze. "Are you hiding her body in here?"

Raze steps back so Evrest can take in the emptiness of the hut.

"You." Evrest jams a finger into Winter's chest, looking like he's about to explode. "You! What did that no good brother of yours do with her? Where has he taken my daughter?"

Raze shoves Evrest's hand off Winter and she drags in a deep breath trying to stop the racing of her heart.

"It doesn't matter where he took her," she says. "They're both dead."

Evrest's brows shoot up, almost like his own men hadn't been responsible for Gray's death.

"The Tournaments are over," says Winter. "You have two people left and neither of us want to win. You can't force one of us to kill the other."

"I can't," he says, still purple in the face. "But if one of you doesn't get out there in that Ring and kill the other, then I'll kill you both."

Winter looks at Raze whose face is twisted in agony, mirroring her own feelings.

"Kill me," she says to him. "Then one of us can live. Kill me and make the Outlands a better place. You can do it. I know you can."

Raze doesn't need words to say he disagrees. He doesn't even need to shake his head. His answer is in his eyes. He puts a palm to his chest.

You kill me, instead.

"I won't do it," she says. "Never."

"Then it's decided." Evrest grabs her roughly by the arm. "The seventh Tournament begins right now. And it's up to you. Either one of you dies. Or you both do."

RAZE

*E*vrest shoves Winter roughly out of the hut and Raze leaps after her, catching her before she sprawls in the dirt. He straightens, intending on scowling at his father. Raze will fight him himself if need be.

The final Tournament will not go ahead.

Winter tucks in closer as they're met by a circle of spear tips, all poised at heart level.

Seven Cy warriors surround the hut, their weapons held high as they glare at Raze and Winter. Their orders are obvious. Lead them to the Ring. Or kill them.

Evrest slips out behind Raze and Winter and walks past the men. "So, what will it be? How many more deaths will there be today? One?" His lip curls in a menacing smile. "Or two?"

Raze takes a step toward him, hatred pumping through his veins. How could this man believe this is what's needed to rule the Outlands? How could Raze have ever followed him so blindly?

The warrior across from Raze jerks his spear forward, the tip coming up against his throat. Raze stills, furious that the pinprick of pressure on his neck is enough to stop him.

"Okay!" Winter cries out as she grips Raze's arm. "We'll fight."

Raze's eyes flicker to the beautiful girl who's putting her life on the line for him. They'll fight? Neither of them wanted that.

Her dark eyes plead with him. "It's our only chance."

"Exactly," sneers Evrest. "It's your last chance for one of you fools to live."

And for Evrest to have his Commander. That's what this is all about. Raze's father wants to have someone to crown, and if it's not Lexis, the child he raised to be his puppet, then it no longer matters who it is.

Raze straightens as he realizes his father needs a winner. That's why he hasn't killed them, yet.

Which gives them an advantage.

He catches his father's cold gaze and nods.

Very well. We'll fight.

Winter lets out a pent up breath as the spears retreat, although they remain pointing at them.

Evrest crosses his arms. "How about we escort you to the Ring?"

Raze releases Winter and they fall into step, side by side. The Cy warriors divide to let them pass, then fan out behind them, the spears now pointed at their back. There will be no escape, no running away.

Winter's hand brushes his own as they steadily make their way to the Ring. Every part of Raze's body aches or stings or throbs, but that one point of contact warms him with the promise that there's more than just pain inside of him. There's also a heart that yearns for this to be different.

A heart that hopes it can be.

They stride past the statue of Cy, and Raze is tempted to push it over. This man is the one who seeded hatred in the Outlands. He bred resentment and hostility and violence. His legacy is these Tournaments.

But Raze keeps walking and jumps into the Ring, ignoring the jolt of agony that rattles through his bones. This is their chance to alter that trajectory.

Winter drops down beside him and they walk into the center of the circle of death. There's a sound behind Raze and he spins around. His father is there, holding the flamethrower. He hurls it at Raze, who catches it instinctively. Its warm metal weight presses into his palms.

"People of the Outlands," Evrest announces. "We have the contestants of the final Tournament."

Faces appear around the Ring, dirty and thin. The spectators' hungry eyes eagerly scan the two of them, and Raze isn't sure what they're looking forward to more. Another grizzly death, or the prospect of the war that is set to come.

After this, the riches of Askala await.

"Your Commander will stand before you at the end of this Tournament," Evrest promises. Several spectators shuffle closer in anticipation. "And that is when the fun will really begin."

Raze shifts closer to Winter, suddenly shocked that this is what he and Lexis were fighting for. War should never be called *fun*. Death should never be celebrated.

Evrest raises a fist. "May the Tournaments serve you well," he intones.

He steps back and a heavy hush falls over the Ring.

Raze and Winter turn to face each other. They've been forced into this moment. They were robbed of a choice to be here. But now that they are, they need to decide what to do with it.

Their kiss from this morning rises through Raze's consciousness. It was tender. Sweet. Passionate.

It was everything that humanity has the potential to be.

Winter steps closer, her eyes seeming to hold everything he's thinking. "We won't fight, Raze. This is where it ends."

He nods, grateful Winter came into his life. She's not weak

like Evrest believes. She's the strongest person Raze has ever met. She chooses what's right, no matter what she faces. Without breaking her gaze, he tosses the flamethrower away. The crowd gasps as it thumps into the sand a few feet away.

They clasp hands and turn to face Evrest. Raze lifts their interwoven fingers, a silent show of solidarity.

"We will not fight," announces Winter. "Death will not choose the leader of the Outlands."

Evrest's face contracts with fury. He steps up beside the statue of Cy. "The Outlands will not be led by those who are weak of heart." He pins them with a rabid glare. "Fight," he growls. "Or die."

Raze shakes his head. Winter tightens her grip on his hand. "No."

The crowd holds its breath as Evrest doesn't move a muscle. This is open defiance. His Tournaments are being opposed. Denied. Challenged by his very own son.

Evrest doesn't say a word as he lifts his hand and flicks his fingers. The crowd in Raze's peripheral vision part as two Cy warriors appear at the edge of the Ring. Both of them are carrying spears. A quick glance over his shoulders shows Raze that every few feet stands a member of his faction. They raise their weapons, pointing them at the center of the Ring.

At Raze and Winter.

Raze's pulse becomes a rolling thunder through his body. The reality that he's choosing not just his own death but Winter's is undeniable in each deadly tip aimed at them.

Winter presses closer to him. "We will not fight, Evrest. It's over!"

Evrest's response is nothing more than a twitch of his hand. A blink later, a spear lands between Winter's feet. She jumps back as dirt explodes over her calves.

The message is clear. If the Cy warrior had aimed for her, if it hadn't been the warning shot it was, Winter would be dead.

And Raze isn't so sure he can be okay with that.

In fact, the idea that Winter should be the Commander suddenly seems like the only solution. She's strong.

She thinks for herself.

And she has heart.

Before Raze can act, Winter yanks the spear out of the dirt. To Raze's surprise she stalks over to the flamethrower. Gripping the spear with both hands, she lifts it high, then slams it down, impaling the weapon.

There's a gasp from the crowd as wood crunches through metal. The flamethrower jerks with the impact, like some beast that's just been pierced through the heart.

Raze doesn't look toward Evrest to see what his reaction is. He already knows.

And it's that knowledge that has him powering toward Winter. He slams into her and knocks her to the ground, the thud of another spear landing in the soil behind them. Pain explodes through Raze as he lands on top of her, but he doesn't move. If there's another spear coming, it'll have to go through him first.

When nothing punctures his back, Raze realizes what he has to do. All those plans to stand up to this were a momentary lapse. He was a fool to think he was anything but a sacrifice.

He can't ask this of Winter.

Raze leaps to his feet, the movement awkward as he favors his good leg, and hauls her up with him. He tucks her behind his back, only to spin around. The spears are still held aloft no matter where he turns. They're surrounded.

"Fight or die," Evrest calls out. He shakes his fist in the air and the crowd repeat the ultimatum, striking up a spine-chilling chant as they say it over and over.

Fight or die.

Fight or die.

Fight. Or. Die.

Then Raze chooses die.

Two steps over and he yanks on the spear in the flamethrower, finding it's wedged tight. He tugs harder but it doesn't move. Grunting with frustration, Raze snaps it in half.

He lifts it, the point aimed for his heart. He mouths two words to Winter. *I'm sorry.*

He contracts his arms, hoping this death will be swift. And if it's not, then he desperately wishes he'll die with dignity, not writhing and screaming in pain.

"Raze! No!"

Winter slams into him, bowling him over and knocking the spear away from his chest. Once more, they crash onto the ground, this time with Winter on top. Dust is still billowing around them as she scrabbles to take the spear out of his hand. "Don't do this," she moans.

But this is what has to happen.

It's what was always going to happen.

He was supposed to die for Lexis. Dying for Winter is just as worthy.

She'd become the Commander.

Raze tries to push Winter away, but it's as if her hands are everywhere. "I won't let you do this," she cries as she swings her arm wide and knocks the half-spear out of his hand. It rolls and tumbles a few feet away.

Raze's heart constricts as he pushes Winter off. Surely she realizes she's not strong enough to stop him.

Winter lands in the dust and Raze scrambles to reach the spear again. He can hear the crowd cheering but it sounds far away. It's as if he's no longer part of their world anymore.

All it'll take is one thrust through the heart and he'll sever that link forever.

Raze has just grabbed the spear when Winter lands on his back. He grunts at the pain but doesn't let it stop him. He grips the length of wood as he tries to push her off again.

But this time, Winter isn't letting go. As he turns and twists, she wraps herself around him. "No, Raze," she says. "Please."

Raze clenches his eyes closed as he pushes with all his might. Winter peels off him with a cry, already clambering to get back to him. Hating himself, Raze grasps the half-spear with both hands and extends his arms. The horizontal length slams into Winter's chest and she tumbles backward, pain and shock stamped across her face.

The crowd roars again. They're getting the fight they wanted.

Except, it's not the fight Raze wanted. He needs Winter to let him go.

Spinning the spear so it's once again pointing at his chest, Raze doesn't give himself time to think. To apologize to her.

To maybe have finally found the strength to speak and tell Winter he fell for her the moment he saw her crying over her friend.

To his shock, Winter appears above him. She drops so she's straddling him and grips the spear aimed for his heart. She yanks, straining with all her might as she tries to take the weapon off him.

Raze draws down, trying to show her this is inevitable. That she's not strong enough. The deadly point creeps closer to his chest. It brushes the leather of his tunic.

But Winter doesn't give up. She arches her back as she strains with everything she's got. "No!" she shouts. "Stop it, Raze!"

The tip pierces his tunic and grazes his skin. One quick yank and this will be over.

Except Winter won't let go. She has tears streaming down her cheeks. Her hands will be on the spear when it slices through his heart.

Raze stops and Winter quickly realizes he's no longer fighting her. She looks down, mouth open as she pants, her lips red and moist from her tears. "Don't," she whispers. "Don't let him win."

"Winter," Raze says hoarsely, just as surprised when the word slips out as she is. He swallows and tries again. "Finish this."

Let him die for this.

Winter's eyes widen at the alien sound of his voice. Her gaze dips to his mouth. "Raze…" she breathes. Her face hardens again as she shakes her head. "Choose to live, Raze. For me." Her eyes bleed with desperation. "For Lexis and Gray and every other senseless death in the Outlands."

What for? He asks her wordlessly.

"We'll prove Evrest can't win. That the Outlands won't be ruled with the threat of death." Winter's lip trembles. "That's worth living for."

Raze is unaware his hands have released the spear until Winter lifts it and throws it away. His heart spoke before he had time to realize Winter's right.

By living, he defies Evrest and everything he stands for.

By living, he's no longer part of this.

Raze's hands come up and cup Winter's face, his thumbs brushing away the moisture that's tracking down her dusty cheeks. He's rewarded with the most beautiful thing he's ever seen. Her smile.

She stands, holding out her hand, and he takes it. Coming to his feet, Raze turns to his father. Glaring at him, he lifts their joined hands.

His father's deadly games have come to an end.

The crowd falls silent, dust curling up around their feet as they shuffle uncomfortably. The Cy warriors lift their spears again, ready for the command to kill the two souls standing in the center of the Ring. Arc is practically salivating.

Raze's chest is so tight he can hardly breathe. Unity and compassion now face division and violence.

All his life, the latter has always won.

"Let there be no more deaths today," Winter announces. "You will have two Commanders or none."

Raze waits, glad he made this choice. Glad he made this statement.

Knowing Lexis would be, too.

Even if it's the last one he'll ever make.

WINTER

*W*inter holds Raze's hand, waiting to see if they're going to live or die. Whatever the outcome, it will be the same for them both. And even though there's absolutely no comfort in the thought of an early death, there's relief that whatever happens, she won't be alone.

Maybe it's for the best if Evrest just gets it over with and kills them now. They can hold hands as they fly to the sky, for real this time, and join their twins in the stars.

Evrest steps down into the Ring, just as a lone raven swoops overhead, letting out a squawk that echoes around the empty sky.

The silent crowd awakens, their murmurs joining the cries of the bird as they strain their eyes. Except, they're not looking up. They turn and stare out in the distance.

"Look." Winter tugs on Raze's hand. "The factions are coming."

People are walking toward them from all directions. The Cragg spectators point as more of their faction approach from the north. The Never move in from the south clutching spears in their nervous hands, flanked by the white-haired People of

Rust. In the western segment of the ring, the People of Cy plant their feet, gasping to see a small group moving in from the east.

Fairbanks.

Brik's familiar hulking shape lumbers toward the Ring, flanked by his motley army of survivors. It looks like he has even more tattoos than he had before.

Raze glances at Winter in curiosity.

"They're not my people," she tells him. "You're my person. My only person."

He puts a palm to his heart, telling her she's his person, too. They're not part of any faction now. It's just the two of them—against the world if they need to be.

Evrest smiles widely, waving his hands for the people to come closer as he stands behind Winter and Raze.

"You're just in time," he says, projecting his voice so that it bounces around the Ring.

Winter clutches Raze's hand tighter, not trusting his father any more than he does.

"It looks like we're late," growls a Cragg. "You told us the final Tournament would be at midday."

"He *invited* them," Winter says under her breath, realizing that whatever this evil man has planned, he wants an audience for it.

"We decided to begin a little early," says Evrest. "Our competitors were keen to get started."

Winter fixes her gaze on Brik. He's practically salivating, no doubt thinking if she wins, he'll be able to seize power for himself.

"We're not fighting each other!" Winter calls out, speaking more to the crowd than she is to Evrest. "I've already told you, the Outlands will either have two Commanders or you'll have none."

"Is this some kind of joke?" Brik shouts to Evrest. "And you wonder why we didn't enter your stupid games to begin with."

"Get on with it!" a woman calls out.

"Yeah!" a man agrees. "Let's get this over."

It's only then that Winter takes in the exhausted faces encircling her. This isn't a crowd hungry for blood. It's a group of people who just want a resolution. They want food for their children. A safe bed to sleep in. The chance to dare to dream about a future.

"We don't need these games," says Winter, letting go of Raze's hand to step closer to the people. "What we need is someone who can lead us to a better life. Raze and I have equally proven our worth to you in these Tournaments of death."

A few people nod, and Winter walks around the Ring, making eye contact with as many as she can.

"Raze tried to take his own life to save mine," she says for the sake of those who just arrived. "But I didn't let him. And do you know why?" She pauses, letting them think this over for a moment. "Because a leader needs to be strong, but they also need to be merciful. They need to know what true love is."

A few people in the crowd join hands with the person beside them. Others grunt as they wait for her to say more.

"You agreed to these games because you wanted to unite the factions," she continues. "You wanted a leader who could give you a better life. Raze and I can do that far better together than either of us can do alone. Which is why we must both win the Tournaments. We aren't the Commanders you expected. But we are the Commanders you need."

Her words are having an impact. She can feel the effect, just as she can see it in the desperate faces.

The crowd throw their fists in the air in triumph, high on the power of having a say in the outcome of these brutal games that have taken so much from all of them.

Winter allows herself to bask in the moment for a few beats of her heart. Something deep inside her drove her here. Was it because she knew this was possible when nobody—not even Gray—believed she had a chance?

The thought of her brother sobers her, knowing she'd take back her decision to enter the Tournaments if she could. Because it was a choice that led to Gray's death, which is a weight she'll have to carry always.

She holds up her palm, and the crowd settles down. "I can lead you to a better life. I will bring you to Askala and we'll take a share in what's rightfully ours. But I refuse to do it alone. There are two Commanders of the Outlands now."

Turning to look at Raze, she locks eyes with him. But something is wrong. Very wrong. He's not smiling at her. He's not even really looking at her. It's like he can see right through her.

"There can only be one Commander," sneers Evrest, removing his hand from behind Raze's back and holding a bloodied knife in the air.

Raze slumps to the ground, and Winter runs to him, every cell in her body screaming for this not to be happening.

"No!" she cries as she reaches him and throws herself on top of him. "Raze!"

He looks up at her with lifeless eyes as blood pools around him.

"No!" she cries again, like she can reverse time by refusing to accept what it's dealt her. Not Raze, too! This can't be happening. It wasn't supposed to be like this.

She gets to her feet, determined that Evrest won't get away with such an act. He wanted a fight in the Ring. But now he's become part of it.

"You chose me over your own son?" she asks, shaking her head as she holds back her tears. "Do you really hate him that much?"

"Oh, I hate him." Evrest wipes his knife on his trousers. "But what makes you think I chose you?"

"I..." Winter looks down at Raze, her heart spilling over with pain, then back at the man who killed him. "I am the last contestant standing."

"She is our Commander," shouts a voice from the crowd.

A murmur of agreement washes over the people.

Evrest shakes his head. "You would have a skinny ghost from Fairbanks rule you?"

"We choose her!" a woman from the Never shouts. "She won the Tournaments. That's the rules. She's the last one left."

"But she's not the last," says Evrest. "There's been another competitor in the Ring this whole time. Have you not seen him?"

Winter picks out Rusty's face hovering near the front of the crowd. Surely, Evrest isn't talking about him?

"Me!" booms Evrest, raising his voice in a way she hasn't heard before. "I am the competitor you didn't see. And as soon as I kill this ghost, you will call me Commander."

Winter's jaw falls open as she tries to find the words she needs to protest.

"You can't do that!" Brik shouts, stepping forward. "Fairbanks rules. This girl is our Commander, and she answers to me."

"You don't even know her name," sneers Evrest. "It's Winter. And just like the season, she's about to become extinct."

Winter grimaces, wondering if her sheer hatred for this man will give her enough strength to kill him. But the guy is twice her size and a trained warrior. She may be able to win a war of words with him, but she's not keen on coming fist to fist.

She looks down at Raze, and her heart aches to be with him. Maybe it is her time. Maybe this is for the best. Because just like the people in the crowd, she's so very tired.

Let this be done.

Rusty steps forward and Winter shakes her head. There's no saving her now. Why does this guy refuse to ever give up on her?

"The rules were clear, Evrest," Rusty says. "The last competitor standing wins the Tournaments and leads the Outlands to victory. That's Winter. Not you."

"She has one more competitor to beat." Evrest raises his fists.

"No, she doesn't," shouts a man from Cragg, climbing into the Ring beside Rusty. "She already won. She's our Commander."

Several more people enter, making it clear that Evrest has lost their trust as they snarl at him.

"If you fight Winter, then you fight all of us!" Rusty punches a fist in the air. "The Tournaments are over."

With these words, more people pour into the Ring and stand behind Winter.

She looks over her shoulder, unable to believe what's happening. When she arrived here, they all licked their lips at the thought of her death. Now, they're calling her their Commander.

The Cy warriors stand loyally with their leader, but there's uncertainty in their eyes now. They have the training. But they don't have the numbers. This isn't a fight they're likely to win.

"The Tournaments aren't over until I say they are!" Evrest keeps his fists raised, although even he's not looking as confident as he did only moments ago.

"You can't change the rules," a Cragg woman says, her voice quavering. "The Tournaments killed Slab. If you change the rules, his death was for nothing. He was a good man."

Winter swallows. Slab was anything but a good man. But this woman has a point.

"*All* the deaths were for nothing if you claim victory now," she says, glaring at Evrest. "You're making a mockery of your own Tournaments, just because they didn't turn out the way you intended. That doesn't make you a leader. It makes you a snake."

"Set a snake on him, I say," sneers a man from Never. "Then we'll put his head on a spear, just like he did to our people."

Evrest flattens his palms and holds out his hands, pasting a nervous smile to his face. "Please, just calm down," he says. "You're not thinking rationally. You're confused. We can—"

"You calling us fools?" Brik sneers. "Because it seems like you're the fool here."

The crowd laughs and Brik puffs out his chest.

Evrest's hands fall as the realization that he's no longer in control washes over him.

"Leave here immediately," says Evrest. "This is Cy land, and you're no longer welcome."

"We don't want this land." Brik takes a step closer to Winter. "This Ring is the asshole of the Outlands."

The sound of sniggering is interrupted by the shouts of a Cragg man. "I'm going to kill every last one of you Cy bastards! We ain't going nowhere!"

Winter turns to look at the army of men and women behind her. People from four factions standing united against only one. It's not quite the unity the Tournaments were seeking to achieve, but it's something.

"We will not fight," Winter calls out, stepping into her newfound shoes of Commander. "There has been enough death already in these heartless games. The sacrifices have been sown and now is the time to reap the fruits. We will give the People of Cy one last chance to join us. We will show them what mercy looks like."

"And if they don't?" a woman asks.

"Then we will take Askala alone," says Winter. "We're responsible for our own future. We don't need Evrest. We don't need the People of Cy."

"And we don't need you." Evrest takes two steps back, keeping his eyes on them like any warrior would do.

Fists pump in the air as the factions cheer and the Cy retreat further.

"Winter is the leader we've been waiting for," says Rusty, putting a proud hand on her back. "Winter is our new Commander."

And now she realizes why Rusty has been helping her this whole time. He was gambling on the long shot, knowing that if she won the Tournaments, he'd be right there by her side. And now that she literally has nobody else left in this world, maybe it's time she gambled on him. She wouldn't be alive right now if it weren't for Rusty. He's the only friend she has left in this world.

"I don't even know your name," she says to him, wanting to give him the respect he deserves.

"I thought you'd never ask." He smiles. "My name's Corbin. Pleased to meet you, Winter."

She cringes at the use of her name and knows there's one final thing she needs to do if she's going to lead this unlikely group of people. She's lost her home, her family, her friends, her everything. To do what needs to be done next, she needs to become someone else.

"I will lead you in the name of all the people who have died," she calls out over the crowd. "People who would have lived if they were in Askala. I do this for Gray. And Raze. And Lexis. And all the other competitors in the Tournaments. But most of all I do this for my sister. Before I left for the Outlands, my mother told me to live the life she couldn't. She wanted me to honor my sister's name. So, from this day on, I am no longer Winter. You are to call me Grace."

Corbin slips his hand into Winter's, and even though it's not the hand she wants to hold, she doesn't push him away.

He lifts their joined hands into the air. "All hail, Commander Grace!"

She smiles as she looks at this collection of factions. They're not her people, not in the way Raze was, but maybe in time she'll learn to feel like one of them.

Maybe, just maybe, she'll do her sister's memory proud.

And as the People of Cy slink back to their huts, she lets go of Corbin's hand to go to Raze, wanting to kiss his lips one more time before she leaves.

She crouches down and leans over him, trailing a fingertip down his beloved face.

She kisses him, softly, certain she can feel the lifeforce within him.

"I love you so much," she says. "I wish you could do this with me."

His eyes flutter open, and she pulls back and gasps.

"I knew you could do it," he whispers, his eyes spilling over with love. "You won."

THE END

Ready for the next installment in The Thaw Chronicles?
Check out Book 10, CONQUER THE THAW, now!

BOOK TEN - CONQUER THE THAW

Only the strongest will lead

The deadly Tournaments are over. A new leader of the Outlands has been chosen.

To hold onto power and seize the riches that lie in Askala, the new Commander must earn respect and build an army. But how can control be taken when everything has fallen apart?

In a harsh world of lies, secrets and brutal betrayals, challenges will be made and rules will be broken. The Commander will need to discover if the real war is against the dying planet or if it's against the people themselves.

A new war has begun. Askala is the prize. Only the strongest will lead.

Lovers of Divergent and The Hunger Games will be blown away by this latest epic dystopian adventure brought to you by USA Today best-seller Tamar Sloan and award-winner Heidi Catherine, authors of the smash hit series, The Thaw Chronicles.

Grab your copy now!

ABOUT THE AUTHORS

Tamar Sloan hasn't decided whether she's a psychologist who loves writing, or a writer with a lifelong fascination with psychology. She must have been someone pretty awesome in a previous life (past life regression indicated a Care Bear), because she gets to do both. When not reading, writing or working with teens, Tamar can be found with her husband and two children enjoying country life in their small slice of the Australian bush.

Heidi Catherine is an award-winning fantasy author and hopeless romantic. She lives in Australia, not able to decide if she prefers Melbourne or the Mornington Peninsula, so shares her time between both places. She is similarly pulled in opposing directions by her two sons and two dogs, remaining thankful she only has one husband.

MORE SERIES TO FALL IN LOVE WITH...

ALSO BY TAMAR SLOAN

Keepers of the Grail

Zodiac Guardians

Descendants of the Gods

Prime Prophecy

ALSO BY HEIDI CATHERINE

The Kingdoms of Evernow

The Soulweaver

The Woman Who Didn't (written as HC Michaels)

The Girl Who Never (written as HC Michaels)

Made in the USA
Middletown, DE
07 August 2021

45555091R00179